Silver Buck

Silver Buck

*To Albert —
my Bother for these many years
my tale of an adventure out of
the old west.*

Lynn Luick

Lynn Luick

Copyright © 2015 by Lynn Luick.

Cover Illustration by Shannen Paradero

Library of Congress Control Number:		2014921893
ISBN:	Hardcover	978-1-5035-2544-3
	Softcover	978-1-5035-2545-0
	eBook	978-1-5035-2546-7

All rights reserved. No part of this book may be reproduced or transmitted in any form or by any means, electronic or mechanical, including photocopying, recording, or by any information storage and retrieval system, without permission in writing from the copyright owner.

This is a work of fiction. Names, characters, places and incidents either are the product of the author's imagination or are used fictitiously, and any resemblance to any actual persons, living or dead, events, or locales is entirely coincidental.

Any people depicted in stock imagery provided by Thinkstock are models, and such images are being used for illustrative purposes only.
Certain stock imagery © Thinkstock.

This book was printed in the United States of America.

Rev. date: 02/05/2015

To order additional copies of this book, contact:
Xlibris
1-888-795-4274
www.Xlibris.com
Orders@Xlibris.com
695354

Chapter One

I was lying in bed looking out the window at the sun rising out of the east just over the mountains my great-granddaddy loved. It was these mountains he had been wandering through for almost half a century that had brought him to this small town of Durango in the southwest corner of Colorado. I had just arrived last night from Kingsville, a cattle town in deep South Texas where I was born; dad worked for one of the state's largest ranches. Mom cleaned the big ranch house the owner lived in and cooked his meals. It was this man that had let me work beside dad after school and every weekend. Because of Big Jim Backo, I graduated from school and have been able to learn about cattle and horses and was taught to shoot any type of gun or rifle by my dad.

After four weeks on the trail, sleepin' on the hard ground with only my horse for company, I thought I could get a good night's sleep, but had lain awake half the night thinking about Jeb, my great-granddaddy, and how I wouldn't have been here if my dad hadn't been gone on a cattle drive to Kansas when my mom got the letter about her grandfather Jeb sayin' he was sick, very sick. So I had been sent, only to find my great-granddaddy had died a week before and been buried only two days before I arrived.

I had never known him, but Mom had told me of his search for gold and silver for fifty years. Now in 1875 all that was left was an old saddlebag of his that was on the dresser across from the bunk I was lyin' in. His horse and pack mule had been sold to pay for his six-foot-hole in the ground.

Saddlebags . . . I was so tired last night I hadn't looked inside my great-granddaddy Jeb's saddlebags. I took two steps over to the dresser where they were, picked them up, and threw them on the bed. I sat down beside the saddlebags and started to open them. The first thing I saw was an old rag. I picked it up and carefully unwrapped what was in it. I looked upon the most beautiful silver-plated Colt 45 with pearl handles I had ever seen. Surprise came across my face, 'cause why would a miner have a beautiful gun like this, and also that 45 was all that was in the old saddlebags.

Laying the gun down, I went over to the only window in the room and looked out over the main street. People were starting to move about. Then I saw her, a pretty black-haired beauty. She was wearing a tight pair of jeans that outlined her figure well, a pretty white blouse with ruffles around the neck and cuffs, and a black pair of Western boots. She went into the dressmaker's shop.

My thoughts returned to the Colt I had laid on the bed. I went over and took my gun out of my holster and replaced it with the pearl-handled 45. When I went to put my gun in my great-granddaddy's saddlebags, I noticed a small rip in the lining of the saddlebags. As I looked closer, I noticed a glimpse of white where the rip was.

Suddenly, there was a knock on the door of my room. I asked, "Who is it?"

It's Dan Walters. Dan Walters is the lawyer I had seen last night about my great-granddaddy. He was the one who had written my mother about Jeb.

"Come on in, the door's open," I said.

He opened the door, and I got the surprise of my life. In stepped the black-haired beauty I had seen in the street not ten minutes ago followed by Dan Walters.

"I would like you to meet my daughter Jenny." She put out her hand and said, "It's nice to meet you. Father has told me so much about you."

I shook her hand and said. "I didn't know Mr. Walters had such a beautiful daughter."

Dan Walters interrupted, "Would you like to join us for breakfast over at the diner, Mr. Taylor?"

"Please call me Buck . . . all my friends do. Besides, Mr. Taylor is my father, I'm just Buck. I would like to join you Mr. Walters, and especially you Miss Walters."

"Thank you. You can call me Dan." "You can call me Jenny." They both said it at the same time. I asked them to give me a few minutes to wash up and I would meet them in the lobby.

We met in the lobby and went across the dusty street to the diner. As we entered the establishment, there were about ten people eating; all eyes turned to us as we were seated. I asked, "Dan, why does everyone seem to be lookin' at us?"

"A lot of people knew your great-grandfather and liked him, so they're possibly just curious about you," Dan said as the waiter came over to take our order.

"I'll have four eggs, six hot cakes, three strips of bacon, and a cup of coffee." I was hungry 'cause I was so tired after my long trip from Texas I hadn't eaten last night. Dan and Jenny just ordered ham, one egg and coffee apiece.

"Did you or any of your family ever hear from Jeb?" Jenny asked.

"No, not for quite a spell, let's see, it seems it was about the time I finished school . . . that was about two years ago. We knew he was looking for silver or gold somewhere in the San Juan Mountains, but we knew it was only an old man's dreams."

Just then the waiter brought our breakfast. I wolfed mine down and was relaxing, looking out the window when I saw an old man looking at me from outside.

"Who's that at the window?" Dan turned to look, but before Dan saw him the old man disappeared.

"Who?" Dan asked, looking puzzled.

"Never mind, he must have just been passin'." Then I remembered the white in the tear in the saddlebags. Suddenly, Jenny asked, "Are you going to be here long?"

"No, just long enough to give me and my horse some rest and see my great-granddaddy's grave. I want to make sure it has a nice marker on it. My mother said that if I found he had died by the time I got here, to see to it. I better be gettin' back to my room. Feels like I've been ran through a gin mill, my bones are even achin'." As I left the diner I noticed how dark it was gettin'. There was some kind of storm building.

When I was across the street and about to go in the hotel, the old man I had seen outside the window in the diner came up to me and, looking around, said, "I'se hears tell that you'se kin to old Jeb!"

"Sure am, I'm his great-grandson Buck. Who are you?"

"I'se be Foster, Jeb and me were kind of friends, that is we met on the trail once in a while and camped together overnight. Could's I'se come and talks to you in you'se room for a while? It might be important to you."

"Shore, come on up." I slapped him on the back and we walked up to my room. As we went up the stairs he kept looking around. We got to my room and I pulled up a chair.

"Have a seat, I'll sit on the bed. What you have on your mind, Foster?"

"This might come as a surprise to you'se, but yours great-grandfather di'nt die too easy."

Puzzled, I asked him, "What you mean by that?"

He got up out of the chair and walked to the edge of the window and peered outside. Then he went to the door and opened it, looked both ways down the hall, then shut, and locked the door. Coming back, he pulled the chair close to the bed where I was sitting and started to tell me a long story.

"Jeb di'nt died of natural cause. He was shot, not by accident. I'se was comin' off one of the trails down the mountain, and hears a shot. When I'se got to where the shot came from, saw two men standin' over his body. Well I'se held back 'cause weren't sure of those two. When they left I'se went down and found Jeb layin' with a hole in his back and all his pockets gone through like they'se lookin' for somethin'. I'se went back to my cabin and hoped no one sees me there."

"Why didn't you go to the marshal with this information?"

"You'se don'ts knows people round heres. They'se don't like peoples like me and Jeb. Think we'se no good, with no family. But I'se knows one of Jeb's family would's show up by the way he talked about your's ma and pa. So I'se knows I'se have to wait and see if one of his family would come. I'se been comin' to town every two or three days lookin. I'se come in last night and saw a horse that looked like it's been on a long trip. This morning I'se seen you'se havin' breakfast with that there lawyer and I'se knows it bound be someone about Jeb."

"Why didn't you come in and talk to me there?"

"I'se don't trust that fancy lawyer or his daughter. He's been buyin' up too many of the claims around here lately. I'se tell you'se one thing, I'se knows he tried to buy Jeb's things 'cause he found some gold or silver somewhere."

"Why do you say that?"

"'Cause his mule was packed down heavy that day he was shot. I'se tell by ways the mules feet left deep tracks in the soft ground. But no one, not even me, knows where he found it."

"Didn't he have a claim filed?"

"Me'se and old Jeb, we'se smart. Knows if a claim was filed, everyone would knows where we'se found anything if we'se ever did. And it's good way to get killed by jumpers. I'se think they'se just tended to wound him and make him tell where it was. I'se thoughts you'se should knows bein' kin. If I were you'se I'se go back to Texas."

"I don't know, this puts a different light on it. I think I'll stick around and try to find out why Jeb was killed."

"If I'se you I'se be careful and not trust anyone. And you'se better make it fast, 'cause looks like a big snowstorm is brewin' up out there. If it starts snowin' in the mountains passes, you'se won't get back to Texas till summer. If you'se needs help I'se have a old place 'bout fifteen miles north of here on the river. I'se better be goin' before someone spots me with you."

"Thanks, Foster, for all the information, I might see you in a few days. So long."

"Good-bye," Foster said and left out the door. I turned around and saw the saddlebags once again.

Chapter Two

As I took the saddlebags apart where they were sewn, I began to see it was a large piece of paper folded up inside. I began to think about what had taken place today; Dan had told me my great-granddaddy was well-liked by everyone; Foster on the other hand said neither of them was well liked by town folks. Then Jenny had asked about how long I was going to be around. I needed to find out more about what was going on around this town, more so now that I had the piece of paper out and could see it was a map of about forty to sixty miles north of Durango. It showed a northwest direction to Foster's cabin on the river, and since Foster said it was about fifteen miles, I judged the rest of the map by that. After the cabin, it showed a northwest direction across the Animo River to Sunlight Peak west to Lizard Head Pass, then northeast to Red Mountain Pass due east on to Red Could Peak. There was a mark halfway down the east side of Red Cloud Peak. There was a note on the back of the map.

"I hope this falls in the hands of a righteous person that will see that it gets to the only family I have, Molly Taylor, Kingsville, Texas. The gun in the saddlebags, if it is still there, I got off a feller that tried to jump my mine. So I am takin' off for Durango with a little ore that I found where the mark on the map is." Signed Jeb Stone.

I had some strong emotions in me knowing I had just read my great-grandfather's last words. I knew now I had to find the people that had killed him. The one way I knew to do this was to find what my great-grandfather had found. This would bring them hot on my trail. I knew one thing, I was going to take Foster's advice and not trust anyone.

I went out of the hotel with a different outlook about this place. It was close to six o'clock as I walked down the dusty street of Durango. On my way to the stables to look in on my horse, I stopped in front of the saloon. I'm not usually a drinking man, but after all the surprises I had today, I could use one. I stepped through the swinging doors and went up to the bar and ordered a beer.

As I stood there I glanced around. There was a large mirror on the wall behind the bar. To the left of the bar there was a door that had a sign on it that said "Private," must be the storeroom or office. As I turned around with my drink in my hand and leaned back with my elbows on the bar and one foot resting on the foot rail, I noticed the wall across the room had a picture of a half-naked woman lying down. Under the picture was a piano with a man playing and the music filled the air. I recognized the tune it was "Oh Susanna." To the right of the piano was a stairs that led up to a walkway that went around three-fourths of the saloon. There were about twelve rooms around the walkway. I saw some men and women going into rooms and some coming out. As I turned around, I thought with a smile on my face, it seemed to be a very lively place.

"You new in town, an't you, mister?" the bartender said.

"Yep, just came in last night. Came to see my great-granddaddy got buried proper."

"Who may that be?"

"That be Jeb Stone, by the way. Where's the graveyard?"

"Well, you go out main about one mile to the north and there she be."

"Thanks, I'm grateful to you."

I finished my beer and left the saloon. As I walked toward the stable, I noticed two men come out after me. One left down the street the opposite way I was going, but the other one was behind me. I entered the stable and lit a lantern, and went over to my horse. I started talking to Blacky, my horse. I had named him that down on the ranch because when he was young he got caught in a mudhole and came out all black from head to tail. He was really a beautiful red stallion. I laughed as I stood there brushing him out thinking of the mud all over him. Blacky nickered like he knew I was laughing at him. When I was through I cut the apple up that was in my pocket and fed it to him, then gave him some oats and hay. As I put out the lantern, I noticed a figure in the doorway. Walking to the door, I saw it was the man that followed me when I came in the stable. As I walked by, he said "howdy." I nodded in reply and then returned to my hotel room.

As I lay in bed I wondered if he had been behind me on orders or if my imagination was gettin' carried away. I woke up the next morning feeling renewed. I had slept like a baby. So I got dressed and went to eat, then saddled Blacky and rode out to the graveyard. It was just off the road in a clearing among the trees. I noticed that the trees weren't the scanty little willows or cottonwood found in South Texas. These were evergreens all of fifty to sixty feet high; they were beautiful. I was beginning to understand what Jeb saw in this raw wilderness.

The graveyard had a white picket fence around it with room for about two hundred graves. Locating Jeb's grave was easy among the fewer than fifty that was already there. To my surprise it had a very nice marker on it with just his name and the year he died. I stood there awhile and let my thoughts wander to the little things my mother had told me about him. With a tear in my eye, I mounted Blacky and went back to town.

I rode straight to Dan Walters's office, tied up Blacky, and went in. Dan looked up. "Hello there, Buck, you look a lot better this morning. Looks like you got a full night's sleep."

"Shore did, slept like a baby."

"That's good, what you up to?"

"Just came back from the graveyard and noticed Jeb's grave had a real nice headstone on it. Wondered if I owe you anything for it."

"Your great-grandfather's horse and mule covered the cost, and there was a few cents left that I used to write a letter to your mother."

"How did you know where to write?"

"We found an old letter in his pocket with your address on it, figured it to be kin."

"Did you find anything more on his pack mule besides what you sold? Like some ore."

"Why no, just some mining tools that we sold, why do you ask?"

"Nothing, was just wondering if he had found anything up in the mountains."

"I guess not, unless someone took it off before my men found him."

"Your men? I thought you were just a lawyer."

"Oh no, I have a ranch south of town and some interest in some claims around here. There's not much money to be made in the law business in Durango right now, but I'm looking to the future, and I see a bright future indeed."

I said my good-byes and headed for the general store which was kitty-corner from Walters's office. I had it in mind to go follow the map Jeb left, 'cause it was clear Jeb wouldn't have been bring ore into town if he hadn't found something worthwhile.

When I stepped into the store, over by the cloth goods stood Jenny Walters. "How'de, Miss Walters."

"I asked you to call me Jenny."

"Well all right, but I never had seen a pretty gal so friendly to me, just an old cow puncher."

"Why, Buck, the way them girls let you get away, so far, they're just insane."

"Well, thank you, Jenny. After you get through, would you care to have dinner with me?"

"I surely would. I'm just about through. I'll go tell my father where I'll be."

"When could I meet you at the diner?"

"Oh, about an hour should do it. Bye now, see you in an hour, Buck."

"Hello, young feller, what can I get for you?" the storekeeper said.

"Well, I don't rightly know, let me see."

"I know how you feel, that gal would make most fellers forget."

I laughed a little, "That's not what I mean. I know I'm going to need about a month's supply of grub, but I don't know what else."

"You'll need a pan to cook in . . . do you drink coffee?"

"Yes, I sure do."

"Then a coffee pot and plate, spoon, fork, and cups. I see you don't need a knife."

I looked down and pulled out my ten incher. "No, this will do me fine. This is what I call my Cottonmouth toothpick. Down where I come from, in deep South Texas, the cottonmouth snakes are so thick around the Nueces River that I use this to stick them with and roast over the fire. A man never would starve if he acquired a taste for snake." With that I put my knife back in place.

"Man, that sounds like one of those tall tales around here. Here, tell these old timers claim there's silver around here you'd have to have a mule for each nugget."

"Well, that's the way tall tales get started. Anyway, maybe you can help me decide. I'm goin' to be doin' some digging along the way."

"Let's see, you'll need two picks, two shovels, some canvas to cover up your pack and for cover for yourself, and some rope to tie it all on your pack horse. What you going to do, look for those one mule silver nuggets?"

I laughed, "Na, just going to try to find where Jeb, my great-grandfather, spent most of his time."

"So your great-grandfather was that old-timer Jeb? Ha, that's funny, he's the one that told me about that silver."

"When did he tell you about it?"

"Oh, about two months before he was shot. I-I-I- mean came down sick. Just a slip of the tongue, so many shootings around here. Well, I think that will do ya, that's, let's see about, make it thirty-five even."

"Can I pick it up in the morning?" I pretended that I thought it was a slip of the tongue. "I need to buy a pack horse."

"Sure, I'll put it in the corner over here. I open at about 5:30, so anytime will do."

I paid him and said thanks and headed for the diner. As I went down the street, I wondered how a nice little town like this could abide with killing an old man living out his last days in the rugged country he loved.

I was about to enter the diner when I noticed Jenny sitting over in the corner. I stopped and watched for a while. Walking over to Jenny was the man that had followed me to the stable last night. Watching closely, I saw her talking to him like they knew each other. Walking over to the table where they were talking, I must have startled them when I said, "Hello, Jenny," because she jumped.

"Oh, Buck, you're here already. Do you know Brady? He works for my father."

"No, only seen him once, like last night when he was following me."

Brady put his hand to his gun and said, "I weren't followin' you."

"Well, you sure like standin' out in the cold for a long time."

Just then he started to draw his six-shooter, but I put my right hand over his gun hand and pushed it back down as I reached with my left hand and pulled out my Cottonmouth toothpick. Just then Jenny shouted, "Brady stop and get out of here, right now."

I relaxed and he threw my hand off and stormed out the door.

"Please, Buck, sit down. I'm sorry about Brady, he has a bad temper. You better watch out for him because he's fast with that gun."

We ordered our dinner and ate quietly. After we finished, I said, "Jenny, I heard some distressing news about what goes on around this town, so I'm going to be leaving in the mornin'."

"Oh, so you're going back to Texas? Well I'll miss you."

"No, sorry, to disappoint you, but I'm not goin' home. I have some business north of here, so I'll be sayin' good-bye now."

With that I got up and walked out the door of the diner. I went about twenty feet and stopped around a corner, then watching the door of the diner, I saw Jenny hurry across the street to her father's office. After about five minutes here comes Brady out of Dan Walters's office going to the hotel. I thought "Well, old Foster might be right about things around here."

I went on to the stable and talked to the owner.

"Do you have any horses for sale?"

"Why, mister, you got a good horse, why you want another one?"

"I need a pack horse for tomorrow, I'm leavin'."

"Yeah, I got some stock in the corral back yonder."

I walked to the corral and looked over the stock. Most looked like they were ready to be plowed under. But one was a nice sorrel with strong shanks and hocks and thighs, with fine withers. I was going to need a strong horse where I was goin'.

"How much for that sorrel over there?" I asked.

"Oh, that's a fine animal, you know your stock."

"How much?"

"Well, let me see (rubbing his chin) I'd say $75."

"And I'd say $50."

"No, couldn't go below $70."

"Well, I can't afford any more than $65."

"That's a deal."

"Will you make sure he gets some good oats and hay tonight 'cause I'm leavin' early mornin'?"

"Shore will."

I paid him along with what I owed for Blacky's board, then stopped and fed Blacky and rubbed him down. After about half an hour I started back to my room in the hotel.

When I entered the hotel, Brady was sitting in a chair against the wall by the stairs, reading a newspaper. I asked the desk clerk how long he'd been there. He told me he had been there about forty-five minutes. I discussed my bill with him and paid up until I left in the morning. Walking up the stairs, I kept my eyes on Brady all the way. I stopped in front of my door and listened 'cause I thought I heard something. Opening the door slowly and peeking in, I saw a shadow and drew my gun, then pushed the door open. I said, "Got you covered." The startled figure put up her hands, then recognizing my voice said, "Oh, Buck, it's only me," then I recognized her as she put down her hands. It was Jenny. I put my gun away and asked, "What are you doin' here in my room?"

"I just had to see you one more time before you left town. I know we only have known each other a few days, but that doesn't matter to me. I have never been this bold before with a man."

She rushed to me and threw her arms around my neck and kissed me with the full length of her tongue. I didn't know what to think, my mind was reeling from the kiss; I had never been kissed like that before. Before my mind came to, she pulled me on the bed and was on top of me trying to open my pants. I regained my senses and pushed her up and said, "Stop it right now, Jenny, we can't do this. It's wrong and I don't feel anything for you."

I was by the window and she was by the door when it busted open with such force it came off the hinges, which caused the intruder to fall on the floor. I looked down and there was Brady lying on the floor with his gun drawn. I stepped over to him and put my foot on his gun hand and took the gun away from him. Pulling him up I said, "What are you doin' here?"

"I thought I heard a fight in here."

"You lie, you knew there was no fight. Now both of you get out of here and leave me alone."

As they left, I heard Jenny whisper to Brady, "You fool, you broke in too early."

I don't know what their plan was, but it didn't work. I could see now why people say beauty is only skin-deep. I had hoped she was a nice and proper girl. I could see now that she wasn't. I put the door back up as good as I could, then went over to the old saddlebags and reached in where it was torn and got out the map. I took my gun belt off and took my knife and cut a slit in the back of my gun belt and folded the map and placed it inside. I turned out the light, got into bed with my clothes on and my gun right next to me and fell into a deep sleep.

When I woke up I took out my pocket watch that my granddad had given me when I was fifteen just before he died. It was fifteen before five, so I got up and washed my face and combed my hair. I fastened my gun belt on after making sure the map was still in place. Picking up my saddlebags and Jeb's old saddlebags, and then my .44-40 rifle, I headed down the stairs on my way to the stables.

Remembering last night, I was cautious as I entered the stable and lit the lamp. There was Blacky and the horse that I had bought yesterday in the stale next to him. I saddled Blacky, placing my saddlebags on him and my .44-40 in the rifle sheath. Then I put a halter and lead rope on the other horse, and mounted and then headed for the general store. Outside I noticed how calm it was, no wind at all and it was becoming a little lighter as I could see the dark clouds.

I went inside and asked the storekeeper about the weather.

"Well, no wind and dark clouds; by late today probably be rainin' here, but up north it a be snowin' in the high country."

"In that case better let me have your heaviest winter coat, and while you're at it, three boxes of .44-40 rifle shells and two boxes of Colt 45s."

"Expecting trouble, are you?"

"Well, you never know and I always like to be prepared for anything, might even have to shoot game to eat."

"What size coat you wear? Looks to me about 46."

"That's about right."

"Here you go, size 46."

"Yea, that fits and buttons up good, thanks."

I got everything out and tied on the pack horse, got on Blacky and said thanks to the storekeeper, and then headed out of town to the north.

As I headed up the trail, I soon came to the graveyard. As I passed, I tipped my hat to my great-granddaddy, Jeb.

When the sun rose higher in the sky, even the clouds couldn't hide the real beauty of the country that was around me. The late fall leaves on the trees were bright red with a touch of orange around the edges. Off in the distance were the tallest mountains I had ever seen. Of course being from South Texas, they could have been five feet and been the tallest I've ever seen. With that I had to laugh at myself out loud. That laugh must have scared the deer that ran out in front of me. A big ten-point buck, but I didn't need any food right now, so I didn't even draw my rifle. It went on about its business.

I was about ten miles out, so I turned off the trail toward the river, because I had decided to head for Foster's and knew it was on the river. I was going to head upriver until I got to his place, so I wouldn't miss it. But just before I got to the river, I stopped and made a fire and got some coffee started and made something to eat. The horses were tied out in the clearing where they could get some of the grass to eat. After I got done eating I packed up everything and started out again.

When I reached the river I turned north, "I should reach Foster's place before dark," I thought to myself. The forest was getting' thicker; I was having to weave in and out among the trees.

Then it started to rain and rain hard. I got my slicker out of the saddlebags and put it on. After about half an hour of steady rain I rode inland, 'cause I didn't want to get caught in a flashflood. I heard when the rain comes down the mountains it gains a force like one of those locomotives and takes everything in its way.

What was that? I stopped to listen, then I heard it again. It sounded like gunfire. I picked up the pace, and just as I reached the top of the knoll, I could see three men with rifles riding around a cabin. I drew my rifle out and started firing from where I was, not intending to kill anyone, but just to run them off. They looked in my direction, but with the heavy rain and the dense forest I don't think they could see me clearly. They took off to the east when I put a couple more shots around their horses' feet.

I went in slowly 'cause I didn't want to get shot at. As I got closer, I yelled, "Foster, if that's you in there, don't shoot, it's me, Buck Taylor." No one said anything. I got to the cabin, and heard someone moaning from inside. I rushed to the, door, kicked it in and rushed inside, but it was too dark to see clearly. Then a weak voice came to me from the far corner.

"Buck, that you'se? It's Foster, I'se been shot."

"Yea, it's me, let me light the lantern and I'll see how bad it is." I found the lantern and lit it and I could see the small, cozy cabin now. Then I saw Foster. I rushed over to him and helped him to the bed, got his coat off and his shirt opened. I could see it wasn't too bad.

"Say, Foster, it's just a shoulder wound, you'll be all right."

"It don'ts feel all right, get me that jug of whisky over there and those clean rags in the drawer over yonder. Hurry boy, you want me to bleed to death?"

As I did as he told me, I said, "I don't think you need that whisky right now."

He grabbed the bottle out of my hand, poured it on his wound, then lay back and took three big swallows of the whisky. "Now, Buck, see if you'se can find that there bullet."

I brought the lantern closer and had a look. "Well, you're the lucky one, it went clean through your shoulder." I took the jug from him and poured more whisky on the wound. He jumped with pain, then fell back on the bunk unconscious. I was glad, now I could bandage the wound without it hurting him. When I finished, he was still unconscious, so I covered him up with his blanket and went out to see about the horses.

There was a small barn. I led Blacky and the sorrel into it out of the weather. When I lit the lantern I saw three stalls over in the far corner. There was a small hay loft, so I went up the ladder; there was a lot of hay and oats. Going back down I saw Foster's mule, "Hi there," I said. "Looks like you're goin' to have company for a few days." I walked over to Blacky and unsaddled him and the sorrel. "Well, Blacky, this is a nice cozy barn." Their ears perked up as I took some hay in my hand and brushed the dampness out of their hair. I got them pretty dry and put them in the stalls, then gave them some hay and oats. Then I fed the mule and got some things from the pack along with my rifle and started for the cabin.

I opened the barn door, and to my amazement the hard rain had turned to snow and the wind had picked up considerably. I had never seen snow except off in the distance on top of the highest mountains. I walked out in it to the cabin and went in to check on Foster. He was still asleep. That's when I noticed how cold it was in the cabin. Then I knew why. The fire in the fireplace had gone out and a lot of the glass was broken out of the windows because of the gunfight a couple of hours ago. So I found some burlap bags and some nails and hammered them over the windows with the butt of my gun. That kept the wind out, but not the cold. Buttoning up my coat around my throat and tying my bandana around my head under my chin, so my hat would stay on and my ears would be protected against the freezing cold, I headed outside to find the wood pile. I stopped around the corner of the cabin and spotted the wood. Then I noticed how much snow had fallen. It had already covered the ground. This was a wonderful place to defend; in the back of the cabin it dropped down straight to a small creek which already had a thin coat of ice. One side of the cabin was built up against a bluff. The only open space was to the front. This made it possible for you to see anyone coming up the trail and very unlikely someone could sneak up on us.

Making about three trips to the wood pile, I got the fire started and had enough wood for a few days. By now it was dark and I was gettin' hungry, so I broke out the grub and fixed enough for both of us. I sat and ate quietly at the window, wondering where those men had gone in this snowstorm and why they were after Foster. The snow was still coming down heavy. It amazed me, this white power snow, how it could fall out of the sky with no let up.

Coming back to reality, I saw a flash of dark on the white surface. It was too far away for me to make out what it was: an animal or a man. But I didn't think it was an animal, 'cause no animal would come out with snow like this. Just then I heard Foster moving and went real fast to check on him.

"How you doin'?" I said to Foster, who was awake now.

"Oh, take more than a claim jumper to do me in."

"You hungry?"

"Sure is.!"

"Well, I got some hot grub on the fire, but first I should wait a minute 'cause think I saw someone comin'. I'm sure it's not an animal I saw 'cause we have a pretty good snowstorm blowin' out there."

I got up and picked up my rifle and went back to the window, but I couldn't see anything else yet.

"I'se knows animals wouldn't be out in snow unless he'd be hungry and it's too early in the winter for that. I'se thinks I'se can get my own grub."

He got up out of bed, and staggered over to the fire.

"Wo, I'se be a little dizzy."

"You all right?"

"Sure, I'se got my legs under me now."

"Still no sign, Foster, you think I was just seein' things?"

"I'se don'ts rightly know, the snow sometimes plays tricks on your eyes when you don'ts know what you'se be lookin' for." He sat back on the bunk and started to eat.

Just then the door burst open and a man rolled on the floor and before I could react, I was lookin' into the end of his rifle.

Chapter Three

"Wait, I'se be all right Dancing Bear!" The man looked toward Foster and blinked his eyes a few times to get accustomed to the light from the fireplace. "This man is friend, he come to help me not to hurt."

With that he took the rifle out of my face and said, "Me not know he friend. True Wind out hunting, heard firing direction of friend Foster wood tepee. True Wind come to village tell us, we come, start snowing, take longer, 'fraid friend Foster died, saw two strange horses in barn."

"This man is Buck Taylor, he'd be kin to Jeb our old friend. He'd come to see Jeb go to happy huntin' ground. Jeb dead, Buck tries to find who killed him and why."

Dancing Bear put out his hand, "Want to shake hand like white man. Jeb my friend, teach me this."

I shook his hand and said, "I'm glad to meet a friend to my great-granddaddy."

"Have two other braves with me."

"We bring them in out of cold," Foster said.

"No, stay in barn, keep look out."

Foster turned to me and told me to get some sleep; that Dancing Bear would keep a look out. Dancing Bear went to the window and sat down. Foster pulled the covers over him and went to sleep. So I lay down with my bed roll and fell fast asleep 'cause it was nearly sunup.

When I awoke, Foster was up and around, and Dancing Bear was just coming in from outside.

"Friend Buck wake."

Foster turned around, "So you'se are. Wants some coffee? Take some of those cobwebs out of your head."

"Sure would, sounds good. Do I smell eggs and bacon?"

"Well, haven't lost you'se sense of smell."

"Put a couple on for me, okay?"

"Sure enough," Foster said.

Dancing Bear came over and sat down beside me.

"Snow and wind stop, no sign men come back. We go to village now."

"I'd like to thank you for comin' and would like to ask how you got your name."

"No thanks necessary, friend help friend always. Got name when little one, father go out four days in woods, far, to find name for me. Come back have big ceremony, told story. Was out in woods two days when came to clearing, stop! Saw bear standing on back legs turning in circle. Father says looks like dancing. I became Dancing Bear. Go now, need help come to village, friend Foster know way. Friend Buck always welcome."

With that little said, he started out the door. I said, "Thank you, Dancing Bear." I went to the window and watched as they went west through the snow.

"Breakfast is ready," Foster called.

I went to the table and sat down and started to eat and think.

"You know, Foster, I have always thought of Indians as my enemies. He called me friend."

"Well, Buck, these ain't just any Indians, these here are Utes, and the Utes are just like any Indians; they were friends to the white man until they started to get pushed off their huntin' grounds. Not that they think they own it, but it's their home and necessary for their survival. When me and Jeb came, we don't try to push or take the land. We started tradin' with them. So they'se trust us as friends, and for a friend they would even die. That is how the Indians is. You'se were talkin' to the chief, so if you'se go to his village everyone would be good to you'se 'cause he liked Jeb lots and any kin of Jeb's would be treated the same as Jeb."

After we ate I went out and fed the horses and Foster's mule. On the way back in I picked up an arm full of wood.

"How are you, Foster?"

"Oh, by day after tomorrow I'll be able to get along about my business and you can get back to what you were doin'."

"I'm been thinkin', Foster; I think I can trust you. You must have been a good friend to my great-granddaddy, so I've got somethin to show you. I need some help. I don't know my way around these mountains. I would have missed your place if it wasn't for the gunfire."

With that said, I took off my gun belt and turned it over and took the map out of the cut I put it in. I threw my gun belt over the back of the chair, and spread the map on the table, "I want you to be my partner and help me find this."

Foster came over to the table and sat down and looked at the map.

"Why, that old buzzard, he found it! Buck this is the silver we'se been lookin' for all these years and my best friend found it. That's why his mule was so loaded down when he was killed. You'se have this, I'se bet whoever killed Jeb is behind you hope'n you'se will led them to it, after they found the silver on the mule."

I told him about what happened in town; that I had liked Jenny a lot but after what had happened I thought her and her father were in on it.

"Buck, you'se find beauty is just skin-deep. Most times, specially some white women. Now Indian women are different, they are always for only the man; what he says is right. They are to please him, you'se can trust them."

"I want you to be with me, Foster; I'll give you 50 percent of anything we find."

"No Buck, that's not right for me. Jeb found it, I'se be glad to help you but I'se take no more than 10 percent. You'se have the map, I'se be yours guide. Anyways, 10 percent will make me rich if it's the strike I'se think it is."

"Okay, we'll start in two days, if you think you'll be all right by then."

"That's fine with me, I'se be fit as a fiddle by then."

We rested the next two days and Foster was his old self again. The wound was healed over and doing fine.

"In the mornin' we'll be headin' out; the temperature outside has gone up and most of the snow has melted."

"Yeah, it was early for that heavy snow. You'se knows, I'se think we should go to Dancing Bear's village, it shows on that there map that it's on the way. It's 'bout one and half days to the northwest."

"I know Dancing Bear is our friend, but why do you want to stop by his village? We have a map and will get there sooner if we go straight through."

"I'se think it be best for you; you need to learn some about the wilderness and they'se be the best teachers in the whole country. You'se see the other reason when we'se get there."

"What do you mean by the other reason?"

"You'se find out, it's be my secret."

We got up early the next morning and saddled and packed the horses and Foster's mule. When I went back inside Foster was ready.

"Foster, you know I think it's colder out this mornin' than it was when it was snowin'."

"I'se figured that 'cause I'se noticed it cleared up last night and it always gets colder up here when it's clear."

We mounted up and headed north up the Animas River on our way to Sunlight Peak. As we came over the first ridge, I couldn't believe the sight of the valley below me. The sunlight was sparkling on the snow that was lingering on the limbs of the trees, making it look like a field of diamonds. This was the first time the sun had been out since I arrived in this beautiful country. The sun had turned this land into a wonderland. I came back to reality when Foster rode up beside me. He started talkin' to me.

"This old sun is sure dryin' out the ground, but we'se have left an easy trail to follow. I'se goin' back to check our back-trail, I'se be back in no time. Sees that peak over yonder? . . . keep headin' to that peak and you'se be right on the trail. If I'se not back by sunset, make camp and keep a sharp lookout. Sees you later."

"Okay, Foster, be careful."

"Sure enough."

After Foster left I kept thinking how anyone could live in this country where it stayed cold for over half a year and snow on the ground for nearly as long. I was used to the opposite, where it stayed above eighty-five degrees for eight months out of the year. Then as the sun crept down toward the horizon, I realized it was the sheer beauty of the country that drew you like a magnet to it and it was beginning to draw me.

It was near dark and Foster wasn't back yet, so I stopped and made camp. I unsaddled the horses and staked them out in a clearin' close by so they could graze freely. I found some firewood that had been dried by the sun all day, so there would be hardly any smoke. The little smoke there would be separated by the branches of the tree under which I built the fire. I got out enough grub for both of us and cooked it up, then got my rifle and sat back away from the fire, not looking into it. If you look into a fire and then have to look into the dark fast, you would be blinded and couldn't see fast enough.

Right then I heard a noise behind me. I turned, but didn't see anything. When I turned back, Foster was standin' there laughing.

"Surprise you, son? . . . wanted to sees how you'se be at night. I'se been out there a while watchin'. You'se be pretty good but you'se be not mountain man, you'll do for the kinds of men which followin' us."

"So, there is someone followin' us."

"Sure is, two men I'se see around town. I'se tailed them until they'se camped and watched them. We'se won't have any problem with them, 'cause you'se know more about outside than they do. You'se may not know about cold climate but you'se knows outdoors all right. Who's taught you?"

"Oh, mostly my father and Jim Backo, whom my father worked for on his ranch. 'Cause the ranch was so large, sometimes you had to be out a week or two at a time. My father would take me with him when I wasn't in school. It was fun to me and I learned a lot. I always wanted to ranch down in South Texas, but seein' this country, I just wonder how cattle would do up here."

As Foster sat down after getting his dinner, he looked at me, "Well, there's some ranches east of here on the plains. I'se not been over there, but I'se heard from drifters passin' about them bein' there. After we'se through here, maybe you'se go over there and see for yourself."

"I might like that if we get out of this all right."

"Sure we will, tomorrow we'se be in Dancing Bear's camp. I'se don't think these fellers behind us will wants much to do with the Utes."

I went out and brought the horses in closer to the camp and staked them. Then I bedded down for the night with my gun next to me.

"Night, Foster."

"Night, Buck, see you in the mornin'."

As I lay there, I heard the horses moving around and nickering. I looked over at Foster as he was rolling out of his bed roll. He saw me and said, "I thinks we'se may have company."

He was to the edge of the trees as I rolled over to get up. I reached the trees, got my gun belt fastened and headed for the horses. When I reached the horses I found they were all right. As I came closer they calmed down when they recognized me. I stayed with the horses 'cause I knew if I went out in the dark, Foster and I might shoot each other not knowing who was who.

Then I heard some shooting over by camp. The shooting stopped and Foster called out, "Come on in, Buck." I reached the campfire and there Foster was standin' over a man lyin' on the ground.

"He's dead, the other one got away." I turned him over. "This is one of the two men that was followin' me in town. I bet the other one is that Brady that works for Walters."

"That's a bet," Foster said. "I'se better keep watch."

"Wake me up in four hours and I'll take over."

"Okay."

I rolled up and went to sleep. I was woke up by Foster shaking my leg.

"Sha, boy, something out there. The horses are sure skittish."

I sat up and got the sleep out of my eyes. Adjusting my eyes to the dark, I couldn't see anything. Finally the horses calmed down, and I said, "It must have been an animal; the horses are all right now. Get some sleep, all right?"

"All right, but wake me up fast if you'se hear anything."

He turned over and was asleep in a minute. Out here in the wilderness you learn to get asleep fast, 'cause you never know when you'll get to sleep again. Nothing happened the rest of the night, so I got breakfast started about 6:00 a.m. The smell woke Foster up a few minutes later. We ate and saddled up, then headed up over Sunlight Peak.

"Man," I said, it sure is high up here, I can hardly breathe this far up."

"It's that the air up here is thinner and when you'se not used to it you'se can't breathe good. Need to go slow 'cause it a be hard on the horses too. If you'se looks down to just beyond the base of the mountain, you'se see Dancing Bear's camp. Don't let it fool you, it's still 'bout four hours until we're there."

Just as I turned in my saddle, I saw a reflection off some metal object on our back-trail. "Foster, we still have someone on our trail."

"I'se knows that all day, but we'se be in Dancing Bears camp before they can catch us. They won't dare come after us in there."

When we reached Dancing Bear's camp about noon, Foster had been right. Everyone welcomed us like we were kin that had been gone for a long time. There were braves and squaws and children on both sides of us all the way to the teepee in the center of the village. Out of the teepee stepped Dancing Bear in his best outfit and the biggest headdress I've ever heard about.

"Glad you come, have big celebration tonight," Dancing Bear said. "Oldest daughter get married to Walking Moose."

"Chief, I'se glad we got here in time to see your oldest daughter, Face Like a Dove, in her time of joy and happiness."

"Bad Jeb not here, you and him like uncle to my two daughters."

"That be one reason why we stopped by. I'se wanted Buck here to meet your youngest daughter."

"Red Bird is helping mother prepare Face Like a Dove for tonight. She be out not too long. You and Buck join men at party now."

We sat down in the circle of men and I watched all of the dancing going on inside the circle. Dancing Bear was the only one sitting higher than the ground. It was a log shaped like a stool. I saw a brave come over to Dancing Bear and speak to him. Then Dancing Bear got up and came over and motioned for us to get up, then he walked away from the circle of dancers. We got up and went over to him.

"What is it, Chief Dancing Bear?" I asked.

"My braves had spotted two men behind you. Braves think same ones attack at cabin before, so they chase them until they sure the men go away."

Foster said, "Thank you'se, Dancing Bear, those may have been the same men. I'se did not think they would come that close to your camp. I'se guess they's not very smart. I'se be sorry we'se brought them that close durin' this happy time in your camp."

"All right, disturb no one. Have seat; not worry tonight." We sat down and enjoyed the rest of the dancing.

The drums stopped and everyone turned to look at the lodge of the chief's at the north side of the circle of dancers. Out came a very pretty girl dressed in a white buckskin with knee-high white beaded moccasins. This had to be Face Like a Dove; behind her came her mother. Then out of the lodge came the most radiant woman I had ever looked upon. Her hair was black as coal looks just before it turns to a diamond, her eyes blue as the ocean far out at sea in the full radiance of the sunlight, and the color and texture of her skin was like a peach just before it ripens on the tree. As they proceeded to the center of the circle, I saw her turn and smile at me. I looked down at myself and wondered how she could be smiling at me. I looked grubby horrid, and had not had a bath or shaved for five days and smelled like a bear in the woods.

Foster poked me in the side, "Sees why I'se wants to come this way."

"Why didn't you tell me about her? Look at me, I'm all dirty."

"It be all right, she knows we'se been on the trail. After the weddin' you'se can meet her."

"No! I can't, not like this."

I watched the wedding to the end, trying not to look her way; afraid she would be lookin' at me. As soon as the wedding ended, I took off for the pond I had seen on the way into the village. It didn't matter how cold it was. I was going to be clean before I saw her again. On the way I stopped and got my razor out of my saddlebags and then dug up some root of a plant I heard the braves talkin' about that was used for soap. When I reached the pond I shucked off all my clothes and jumped in the ice cold water. I was glad it was a little above freezing or the water would have been iced over. I was in shock from the cold water around me. I slowly became used to the water as I lathered up with the soap root. With my hair full of soap, I turned around and there was Foster.

"I'se had a hard time findin' you'se, why did you run off like that? Wants you'se to meet Red Bird, Chief Dancing Bear's daughter."

Nothing could have stunned me more; there beside Foster was Red Bird. I was speechless.

"Red Bird, this is Jeb's great-grandson, Buck . . . Buck, this is Red Bird. I'se guess I'se leave you two alone now!"

"Foster, don't leave me like this, my clothes are way over there on that bush."

"Never mind, I wash clothes for you."

It was Red Bird talkin' to me. I didn't know what to think or do. Remembering the soap in my hair I went underwater. When I came up Red Bird was in the water with my clothes, beating them on the rocks to get them clean. Then it came to me, her dress was on the bank of the pond; she was naked. Finally I said, "Red Bird, you don't have to do that, I can do it."

"No, I do it! Father get mad if I let guest do women work. I build fire on bank and dry clothes for you."

With that she just walked out of the pond without a stitch on her body and put her dress back on and walked off saying, "Be back in minute, you stay in water or you freeze out here."

My mind was reeling from the site of her perfect body when she appeared with a blanket over her shoulder and an arm full of firewood. She built a fire and hung up my clothes.

"Time to get out, you freeze to death."

My mind was full of so many thoughts I had forgotten about the cold. My attention came back to her. She was standing holding up the blanket for me to get out.

"Well, just turn your head."

"Do not be silly, see men all time when take bath, hurry, you freeze."

I had to get out, I was turning blue, so I closed my eyes and got out. I felt her put the blanket around me, her arms were so warm and dainty. I opened my eyes to see her looking down inside the blanket at me.

"Cold water make Buck small, but must be getting warm, Buck is rising to sky." Then she laughed.

Embarrassed, I pulled the blanket away and wrapped it tight around me and sat close to the fire.

"Buck mad at me, I hope we can be good friends."

"No, Buck not mad, just embarrassed, I'm not used to women being around when I take a bath."

"Glad Buck not mad. I like Buck . . . Buck like Red Bird?"

"Sure I like you, you're beautiful. I never saw a girl's body before, it surprised me to see you like that."

"We used to, we see each other all time, when take bath or play in water, warm time of year. What is beautiful? Is good, means you like what see?"

"Yes, I like what I see. Beautiful is like the flowers in the warm time of the year or like a fawn standin' with its mother nursing."

"I understand. Clothes dry, better get back. Father worry."

I got my clothes back on without further embarrassment, and we put out the fire and walked back to the village hand in hand. As we approached, Foster saw us and started grinning. The new married couple was fixing to leave. I went over to Foster as Red Bird said good-bye to her sister and new brother.

"Well, boy, looks like you'se and that pretty little thing hit it off all right. We'se better be on our way early in the mornin'."

"You were right, Foster, these girls are surely different than white girls. They say what's on their mind and don't hide anything. I sure would like to stay around longer."

"We'se could, but we'se got this map to follow and this time of year the weather is unpredictable; we'se could be snowed in those mountains 'til summer if we'se don't leave. You'se can come back."

"Okay, I know we should go."

I walked over to where Red Bird was standing waving good-bye to Face Like a Dove and Walking Moose.

"Where are they goin'?"

"To honeymoon lodge, about two miles away. Custom say they stay away for week, not come out lodge. Not hard if in love. Try make baby."

"Red Bird, do you have anyone you're in love with, I mean, ah well, we have to leave in the mornin' and I wanted to know if it's all right if I come back to see you when we get done. I hate to leave so soon."

"Not in love with anyone 'til today when meet you. Come back maybe we go to honeymoon lodge, try to make baby."

"Red Bird, you embarrass me. I like the way you say what you think and feel, but I'm not used to girls like that."

"Why, white girls not tell truth?"

"Well, they pretend not to like things like that until after they are married. Well, I better get to bed. Foster and I have to get up early in the mornin'. Good night, Red Bird."

"Good night, Buck."

Foster was already asleep when I got back to where we were sleeping. Getting my bed roll and spreading it out I thought how happy I felt inside, I had never felt like this before. I think I'm in love for the first and last time in my life. With Red Bird in my thoughts I rolled over and went fast to sleep.

When I woke up, I saw Foster was already up. I smelled bacon and eggs and coffee. I got up and there was Red Bird.

"What are you doing here?"

"Come say bye to you. Foster says you like these things to eat in mornin', I fix for you. Woman fix for man she loves and man eat if he love her."

So I ate everything 'cause I did love her; I knew that now.

Foster came over to us, "You'se better say your good-byes, we'se have to get now."

I looked her in the eyes and they told me to take her in my arms and kiss her. As I let her go, I said, "I love you, Red Bird, I'll be back."

I mounted up and headed north beside Foster.

Chapter Four

As we went up the next ridge, I looked back, down at the peaceful village where the woman I loved was. I could see smoke rising from the campfires into the sky that was showing the first light of a new day. Foster snapped me out of my daydream.

"Come along, boy, we'se got a long haul 'head of us. This weather ain't goin' to last forever. Come along now."

I hurried and caught up to Foster; now we were out of sight of the village.

"You'se got to get your mind off that there filly. She'd be there when we'se gets back."

"How you know what was on my mind?'

"You'se forgot I'se be young once, even now I'se get the urge once in a while. But you'se could get killed if your mind's not on what you're doin, 'cause those fellers Dancing Bears braves ran off goin' to be watchin' for us somewhere up the trail."

"You don't think they gave up by now?"

"If's you'se be a unlawful man would you'se give up if you'se knows there be hundreds of thousands of dollars waitin" for you? All you'se have to do is follow two fellers to it, then kill them. Their mistake was showin' their hand too us so soon. That might be their down fall if we'se be careful and keeps our eyes peeled for them."

We rode on slow and steady all day. We had to because the trail we were taking was so narrow in some places we had to get off our horses and walk them along. It was a good seven or eight hundred feet drop in some places. We also had to be careful, some of the places were bare of trees which left us open to rifle fire. It didn't make sense to give them any free shots, if it could be helped. They were going to have to work to get us.

Late in the afternoon we stopped at a small stream to let the horses water and get a drink ourselves.

"Foster, should we stop here for the night? It's well covered, there's water and grass for the horses."

"I'se think you'se right but let's go on the other side of this stream about hundred feet up over there."

"Why?"

"'Cause you'se never knows when its goin' to rain up there in the mountains and by mornin' we'se couldn't get across 'cause of high water."

We walked the horses across the stream a few hundred yards, to where there was some good grass for our animals, and made camp for the night.

"You know, Foster, I'm not use to these mountains, I mean, like you said, you have to think it might rain up high. Down in South Texas, you don't have to worry about things like gettin' ambushed or raining up high. Why, it's so flat you nearly have to push the water to make it flow downstream, and well, each tree is about two miles apart, so you can see anyone within range. You ever been to Texas?"

"Nope, closest I'se ever been is eastern New Mexico, but Jeb tolds me lots about it when we camped together likes this."

Foster got the grub out and cooked up some tasty viddles. By the time I finished washing the dishes and putting them away, it was dark.

"You think we should stand watch tonight to look out for those hombres."

"No, I'se think the horses will wake us if anyone or anything comes around. We'se pretty light sleepers."

"I'm goin over to see Blacky, I haven't spent much time with him lately except on the trail; I found this on a bush today, closest thing to an apple I have."

Blacky started fussing when I came up; I cut up the fruit into pieces and he ate it right down.

"That's a good boy, you made friends with the sorrel yet? We're goin' to have to name him. Let me see, how about Lagger, 'cause he's always behind us on the trail. Lagger it is." I went over to the sorrel and rubbed him behind the ears.

"How you like that, Lagger?" His ears perked up as if to tell me he liked his new name. I said 'night to Blacky, Lagger and the mule; then went back to find Foster fast asleep. I climbed in my roll with boots and coat and all 'cause it was downright cold tonight.

"Buck, wake up, we'se have to get goin."

"What's a matter, we haven't had breakfast yet?"

"No time, hurry get the horses ready."

"Something wrong, isn't it?"

"Yea, I'se think there's a blizzard comin'."

"Why, there's not a cloud in the sky," I said as I went to get the horses ready. I was gettin' on Blacky when Foster came in a hurry and told me we better get.

"Son, let's hurry, if what I'se feel in my bones is true then we'se may be in trouble if we'se don't make it through Lizard Head Pass by noon and that's just 'bout how far we are from it."

"Okay. I'll take your word for it."

We were on the trail for two hours when the dark gray clouds began rolling in. "The closest I've come to seeing something like this was a blue norther we get in Texas, but we never got snow with it. I've seen it drop from eighty to thirty-five in two hours."

'Well you'se might get to see it drop from forty to twenty below zero by noon. If we'se be lucky the snow won't come 'til we'se through the pass. Look Buck, up ahead, there, see those two high peaks? That a be Lizard Head in between. When we'se reach that pass we'se be 'pretty near two miles up. We'se get caught in there, we'se just might hang it up, we'se be buried alive with our horses under us."

"It gets that bad? I never knew it a be that bad up in these mountains!"

"Well it is, down in Durango it can snow two, three inches and up here it a be twelve to eighteen inches with the drifts up to fifteen to twenty feet, depending on how hard the wind blows. Better not talk anymore, may need that energy later if it starts snowing."

Right after Foster said that, the wind picked up and started blowing thirty miles an hour. I could tell the temperature was dropping rapidly. It must have fallen a good twenty degrees already. Then it started raining like cats and dogs. It was coming down harder than when I came up to Foster's cabin. I stopped and got my slicker out, and so did Foster. Then we started moving again, trying to keep the ice from building up on us or the horses. The rain turned into hail. I thought to myself, "Hope these don't get any bigger, they'll knock me off Blacky." I looked back to check on Lagger; he was having trouble keeping his footing, so was Blacky and Foster's mule up ahead of me.

"Well, son, I'se think we'se be in trouble now, hail usually means snow next."

We were having to yell at each other to be heard over the wind.

"Foster, look, what is that up ahead?" He turned around in his saddle to look.

"Oh my lord, better start praying, Buck. That's the pass and it's already blocked with snow and it's comin' this way; sure enough it be a blizzard of all blizzards. Our only chance is to head for the top of the mountain over there or we'se be buried. Throw me your rope and hang on for dear life. Whatever happens you don'ts let go of that pack horse, that's our only food."

Foster pulled up and I hurried beside him.

"You'se never been through one of these so let me warn you'se. You'se won't be able to see me at all for the snow. Pull you'se hat down over your eyes and hang on to both ropes for all you're worth. You'se ready?"

"Okay, Foster, I trust you, let's go."

We headed up and up, by now I couldn't see anything. I could fell a pull on the rope in front and in back of me. Blacky was real nervous, I could feel him shaking under me. I think I was more scared than he was, my hands and feet, not to mention ears and nose, felt like they were going to fall off. This went on and on, felt like for days, but I guessed it was only three or four hours. It would be getting dark soon. I didn't think it mattered anyway, 'cause I could barely see my hand in front of my face.

I felt real sorry for the horses; it was up to their knees already, and it looked as if the snow wasn't going to let up one bit. Then there was a tug on the rope, so I looked up and didn't know what to think, after being like in a little box for hours by myself. I could see Foster, barely, but I could see him. I rode up to him.

"Boy, Buck, we'se got lucky, look ahead there."

I looked, but didn't see anything. "What, Foster, I don't see nothin'."

"Waits you'se see it in a minute. Follow me close and don't let go of the rope yet, it may start blowin' hard again."

I kept an eye ahead but all I could see was a clump of bushes sticking out of the snow.

"We'se here."

"Where are we, Foster?"

"See that clump of bushes, we'se get off and start digging like it was gold down there."

I trusted him, although at the moment I thought he was goin' crazy, so I dug in the snow, I couldn't feel my hands anyways. And then lo and behold, there was a cave behind those bushes.

"Well, boy, what you'se think of old Foster now?"

"I could kiss you," I yelled over the howling wind.

"Don't do that, just go in and hope it's big enough for the animals. We'se goin' to need them if we'se goin' to get out of this one."

I dug snow out of the entrance and hurried in. It was dark inside, so I reached in my pocket and got some matches out, hoping they were dry. From outside Foster yelled, "Look out for bear, Buck."

"What, Bear?" hastily I struck the match; it lit, no bears, thank the Lord. Now I could look around better with no fear. The cave went way back. I yelled out, "Bring them on in, it goes way back in." Foster came on in with the animals.

"We'se lucked out son, for a while. Let's get a fire started, if we'se can find any wood."

"Here's a little over here. Not enough for very long."

"It a do for now."

We got it started and then looked farther back in the cave.

"Look, another room, bigger than the outer room."

"We'se really lucked out. Look a whole pile of firewood. This must have been used by someone one winter."

"Foster, I found who used it. There's some bones laid out in a body form."

"Sure is, well we'se can't do anything for him now. But we'se better get busy or we'll ends up like that."

We got started building a fire in the inner cave, which had two smoke holes, which was another piece of luck. Then we unsaddled

Blacky, Lagger, and the mule. We got them as close to the fire as they would come, 'cause we didn't have anything to dry them off with.

"We got food, Foster, but what are we goin to do about feedin' the horses."

"Just you'se hope this don'ts last too long and the temperature goes up and melts the snow enough so they can get down to the grass."

"How about water?"

"We'se can just bring in snow and melt its by the fire in our's hats if need be!"

As foster was talking I went over to look out, but the entrance was already covered with snow again.

"Look, Foster, it's covered with snow."

"It's all right's be warmer like that, we'se get air from the hole over in the back of the cave. I'se been snowed in like this before. Let's eat and gets some sleep, it's already way after dark. We'se think about our problems after we'se get some rest. Let the fire go down in the animals cave, they don'ts need as much heat as we do."

We ate and then rolled up in our bed rolls. It wasn't easy to sleep. Blacky and me been together ever since he was born. It would be hard to sit here and watch our animals starve to death. I finally got to sleep after deciding to do everything possible and that's all that could be done. Me and Foster would be lucky to get out of this alive ourselves.

Waking the next mornin', or at least what I thought to be mornin', it was dark as night in the cave. The fire was out; I began feeling my way to the wood pile to get wood and start the fire again, then put on some coffee. That got Foster up and about. Didn't start any breakfast 'cause I thought we ought to stretch the food as far as it would go.

"That's smart, Buck, you'se knows what to do all right . . . don't have to worry about that."

"Sure, but don't know about the animals."

"That's a problem that has to be solved if we'se goin to make its out of this. I'se tell you what, every day we'se dig a hole to the outside to see if the storm has stopped. If it has let up, one of us will go out and look for grass, thinks it should be me's 'cause I'se knows what to look for."

"We both can go so you can show me what to look for, be my teacher."

"No, 'cause it's dangerous out there; if I'se don't make it back you'se still have a chance. I'se tell you'se some things to look for over the next few days so you will have a better chance if I'se don'ts come back. Right now we'se better rest all we can."

We sat around all day. It got very boring; I had to walk around, so I went and dug out a hat full of snow, let it melt by the fire then gave it to the horses and mule. I had to make about ten round trips before the animals were satisfied.

We dug to the outside later in the day, but the blizzard was still blowing as hard as ever. This went on for three days and nights as far as we could tell. It gets a little confusing when you can't tell night from day. My pocket watch wasn't much good; I knew the time but couldn't for the life of me tell if it was night or day.

During this time Foster told me things to do and not to do. Like when you go out make sure there is ground under the snow 'cause sometimes the snow forms little bridges that looks safe but are deadly. Take a piece of cloth and make little slits in it to look through 'cause the bright sun reflects off the snow which could be blinding. This is called snow blind. Look around large boulders for grass, because wild animals couldn't trample it down in the summer and fall; this is where the grass would be the tallest and easiest to get to. Be on the lookout for game because they are hard to spot, their winter coats blend in with the snow. Most of all, be on the watch for wolves, they're hungry this time of year. They usually don't attack humans unless their hungry. I tried to remember all of this and more. Foster taught me a lot in a very short time.

On the fourth day, I dug out of the cave and there was light shining above.

"Foster look, the sun's out; I said diggin' all the way out, the winds stopped blowin' so hard."

Craw in out of the hole I dug, Foster stood up shading his eyes.

"So it has, I'se get some things together and go out lookin' around awhile, it looks about one o'clock, I'se have two or three good hours to look around. You'se stay here with the animals, I'se try to find something to make snowshoes out of."

With that he packed up some gear and found a long stick in the cave to punch through the snow with, then took off. I tried to fill the hole back in as good as could be done, so the cold air wouldn't come in. Two hours went by. I kept hoping nothing had happened to him, 'cause it would be nearly impossible to get out of here with no help from anyone. As I sat by the fire, my mind began to wander back to Red Bird. It seemed like a year had gone by instead of just two weeks. Remembering Red Bird and her people put my mind at ease. That's when I dropped off to sleep. In my dream I could see myself on Blacky riding among a large herd of cattle. Coming through the cattle up to a large house, standing on the front porch was my beautiful Indian maiden, Red Bird. Beside her were two small children, one girl that looked like Red Bird and a boy about a year older than the girl that was the spitting image of me. Stepping out of the saddle, I took them in my arms to kiss them. A draft of cold air brought me out of a dream world into reality. Foster was shaking me.

"Buck, wake up, Buck, wake up."

"You're back, I fell asleep."

"The fire's out, you'se nearly froze. I'se get a fire goin'. Come over and get warm."

Getting to my feet, I went to the fire and started to warm myself.

"What time is it? How long you been gone?"

"It's after dark already, been dark for hours. I'se didn't find much of anything, some dried out grass, maybe enough to last a day or two. Think I'se knows where the horses can be taken through to some better grass. They'se have to dig for it. It snowed so much I'se nearly got lost, everything looks so different. Looks what I'se found, we can make snowshoes."

"What do snowshoes do?"

"They make your feet like webs, so we'se be able to walk on top of the soft snow instead of sinkin' up to our knees. I'se goin' to eat a little then get some sleep, we'se take the horses out day after tomorrow after the snowshoes are built and ready for us to use."

"Okay, Foster, get some sleep, I'm goin' to see to the animals."

I went into the next room of the cave and built up the fire, then sat and watched the horses and mule munch on the little bit of grass that Foster had brought back. At least they got something in their bellies after four days, but not enough. I went back to where Foster had fallen asleep and set back to think, and I wrapped a blanket around me. That dream I had was so real, I can't get it out of my mind. But if anything was going to keep me alive, that dream was it. I fell asleep again thinking about Red Bird.

For the next two days we just ate a little, drank some coffee and slept off and on.

"We'se be goin' out today, don'ts saddle the horses, we'se cant's ride them anyways. Looks what I'se made for our feets."

"So that's snowshoes? Show me how to put them on."

"You'se just put your's feet in here like this, then bring this over like a strap to keep them on. Get the horses and I'se get my mule and let's go out. Don'ts forget the cloth around your eyes."

We dug the snow out of the entrance enough so the horses could get out. It was good to be outside again and the animals were elated to be out. I saw what Foster meant about the sun reflection off the snow. It would have been blinded without this cloth over the eyes. The snowshoes worked so well, I could tell 'cause the horses were sinking in the snow up to their knees. We had to go slow 'cause of the animals bogging down in the snow. It took an hour to go a mile. I could see that Foster was following the trail he had took before; I could see his tracks in the snow. I caught up to him.

"Man, it's cold out here, what you think it is?"

"Its must be at least twenty below zero. That's why you'se never wants to stop movin' for very long, you'se freeze to death right where you'se stand. See's that stand of trees over yonder? I'se think that's the frozen pond I'se found the other day."

We reached the frozen pond, there were big boulders to the north of the pond which kept the snow from getting, so deep.

"See those boulders? We'se starts diggin' down in the snow beside them, the horses may get the idea that there's grass down there."

I started diggin' on one side and Foster on the other.

"Come, Blacky, dig."

He watched me for a minute, then like a blow to the head he was beside me pawing the snow. Then here comes Lagger, and he started on the other side by Foster. We were down to the bottom and there it was, all that lovely grass. Then I took my rifle butt and broke through the edge of the pond. The water trickled out and the horses had to drink fast before the water froze again. Reaching in my pocket, I found two long pieces of rope that I had tied the pack on at the store in Durango.

"Look, Foster, I found these in my pockets. We can cut a lot of grass around here and tie it on the animals."

"Boy, you'se goin' to make a mountain man yet. That's the best idea I'se heard yet. We might find a rotten tree so we'se can take back some firewood to."

We hurried and loaded the animals with the grass then started back to the cave. I could hardly feel my feet and hands by the time we were only halfway back.

"I'se wants to make a little side track here. The first time out I'se set some traps."

"All right, but let's hurry, I'm freezin' out here, seems like the wind picked up."

"Sure is pickin' up, here we'se be. Why, there's nothin' here, looks like wolves got our game out of the trap. Looks like four or five in the pack. We'se better get haulin' back before those wolves spot us."

The animals started getting jumpy. I turned and there they were right on us. Drawing my gun, I got off three shots; with two wolves down and dead, the others took off. We stepped up our pace and came within sight of the cave and Foster stopped.

"Buck! Over there, a dead tree! We'se needs more firewood we'se goin' to be out by the time this one's over. We'se got to stop and take a chance."

"All right, but let's make it fast."

The tree was so rotten that it fell into pieces when I pushed on it. We gathered up the pieces, and loaded them on Foster's mule. Foster led the way 'cause he had found the cave before in the dark, and it was pitch-black now. He found the entrance and we dug in. The storm was already whistling around us as we led the horse inside. Unloading the grass and storing it in our section of the cave, 'cause it was going to have to be rationed just like our food was. Foster and I had only been eaten one meal a day, and I wasn't a heavy man, so this couldn't go on too much longer or I would be skin and bones. We got the fire going after we rubbed down the animals with a small amount of grass to dry them off.

"You'se knows, Buck, I'se seen lots of fast draws but when you'se killed those wolves, thats be the fastest I'se ever seen."

"That wasn't fast at all, my daddy would had been ashamed. If it would had been warm weather, I'd have gotten all four before any could have gotten away. Let me tell you what my daddy told me. He said never use a gun unless need be and only when there's no other choice, never show off with your gun, 'cause once someone knows how fast you are that gives them an advantage over you. They know what to expect and can find a way around your fast gun. See, Foster, if it hadn't been for those wolves coming upon us sudden like, you may not have ever known how fast I was. I'd appreciate it if you don't ever tell anyone 'cause you never know who we're goin' to be up against when we find that mine."

"Count on me, son, I'se never tell if you'se says don't. Besides, way that storms blowin' out there we may never get to see anyone again . . . Don't look so down, I'se was just funnin', I'se been in worst spots than this before. In fact one time with Jeb, it was winter, just like this, it was over northeast of here at a place called Pike's Peak, about 1840. Anyway, it was about twenty below zero with wind blowin' 'bout thirty miles an hour when I'se stepped down in the snow and it gave way. Must have fell over a hundred feet; lucky for me it was deep snow or I'se would have been dead. Well unlucky I'se was, 'cause I'se hurts my ankle so bad I'se could not get up and the snow was so deep I'se could not even crawl. My mule was up there somewhere, I'se thought I'se be a goner. In that kind of temperature I'se be dead in an hour or less. I'se try to move but just would go deeper in the snow. But that day luck was really with me because I'se had fallen right on the trail Jeb was on. When he found me I'se was already unconscious, but he tied me to the back of his mule and took me to his small cabin. He told me later that he found me 'cause my old mule was bellowing so loud he could hear him over the wind. That's when he saw the place where I'se fell through the snow. Sure enough, that's how we'se first met and were friends ever since."

"That's thirty-one years ago, you all knew each other a long time. Why, that's before I was born."

"Yes, I'se remembers the day when Jeb got the news you'se been born. We'se went into town and he bought everyone in the saloon two rounds with a little bit of silver he had found. Tell you'se the truth, that is why I'se come with you'se, figures I'se owe Jeb that much. Didn't want you'se gettin' killed like him. Now that I'se got to know you, I'se like you'se a lot; I'se see a little bit of Jeb in you. Now I'se owe you'se to for my life."

"Why you say that?"

"'Cause those wolves would have sure made me their dinner if you weren't there and don't you'se forget back at my cabin, those guys would have kilt me for sure."

"You don't owe me nothin', I just happen to be in the right place at the right time, that's all. I'd be glad to do it again. Anyway I've learned a lot about my great-granddaddy; he wasn't a fool like some people thought. He had a dream and didn't stop 'til he realized it come true. It nearly really came true for him and I'm goin' to see that it does through me. Hopefully he's watchin' from somewhere up there and maybe his boss will help us get out of this fix we're in somehow."

"Buck, he sure would be proud to hear you talkin' like that. Believe me, he surely must be helpin' in some way or we'se be dead already."

"I don't know why you think you owe me for savin' you. If it wasn't for you, I'd be buried alive in that first snowstorm, not to mention findin' this cave that saved us and the animals."

"Yea, well I'se guess that's what friends are for, to help each other when need be. We'se better get some rest now, we'se don't have much grub left maybe enough for a week. After this storm, if it clears, we'se goin to have to try makin' it to Telluride and hole up for what looks like a long winter. With this kind of snow we'se be lucky to make the thirty-five miles in ten days. If we'se make it there we'se be all right and it's direct west of Red Mountain Peak where we'se be headin'."

We got to sleep that night, but the storm kept on raging like the weather was out of control. I'd never seen anything in my life that could come close to this. It was so cold, even in the cave one side felt like a frozen lake, and the other side was roasted by the fire. We both had to keep turning like a roasting pig at a party.

This went on for a week. We had been cooped up in the cave for three weeks. It had been four weeks since I had seen Red Bird and nearly six weeks since Durango.

"Merry Christmas and happy New Year's, Foster."

"What's a matter, you'se be loco or what?"

"No, sir, I just been figurin' and I think we missed the holidays. It must be January by now."

"You'se knows, come to think on it, I'se think you'se be right, Buck, so Merry Christmas and Happy New Year's to you'se too."

The next morning we woke up, and I went to feed the animals. They were losing lots of weight, so I melted some snow to give them. I yelled to Foster, "Come here, Foster, hurry."

Hurrying over to where I was, he grabbed his rifle on the way.

"What is it, son?"

"Listen closely."

"I'se don't hears nothin'."

"That's it, the wind, it stopped."

"Hurry, let's dig out."

We got the snow out of the way, one last time I hoped. Sure enough, there it was; that big beautiful sun hurting our eyes. It was so bright, and not a breath of wind was moving. We started jumping up and down with joy.

"Buck let's get a move on. You'se feed all the grass to the animals, we can't take it with us, and they're goin' to need the energy for the trip. After that, get them packed and ready to go. I'se goin' to fix us up a good hot breakfast. We leave in an hour."

I was humming while getting the animals ready. Then Foster called.

"Come and get it before I'se throw it away."

Going to the other room of the cave I sat down and started eating. Then Foster spoke up.

"I'se know you'se happy, so am I'se, but we ain't out of the woods yet. If we'se be very lucky we'se could make it to Telluride without another storm hittin' us."

As we finished our grub, I said to Foster.

"Well, you know right now I feel very lucky, just like Jeb and the Lord are sittin' right on my shoulder."

"I'se know how you feel, been feelin' the same way, like there's a warmth around me."

Chapter Five

We left the cave with a good feeling around us; the sun was out, the wind wasn't blowing and we were having an easy time of it with the snowshoes that Foster had made. I couldn't say the same thing for the horses. Every time they took a step, they went up to their knees, and sometimes all the way to their forearms quarter in the snow. It was a slow process working our way off the top of the mountain.

"See that over there, Buck? That's why we'se had to go up the mountain instead of through the pass."

"You mean that's Lizard Head Pass? It looks like part of the mountain."

"Believe it or not, the bottom of that is six hundred to seven hundred feet below the top of this snow fall. If we'se been caught in there in that storm, nobody would have found us 'til spring."

"I believe you, but bein' from where I'm from, it's hard for me to image just how anything so wonderful and beautiful as this country is can be so deadly."

We were off the top of the mountain and were now going down a narrow trail. Foster was in front, pushing the snow off the trail so the horses wouldn't have as much trouble going down. If we slipped, it was a long way to the bottom. "I'se hope we'se hits the bottom before nightfall. I'se don't want to get caught on this trail all night. We'se have to sleep standin' up, 'cause we'se wouldn't make it down in the dark."

So we went winding down the mountain. I was watching Foster's every move; I wanted to learn all that could be learned from my old friend. When we stopped for a breather I got to look out over the valley below. It was like a wonderland of snow; even the trees were covered with it. Then something caught my eye.

"What's that over there?" As I pointed, Foster looked up.

"That a be where we'se be headin', that's Telluride, but don't be too happy, it's still about twenty-five miles. Come on, we'se got to get off this here mountain before night."

So we went on and on, slowly working our way down the trail. I took another look toward the town, but could not see it anymore. We were getting below the tree line, and just before dusk we were standing in the valley that had been below us that morning. My legs and arm muscles were sore because of all the weeks spent sitting around the cave.

"We'se make camp under this here ledge, it will protect us a little. Let's try to find some wood. It's goin' to smoke a lot, 'cause it will be wet, but I'se don'ts think anybody that's lookin' for us goin' to be out in this weather. If they are their not in their right mind, I'll tell you that."

We gathered up enough wood for a fire all night. We weren't in the open, so we didn't have to worry about the wind chill. We found some trees that were thickly grouped to tie the animals under and keep them out of the wind.

The next morning was the same bright day. We got ready and left early. Anyway we didn't have any food and moving kept our minds occupied and our bodies warm, if that was possible in these icy surroundings.

This went on for two more days; no food for us or the animals; we had to eat snow for water. Then on the fourth day we spotted some tall grass sticking out of the snow. We dug down and the animals ate their fill. As they got done, I spotted an object moving in the distance from where we were.

"Foster, look, what is that? You see it?"

"Can't make it out . . . let's get goin'."

The snow wasn't as deep now; we could go around the deepest drifts, so we took off our snowshoes and mounted up.

Blacky was in poor shape; his bones were sticking me through the saddle blanket. It still was slow but not as slow as walking. As we got closer to the moving object, I stopped to look.

"Look, Foster, it's a moose!"

"Yep, that thing must be nearly dead, look how thin he is and movin' so slow."

"Well it's either him or us."

Taking my rifle, making sure it was still working, I aimed and shot it through the head. He went down, and didn't move at all. We butchered it and packed it on Blacky and started walking again. If we took time out to gather wood, start a fire, and eat we would loss valuable daylight. We kept walking to keep warm; that short time in the saddle made me feel like I was goin' to freeze. We planned to eat when we stopped for the night.

That night we had a feast, or at least to us it was after four days without anything.

"You'se know, son, if everything goes all right we'se goin' to be in town day after tomorrow sometime."

"You really mean it? I can't believe that town I saw from the mountains is this far. It sure is a big country."

"This here is God's country, if you'se learn to live with it and not fight against it you'se be all right. Now let's get some sleep and get an early start."

"Sleep? I haven't got that much sleep because of trying to keep from freezin'."

"Know what you'se mean, it's hard but I'se think this here country is worth it. Wait 'til spring and summer, you'se love it. Good night, Buck."

"Good night, Foster."

* * *

Next morning we ate fast 'cause we weren't going to stop until we hit town. We could tell we were near town when we came to a road, it had been cleared and there were tracks, wagons and horse tracks. We kept going, we were still walking 'cause the animals were in bad shape to be ridden.

"We get to town and get the animals to the stables, I want a hot bath and shave if possible."

"I'se wants a drink of beer, I'se gettin' tired of eatin' snow for something to drink."

"I don't drink much, but wouldn't mind a beer myself. I'll join you for that drink, then my bath comes next. Don't worry about money, Foster, I got plenty for both us. We'll get a room at the hotel."

"Okay by me, not used to a hotel bed, but for once it might feel great."

As we looked up ahead, there it was. The town was nothing fancy but it sure looked great to me.

"Don't like towns much but this one's a sight for sore and nearly blind eyes."

"Know what you mean . . . mine feel strange too."

"Like I'se told you'se it's the snow even with the rags around them, but they'll be all right after a couple days of rest."

We were on the main street now and everyone was looking at us. As we headed for the stables, a man came over to us.

"Hello there, I'm the sheriff of Telluride. Looks like you fellers and your animals had a pretty ruff time of it." I let Foster speak up; I didn't know how much to be let known after the last town I was in.

"We'se sure did, got caught on the other side of Lizard Head Pass in a storm a few weeks ago. Got lucky, we'se found a cave near the top."

"You're sure lucky. You should be dead, that was the worst storm I ever remember."

"Well sheriff, we'se better get to the stables, our animals are in bad shape. We'se see you around, we'se goin' to be around town for a while. So long."

"By the way what's ya'll name."

"I'se be Foster and this here is Buck."

We got to the stables and gave the owner a twenty-dollar gold piece.

"Mister, you take care of these animals and get them in shape. Give them some oats and hay and if you rub them down good, there'll be an extra ten dollars more for you. They had a hard time of it and they've been good to us. I'll be back in the morning to check up on them."

"Thanks, son, I'll take real good care of them. You can count on me."

"We'se better get along, Buck, I'se be ready for that beer."

"Me too, let's go."

I noticed, as we walked down the street, how muddy it was from all the wagons, buggies and horses going in and out of town. The snow was all piled up along the wood walkway in front of the stores. I guessed it was the snow that had to be shoveled off the walkways. There was no snow on the roofs of the buildings because of the wood stoves that would be going continuously in the stores. The temperature was still in the low teens.

Telluride was a very small town; it consisted of only one street, the main street, with the stables and the blacksmith shop at the far end going out east to the sheriff's office at the west end and in between was the general store, dress shop, barbershop, and the bank. I mustn't forget the saloon that we were standing in front of or the hotel next to it.

"You go on and get your beer I'm goin' to the hotel and register us for two rooms. I'll join you in a minute. While you're at it, Foster, see if they have any food to eat and order some for me."

"Take your time, I'se got some catchin' up to do. I'se be dry as a bone."

We parted. He went to the saloon, and I went to the hotel. Walking through the doors it was noticeable that this was a nice and clean hotel. To my left was an inside door that led to the saloon; this was convenient for Foster who would possibly spend a large amount of time this winter in there. I walked up to the counter, but no one was there. I hit the bell a couple of times and out comes a man about forty-five with a bald head and skinny as a rail. Reaching in his pocket to put his thin metal-rim glasses on, he looked up at me.

"May I help you, young man?"

"Yes, sir, I need two rooms for me and my partner, he's in the saloon right now . . . next to each other if possible. Quiet also."

"Sure enough, you'll have the place nearly to yourself this time of year. We hardly get any visitors this late in winter. This is the most we had in four or five years, I recollect. Sign here."

"I'll sign for my partner too, if that's all right."

"Sure thing."

Glancing down, I signed for us both, then noticed the name above mine. "How long this feller been here?"

"Let me think, been about . . . now I remember it was the day we got that first blizzard that closed the pass. Him and his friend been here ever since. No place to go until spring thaw unless you live in one of the ranches nearby."

He turned around the register and looked at the names.

"Buck Taylor and Mr. Foster. You the fellers came over the pass, the sheriff was telling me about? That's a real accomplishment; people be talkin' 'bout it around for years to come. I been here twenty years and nobody done it in that time."

"We were real lucky, that's all there is to it, but I better get over to the saloon. Hadn't had anything to eat since yesterday."

"Don't forget your keys. Here they are, room 101 and 102, right in front above us here."

"Thanks, oh yeah, can I get a hot bath somewhere around here?"

"Sure thing, be waitin' in your room in about half an hour. By the way, ya'll staying 'til spring, right?"

"Looks that way right now. I'll be back in a while for that bath."

I went through the side door into the saloon. There was Foster at the bar.

"Let's set at the table over there. Bartender bring me a beer over there." He waved his hand indicating that he would. Me and Foster had a seat at the table.

"You know, Foster, you never told me your last name. I just signed you in as Mr. Foster. Don't even know if that is your last name."

"Foster is my last name, but let me see, been forty years since I'se thought of my first name. Thinks it's, I'se think John, yea that's it, John."

"It didn't seem to matter until I went to sign you in. By the way here's your key."

The bartender brought us our dinner and some more beer. This was to me like one of our big barbecues back home, after what we've been through. There was ribs, salad, beans, and believe it or not some peas and carrots. Unbelievable in this snow-bound place. As I looked up to speak, I saw the man that was registered at the hotel.

"We're goin' to have to be careful," I said in a whisper.

"Why you'se whisperin' like that?"

"Foster, two men in the corner over there."

He glanced over his shoulder, "What about them?"

"I saw their names on the hotel register. One I know, it's Brady, the one that works for Dan Walters in Durango. The other one I don't know. They got in the day before that snowstorm closed the pass."

"They'se must be the ones Dancing Bear's men ran off from his camp, when we'se were there."

"We had a run-in when I was in Durango, so he don't like me very much. Be careful, he's mean. I'm goin' to go to my room now, got a hot bath waitin'. You can take one after me if you want."

"No's, thanks, I'se not due 'til spring."

I laughed, and headed to my room, keeping an eye on the corner where Brady was sitting until I got out of his sight. As I passed the clerk at the desk, I asked, "You get my bath?"

"Yes, sir, some soap and towels too."

Putting my saddlebags over my shoulder and tightening my grip on my rifle, I went on up the stairs to my room. I looked, and had the key for 101 in my hand, so I unlocked the door and went in and locked it again. There it was, that beautiful tub of water. Putting' down the saddlebags and rifle, within reach of the tub, I started undressing. Put my six-shooter over the chair and got my clothes off and got in the tub. Could feel my feet and legs tingle from the warmth of the water. After weeks of freezing, this was like heaven above. I just laid back, shut my eyes, and relaxed.

I must have fallen asleep because there was a knock on the door that startled me. I grabbed my rifle.

"Yes, who is it?"

"Mr. Taylor, I have more hot water for you, but the door's locked."

"Just a minute."

I got out of the tub, wrapped a towel around me and opened the door a little. The woman pulled the door all the way open and came in and dumped the water in the tub.

"That's all the water you're going to get so you better hurry up before it gets cold."

"Well, get out so I can."

"Go ahead, I've seen a man naked before. If there's anything else you might need I'd be happy to oblige you."

With that she pulled my towel off and lifted up her skirt. I jumped back in the tub.

"No, thanks, I'd be needin' none of that."

"Huh!" she said.

Silver Buck

She went storming out of my room, and I locked the door once again and finished my bath. I then shaved and washed my clothes and hung them to dry. It was cold, but my clothes were dirtier than I was, so they needed washing also. I went on to bed, 'cause I was sure Foster would be drinking all night, and went to sleep.

When I woke in the morning and walked over to the window, it was a cloudy, gray day again. I had to go check on Blacky and Lagger, so I got dressed and went to Foster's room and knocked on the door.

"Who is it?"

"It's me, Buck."

"Why, come on in."

I walked in and there was Foster in bed with the girl that tried to get in my bed last night. She was laying there naked from the waist up.

"Sorry, excuse me."

"That's all right, just one of the whores around here. Told you'se back on the trail I'se sometimes gets the urge."

"Well, I just stopped by to tell you I'm goin' to eat, then check on the horses. Oh, by the way, it looks like snow again."

"Let it snow all it wants now, we'se got all the comforts of home. You'se goes on and check on the animals. Make sure he takes cares of my old mule too. Meet you'se later in the day."

"Sure, you should keep the door locked, you know who's down the hall."

"Hey, doll, goes lock the door."

The woman got out of bed all naked and came and shut and locked the door. I stood there with my eyes bugged out. Red Bird was missed very much. Trying to rid my mind off those thoughts, I turned and went down and ordered breakfast. I sat there and enjoyed my meal, relaxed and clean. The last month now felt like a dream. Then my thoughts turned to my mother. She was surely wondering what happened to me. Going next door to the hotel, I asked the clerk for some paper and a pencil. I went back and sat at the table and wrote my mother what had happened and that I was going to stay a while until late summer. I told her not to worry about me, that I had met the girl of my dreams and I hoped she didn't mind, but she was the daughter of a Indian chief.

Buttoning up my coat, I went over to the general store.

"Excuse me, but do you think this will get through?"

"Good thing you came in today, the mail is just going out, first time in over a month. Let's see, oh yeah, Texas. Might take a while, but it'll get through."

"Fine, how much is it?"

"Two cents. Well, how you like being the talk of the town, being out there a month and live to tell about it?"

"I didn't know it was the talk of the town, but I'm glad to be here alive, that's for sure. Thank you, but I got to go see about my horses . . . they were in a lot worse shape than I am. We're goin' to need some supplies in the spring."

"I'll be glad to help you anytime, just let me know."

I walked down toward the stables. With the cloud cover hardly anyone was out 'cause it seemed much colder without the sunshine to warm the soul. Upon entering the stable, I saw Blacky and Lagger.

"How you boys doin'? You all look a little better, but you got a lot of weight to put back on."

"They'll be all right with some good care. Their coats was sure in a mess."

"Here you go, Blacky, and here's one for you too, Lagger." I cut up two apples and let them eat them out of my hand.

"How about the mule? I want him taken care of just like the horses. They're goin' to have the rest of the winter to get back to normal."

"Oh, that's good, they'll be in fine shape by then and you don't have to worry about that mule, he's strong as an ox."

"Well that's good, I'm goin' to get now."

As I left, I rubbed Blacky and Lagger behind the ears and went out down the street. The thick gray clouds were rolling in fast from the northwest over the mountains. Walking as fast as my legs could carry me, I went straight to the barbershop. When I opened the door, the barber was giving someone a shave, so I sat down to wait my turn. It's something how nearly all the barbers look alike with the large handlebar mustache with side burns nearly to the chin. Then there was the way they dressed with a white shirt and a garter belt on the upper part of the arm and that funny part down the center of the hair which was turned up on the ends and the black shoes and black pants.

"Hey, mister, it's your turn."

I had been daydreaming, then I saw Brady walking out the door. "Better watch myself, I could get killed like that," I thought to myself as I got in the chair. But then Brady wouldn't be the type to shoot someone in front of a witness, his type shoots in the dark, in the back. I still better be more careful.

"Well, gent, what'll it be?"

"Oh just make my hair look neat and give me a shave. Gave myself one last night but I was so tried don't think I did a very good job of it."

"I'll fix you up all right. You do have a few cuts, what you use, your knife?"

"No, but my razor is pretty dull. Been up in the mountains for a while."

"So you're the one that made it over the pass. Everyone in town knows about that. Hear tell you're goin' to stay in town all winter."

"That's right, sure does get around fast."

"Well, you got to understand this here is a small town so we don't have much to talk about in the winter, 'cause we're snowed in most of five months. We get pretty well excited when someone makes it in to town. We got some mail in today, that's even unusual this time of year. From the looks outside we won't get any more 'til spring thaw. That's it," he said as he let me out of the chair.

"How much I owe you?"

"It's on the house this time; it's a privilege to talk to someone that made it over the pass this time of year. Bring me that razor of yours before you leave this spring and I'll sharpen it free." "That's sure neighborly of you . . . thanks."

"Don't think nothing of it, but next time you're in here, mind tellin' me how you managed it?"

"That's a deal. You can count on it. So long now."

As I went out the door, I saw the barber knew what he was talking about. It was starting to snow again and that wind was blowing the snow in big swirls up in the air then down to the ground. I buttoned my coat up to my neck, put my hands on top of my hat to hold it on, and headed into the whistling wind across to the hotel. I made it just in time; that wind had taken the breath out of me. I pulled the door open and stepped through. The wind pulled the door out of my hand and slammed. Leaning back against the door, I said to everyone who had stopped what they were doing to look what caused the door to slam.

"Think we're in for a bad one this time."

I walked over to the desk for my key while everyone went back to what they were doing.

"Need my key," I told the desk clerk.

"Here you go. You know this looks like the storm that's going to keep us all in 'til spring."

"I won't mind, I'm pretty tuckered anyway."

I waved a thanks to the desk clerk as I went up the stairs to my room and thought I should go check on Foster. I walked over to his door, but just as I started to knock, I heard voices coming out of his room. That old devil, he was still at it with that whore from last night. I decided to go on to my room and call it a day.

I woke up during the night, and didn't know what woke me until I heard the now-familiar whistling whirlwind outside. It seemed that the wind came right through the walls of my room. I really felt cold, so I put on all my clothes and climbed back in bed, but couldn't go back to sleep. That wind was creeping into my mind and would not leave until finally I let my mind go back to the happy days on the ranch. That got me relaxed and drove me into a deep sleep. Morning came, so I thought, but it was black and still night outside. I lit a lantern so I could see what was going on. I looked at my watch, and sure enough it was eight o'clock. Walking to the window, I couldn't see anything, then it came to me: it's snow out there, that's why it's so dark. The snow had blown all the way up to the second floor and covered up the window. This must be what they meant when they said snowbound. At least it felt warmer inside since the snow blocked the howling of the wind out. I decided I might as well go back to bed. I still hadn't recuperated from our ordeal in the cave yet.

When I woke I went downstairs and the few people that were registered in the hotel were milling around. I stopped and had a seat at the foot of the stairs to listen to some of the conversations. One woman was saying, "We'll all die in here." And another, "By the time this storm quits we won't be able to dig out to save our lives." Then the third person in the group, "We'll starve to death." Here the hotel clerk spoke up.

"We won't starve, the saloon next door has plenty of food for all of us. That's why we put a door on the inside of the building leading to the saloon. Besides, let's see, there are only nine of us, we got enough food next door for two weeks."

"But how about being buried in here? We won't get any air." This is when I spoke up. "May I speak? The snow piled up like that will keep us warmer and as long as the fireplace is kept goin'. The snow won't be able to cover up the chimney."

"Listen to him. He knows, he's the one that was trapped up in the mountains." The hotel clerk said.

"Now let's all relax, we'll be all right."

I went back up to my room. I figured I might as well rest while I could. Going into my room, I could hear Foster snoring. That made me feel better 'cause I'm sure he knew what was happening, and if he wasn't worried, I wasn't going to fret about it. So I relaxed in my room, only coming down to eat a bit. This went on for two days.

When I came out of my room, standin' there in front of me was Foster.

"Foster, finally you decided to join me again? Thought you went into hibernation with that gal."

"Nope, you'se can only take so much of them there females, but I'se sure we'se be snowed in so she'se made herself at home 'til I'se ran her off this mornin'. Anything been happen out here that I'se should knows?"

"Not much . . . when we first got snowed in, some people got upset, thought we were goin to die in here."

"Why, this place is like heaven compared to where we'se be in the mountains. That's why I'se stayed in here, nothin' I'se could do."

"I got them settled down and everyone believed me because of what we went through."

"Good, now let's goes get something to eat, this old bear's kind of hungry."

We were sitting in the saloon eating when we heard a commotion in the hotel lobby. I went to see what had happened. The man Brady was with was there, digging out the snow that was piled up in the doorway and he was yelling at everyone to leave him alone. He was saying he couldn't stand it in here anymore and he was leaving. To make sure of this, he had his gun out, threatening to use it on anyone that tried to keep him from leaving. Even Brady stood back and let him alone. Then he was gone, disappearing into the snowbank. Someone closed the door and said, "Well, he want last too long." Then everyone went back about their business.

"Some partner you hooked on to, Brady," I said.

"You . . . you just better stay out of my way, hear me good," he snarled.

"Sure, have it you way, I'm not lookin' for any trouble until it comes to me, then I'll finish it all at once." With that I turned my back and walked back to join Foster.

"What's that all about?"

"Oh Brady's friend went loco and dug his way out. Even held a gun on Brady, never seen the like!"

"I'se guess some people just can't stand bein' cooped up and goes crazy."

"We better be careful, from the way Brady was talkin' he might do something crazy too. Let's stay on our toes."

This went on for a couple more days. Then out of the blue someone came digging their way into the hotel. It was the sheriff.

"This one's pasts, now we'er goin' to need everyone outside to help haul away the snow to the far side of town."

Everyone was shouting with joy and grabbed their coats and headed outside. When we were standing in the warmth of the sun, everyone just stood there awhile like it was a dream come true. Then I noticed all the wagons—about four of them.

I asked, "Sheriff, where did the wagons come from?"

"Well, the storm stopped yesterday and some of us that were holed up in the general store got some shovels and dug out. First place we knew we had to get into was the stable, and by the end of the day, we were in there. Then this mornin' we got the horses and wagons out."

"I have to go see about my horses."

"They're all right, they're right over there. We had to use every animal to get rid of the snow. Lucky for us, Grant, the stable man, got snowed in the stable. Your animals are in fine shape. Now everyone get to work."

I went over to Blacky and Lagger and rubbed their heads and told them, "Now we all have to help, so I want you two to do your part." They nickered at me and everyone went to work, half filling up the wagons and the other half unloading them on the outside of town. By the end of the day we had the town pretty well cleared of snow. Everyone was so tried they all dragged off to bed by sundown. That's when I saw a blanket on the ground and went over to have a look-see. It was Brady's partner.

"Found him under the snow when we first dug into the stable. Guess he was after a horse." The sheriff was telling us.

"He went crazy in the hotel a few days ago and lit out."

"They'll do that sometimes."

I went back to my room, said good night to Foster, and fell asleep across my bed with all my clothes on, too tired to get them off.

This situation went on all of February and March. I never in my life knew it could snow this much anywhere in the world. Everyone was sure getting a workout loading and unloading those wagons after every storm. That worked out good for me, because I was used to hard work and this kept my muscles in shape for the hard summer ahead, if we found great-granddad's mine.

Then early in April I asked Foster, "Don't you think it's about time we lit out of this place, we've been here goin' on three months now? It hasn't snowed for a couple of weeks now and I bet you it's at least forty-five degrees."

"That's all true, but I'se be sure there's one more storm out there, just look at the ground, you don't see those spring flowers yet. That's what I'se be waitin' for. If you'se don't believes me, just ask anyone that's been up here any length of time and he'll tell you'se what I'se mean."

"It's not that I don't think you're right, I'm just tired of waitin' in this place."

"I'se know, but it won't be much longer, maybe a week or two. Why don't you take Blacky and Lagger out and exercise them every day? They need to get in shape for the long haul."

"That's a good idea, I'll go out tomorrow and look around this country."

"Just don'ts go out too far, remember what I'se said about a storm."

"All right, not too far."

The next morning I got up early and saddled up Blacky and put a lead rope on Lagger, then headed out of town to the east. Blacky was real playful; I could tell he was really excited about being out in the open spaces again and I saw the same wonderment in Lagger. So when we were out of town about five miles, I dismounted and unsaddled Blacky and took the leader rope off Lagger and turned them loose to run in the fresh, wild and cool air. As I watched them, they reminded me of young wild colts just running having a good old time. The mud would go flying as they took off across the fields. The snow had disappeared but had left in its place the most important thing in the world, WATER! Up here water was very important; it helped everything: the trees grow bigger, the flowers grow more beautiful, animals and humans alike needed the water to survive in this big world. And from up here in the Rockies the world looked enormous and forbidding.

Blacky and Lagger came back after a while and I saddled up and moved on across the land that was beginning to grow on me as much as my passion for Red Bird. As I came to the top of a ridge and looked out over the valley below, I stared in wonderment at the peaceful valley below. Then I noticed a river in the middle of all this beauty that was raging out of control. It was taking whole trees up by the roots and tossing them around like toothpicks. It was a mysterious sight to behold and it was to my satisfaction to behold the beauty and danger all at the same time.

"Well, Blacky, we better be gettin' back, I promised Foster we wouldn't go too far." We turned around and headed for town. We came down the main street heading for the stable when I saw Brady coming into town from the other direction.

I got the horses rubbed down and fed, then went to the hotel. There I found Foster having a drink in the saloon next door. When he saw me he said, "There you'se are, how 'bout a beer, Buck?"

"Sure, why not?"

As I drank my beer I asked, "Did you happen to see Brady today?"

"I'se saw him go out after you'se did this mornin'. So I'se followed him and he was nosin' after you, but I'se came back to town when he started back. I'se think he just wanted to make sure you weren't leavin' town."

"Sometimes I wish he would force his hand so we could get him out of our hair. Well, I'm goin' on up to bed after I eat, so I'll see you tomorrow."

Each day I took the horses out to exercise and they were looking as good as they did before winter. Their coats had a certain luster to them now. I did this for a week and then I woke up to a lightning and thunderstorm. I couldn't believe it was happening and then came the snow and it came down hard, and there came the wind again. Foster had been right, I would have hated to be caught out in this. It made me glad that Foster was with me or I would have been out on the trail right now. But this storm seemed different somehow. I didn't know why but it did. Sure enough, by late afternoon it had stopped. This time we didn't even have to shovel snow 'cause it melted as fast as it fell. The reason was that it was around forty degrees.

Next morning Foster came to me and said, "We'se better get ours things together 'cause we'se be leavin' tomorrow."

I became very busy going to the general store to get all the foodstuff together, paying all the bills. I gave the man at the stable an extra twenty dollars, 'cause the horses really looked great. He was very grateful. I went back to the hotel and settled our account there, and went to my room to go to bed for an early start. But when I was going into my room I heard a noise comin' from Foster's room. I thought! Oh well, he's at it again. Then as I got closer it didn't sound right, so I knocked, and no one answered. I busted in the door and there was Foster all tied up. I got him untied.

"What happened, Foster?"

"That there Brady broke in and got the jump on me, it makes me so mad! He looked through everything. I'se think, but how he know we'se have a map? All the time he was here, he kept askin' 'Where is it? Where is it?' I'se just kept sayin' I'se didn't know what he be talkin about. Actin' dumb, you'se know."

"If you're all right, I'll go see about my room."

I left and when I entered my room it was like a tornado had hit right in the middle of the room. Far as I could tell nothing was missing so I went back to Foster's room.

"Well, he didn't take anything. I have the map in its safe place. I wonder how he knows we have a map. I better look for him."

"That's no use, he'd be out of town watchin' the trails for us. He must had known we'se leavin' when you started payin' off all the bills. We'se better get some sleep now, we'se leave early in the mornin'."

Chapter Six

It was hard to get to sleep. It was exciting thinking about the days to come. We had a long ride ahead, but there was a good feeling inside of me that couldn't be explained. Just a feeling, just a feeling. Suddenly, it was morning. I told Foster I'd meet him in front of the general store, then I left for the stable. I got the horses ready and shook hands with the stable man, who was responsible for the fine shape our animals were in, and thanked him again for a job well done. When I reached the general store, Foster already had our supplies on the walkway. As we were loading our supplies on Lagger, the sheriff came over and started a conversation with us.

"I want to thank you boys for all your help with the snow this winter. I think I speak for everyone in town when I say you all are a real asset to any town and we wish you could stay and make this your home."

"Thanks, Jim, but it's us that should thank all of your people that took us in when we needed help."

"You all paid for what you got and that helps these people in the slow time of the year. By the way, I heard about what happened in the hotel last night. Sure am sorry about it. Did he get anything?"

"No, I'se guess he was just after money."

"That makes sense, because he left without paying any of his bills around town and his partner died during the winter and left all his debts also."

"I wasn't goin' to mention it; but since those two left lots of people in a bind here, I'll tell you that those weren't our friends but we saw them before in Durango. So you might contact a Mr. Walters about their debts, 'cause I'm sure they worked for him. He's the only lawyer in town, so it shouldn't be hard to get hold of him."

"Thanks, I'm glad to hear that. Were those boys after you?"

"We'se not sure, we'se give them the benefit of the doubt . . . We'se leave it at that."

"All right, I won't press it any further."

"Thanks, Jim, we may be back through when we head back to Durango."

We mounted up and pulled out for the east, on our way to Red Cloud Peak.

"Foster, I forgot to tell you, about two weeks ago when I was out with the horses there was a river that we might have trouble gettin' across, it's a couple of hours out of town."

"There's not any river between here and Red Cloud Mountain. Must be's that pesky little creek. That's the one I'se lost one of my mules in years back. This time of year it's big as the Rio Grande, but by next month you won't even know it's there. It's the snow meltin' off the mountains that's all. We'se get over it. It doesn't even have a name."

"You mention the Rio Grande, that's the river that ends at the Gulf of Mexico about a hundred miles south of where we live down in Texas."

"It may end in Texas, but it starts in Colorado. In fact it starts in the Red Mountains where we'se be headin'."

"Well I'll be, it's a small world, isn't it?"

Sure enough, when we reached the creek it was only half the size it was when I was by there.

"I don't understand, it was lots bigger when we were out here before."

"Well, you'se see, Buck, it's like this, when the snow melts it melts around here in the foot hills and a little ways up the mountain. The top three-fourths of the mountain is still frozen. This allows the creek to go down before more melts. But in some years the temperature goes up too fast and all the snow melts at once. This is bad 'cause it makes the creeks and rivers flow so much that animals get caught in it and they drown. But not this year, look, we'se can nearly wade across."

"I'm catchin' on slowly but surely."

"That the only way to learn; by watchin' and listen' all the time."

We rode on and on with the mountains above, stretching up into the clouds in the sky, and the valleys below, looking greener by the minute. The birds were calling to each other in the process of building nests for the young that would be coming any day now. We didn't have to worry about wolves or bears now; it was spring and there was plenty of game and vegetation abound. Tonight we would camp in the foothills of Red Mountain. Foster had rode off a few hours ago, to check our back trail for Brady, and he had pointed me in the right direction. These lovely, lonely mountains were slowly becoming my home.

I was riding Blacky slowly through the trees, keeping a lookout for sign that might mean trouble: a broken limb, grass broken down where someone might have sat or stood for a while, or grass eaten down in one place where a horse might had been tied. Also, the horses would let me know if someone was around if the wind was blowing in the right direction.

It was just about sundown when I made camp to wait for Foster. It was a beautiful sunset, the sun was a big fiery orange ball as huge as I'd ever seen it. When the sun was gone, the warmth that it had brought was also gone. There were patches of snow on the ground. I must have been goin' up higher into the mountains all day. Foster came dragging into camp just at dark.

"What's the matter, Foster?"

"Should had went out ridin' with you'se every day! My butts like a raw piece of meat. That's what that town livin' will do for you'se, made me soft."

"Well, here's some coffee for your insides and some grub for your stomach. Have a seat."

"If it's all the same to you'se I'se rather stand."

I started laughing out loud. "That's not town livin' that's stayin' in bed all day with the whore you took up with."

"All right, boy, don't get sassy with me."

I sat back drinking my coffee and looking over at Foster once in a while and grinning to myself.

"Say, Foster, did you have time today to see if Brady was behind us or not?"

"My mind was on other things down yonder, but I'se manage to keep an eye peeled for him, but he never did show his face."

"You think he's out there, don't you?"

"Yea, I'se do, 'cause if Jeb's mule was loaded with what I'se think, then they'se knows better than us what it might be worth and they won't be givin' up so easy."

"I been thinkin' all day while you were gone, that we been goin' right straight to the place marked on the map and remember they were in Telluride before that first storm that trapped us. So instead of bein' behind us, he maybe in front, waitin'."

"Boy, you'se sure have a head on you'se . . . maybe right as rain."

"Now figurin' he might be in front of us, that pass there ahead, has a lot of places to watch us from until we are right on the spot where we're goin'. That's why I stopped here and waited for you."

"Did you'se have a idea? If so, I'se be ready to listen."

"Knowin' the way you can get around these mountains, you might know a way to go around and come in from the other way to miss the pass altogether. We could avoid any trouble that way. What you think?"

"Let's see, there is a way over the top; it's about three thousand feet higher than the pass. The horses might have a rough time, but if it's not icy up there we'se might make it. We'se might take an extra day."

"You and Jeb waited all your life for a big strike, and we don't want to let it known where it is until we can get in and see for ourself if it's worth the trouble and can file on it."

"What'd I'se tell you about filin', then they know where it is."

"But Foster we can take out one big load. With that we can hire honest men to help us. If we can get in and out without bein' seen. If we have to, we can send for a territorial marshal from Denver. See Foster, if Dan Walters is involved, and I think he is, if we keep the find to ourself, then he can keep at us with no interference from anyone."

"I'se can see your point, I'se goin' along with your thinkin'."

"Let's get some sleep and get an early start."

We got to sleep, but it was a cold night and we didn't want a fire, because Brady might spot us, and we wanted to keep out of sight if possible. In the morning we ate beef jerky and started up the mountain. The terrain was rocky with patches of snow here and there. Proceeding with care and caution, we were three-fourths of the way up before mid-afternoon. Then we hit the snow, not real thick but enough to slow us down. Fortunately there was no ice on the ground. The snow slowed us down, but ice would put a stop to the horses dead in their tracks. We were working our way around the side of the mountain when dark fell, so we had to make camp where we were. This night wasn't going to be very pleasant because it was solid rock where we were and no cover. This far up the vegetation was very, very thin or nonexistent.

"Better get some rest, tomorrow will be the hard part."

"What you call this?"

"Today we'se were playin' around."

"Oh really? I just hope it warms up."

"It will when we'se get to where the mine is. It should be below the snow line if the map is right, and I hope it is."

In the morning we got going early. Going down was harder than coming up. With the snow starting to melt, the rocks were becoming slippery and hard to maneuver on. Some places the horses didn't want to move, so Foster had to pull and I had to push. We had to do this three times. The worst was the mule; he just didn't want to budge a foot which was all it was to be over the break in the ledge. Foster was pulling and I got down under the mule's hind quarters and pushed up as hard as I knew how. He got up and went straight ahead knocking Foster over the ledge.

"Buck, hurry, I'se just barely hangin' on!" I turned and saw or didn't see Foster but his fingers holdin' on to the ledge.

"Hold on, I'm comin'."

I jumped over the break in the ledge and grabbed a hold of his hand just when he let go. This nearly pulled me over, but I got my footing and pulled as hard as possible. Finally getting him up on the ledge, we sat back and got our breath.

"I'se thought we'se be goners when you grabbed me, you'se got plenty of strength in those shoulders of yours."

"Now I'm glad my dad used to let me bulldog those steers at the roundup. Our roundups would take three to four weeks and the first couple of days my arms and shoulders would feel like they were goin' to come out of the socket, but after the soreness was gone it was all right."

"That's my luck, that you be strong as an ox. That dumb old mule nearly kilt me and you too, we'se just about ran out of luck on that one. We'se be over the rough part now. By noon the snow line will be behind us."

While we were resting I got the map and looked it over carefully. I didn't want to miss anything that we may have overlooked.

"Look Foster, I know we seen this before, but look at that X on the map. Do you think he might had marked that on a rock or something that would look natural, not out of place?"

"Possible and practical, we'se better start in a wide sweep of this whole side from here down. We'se separate but we'se kept in sight of each other."

"You rested up enough now?"

"Sure, let's go. I'se be ready to get rich."

We started making wide sweeps of the area, keeping in sight of each other so if one of us found the mark we wouldn't have to shout. Sound carries a long way in the mountains, where someone might hear. What could he have used for a marker? I racked my brain and kept on looking I thoughts of branches, or bones but these things might be disturbed by wind, rain or wild animals. What could be used that would be hard to move yet not easy to see unless you were looking for it? Walking over to Foster, I was disappointed.

"It's near dark. We might as well camp and get a fresh start in the mornin'. Did you see anything?"

"No, nothin', but we'll find it. You didn't expect to come all this way and just walk right up to it, did you?"

"Well, I didn't know what to expect, but your bein' with me gives me encouragement to go on lookin'."

"That's a boy, keep on thinkin' like that and we'll find it for sure. Been doin' this for thirty years and I'se just keep a lookin'. That's all can be done."

The next morning we mounted up and started our search again, working our way down the mountain. I must have dismounted fifty times looking behind bushes and on and under ledges and in caves but found nothing. We stopped at noon to eat. We risked a fire for some hot coffee and a nice hot meal. The animals needed a rest also;

there was a stream running down the mountain from the melting snow up above, and down on this level there was grass for the horses to eat.

"You know, Foster, that X on the map is about halfway down. There's a feelin' inside me that we might have just rode by it and not noticed. After we rest, think I'm goin' to take a ride and backtrack a little ways 'cause we're over halfway down this damn mountain."

"Couldn't hurt anything, that's for sure. It's lots more work lookin' for something and knowin' it's there than lookin' and hopin' it might be there. If that makes sense at all."

"That has to be it."

"What!"

"We're lookin' for some sign a man left, but from what you told me of my great-granddaddy, he would make it look as natural as possible but still point the way. I'll be back. I'm goin' back up the mountain a little way. I'll come and get you if I find something . . . if not meet me back here at sundown, all right?"

"Sure thing, good luck."

Me, Blacky, and Lagger started back up. I didn't know exactly what I was looking for, but I think I would know if I saw it. I began making wider and wider circles, working my way up. After about three hours of this I was about to give up; my legs and back was hurting from getting in and out of the saddle all day when I spotted something reflect the sun into my eyes. It came from behind some brush up against the side of the mountain about hundred feet above me. As I rode on over and jumped off Blacky, my soreness had turned into excitement. Pulling the brush away, I saw what we were looking for. The X was right in front of me. There was Jeb's pick and shovel turned across each other to make an X. There was also a large rock at the place where they crossed and smaller rocks lined up to form an arrow. This arrow was pointing to the side of the mountain. I didn't have time to look now. Tying Lagger to a nearby tree and jumping on Blacky, I took out down the mountain to find Foster. I couldn't go too fast; I was afraid Blacky would stumble and throw me. Finally I reached the place we were going to meet, but he wasn't there yet. I took off down the mountain, looking both ways to make sure I didn't miss him. I had to chance it and yell because I couldn't see very far because of the heavy timber.

"Foster, where are you? Foster it's me, Buck!" Keeping this up for about thirty minutes, I spotted him off his mule getting a drink out of a stream. "Foster, Foster, Foster!" I yelled as I rode up closer. "I found it, I found it."

"Calm down, boy, what's you'se say!"

"Foster, I found it." Tears of joy were rolling out of my eyes.

"Where?"

"Up there where we passed this mornin'."

"Where's our supplies?"

"Up there, I left Lagger tied to a tree so I could find the spot again."

"Let's go now! Blacky can rest later. We'se got to make sure our food is all right. We'se found out earlier that sometimes food's more important than silver or gold."

We rode as fast as we could; this part of the mountain was steeper than any other part we had been on. Blacky was tired but he kept on going up and up, and then we saw him standing there like nothing was happening at all. Lagger was a pretty sight to behold.

"There he is, Foster!"

We jumped off and hurried over to him.

"Well, I'se be! How you'se like that."

"Yeah, I would have missed it again, if the sun hadn't shined on the metal shovel. Let's go see what's back there."

"It's dark already, Buck, we'se wouldn't be able to see anything. We'll go in, in the mornin'."

"I'm too excited to wait."

"Look at it this way, if we'se open it up now and someone jumps us, they'll find it."

"All right, but I won't sleep a wink."

"Me either, one of us should stay on watch from now on. Brady may still be out there, you know."

"Yea, I know. I'll take the first watch after we eat,"

We started a fire, but we used real dry wood and built it in a sinkhole surrounded by rocks. We finally got to eat a hot meal and drink some hot coffee. This tasted so delicious for it was still very cold at night and it warmed our insides. Foster went to sleep, and I sat with my back against a rock with my rifle across my lap cocked and ready. Sitting there, my mind started to wander and search for the reason I had been led to these mountains far from my home. When I was down in Texas on the ranch I thought of myself as a man, but now I knew different. Now the truth came to mind. I came from Texas a boy; now this country and these mountains have molded a man out of that boy and now that man will never leave Colorado until the end of his days on earth. Now that I had made my decision, my mind could relax, so waking Foster up to take the watch I fell right to sleep.

Waking up to the smell of bacon, eggs, and coffee, I jumped out of my bedroll and went over to the fire.

"What you doin', Foster? Anyone within three miles can smell that cookin'."

"Sit down and have some breakfast, Buck. While I'se was on watch last night it came to me that we found the place and if we'se goin' to be up here for a while we'se has to eat. We can't hide forever and might as well have a showdown now than later. Anyways, don't think Brady be dumb enough to try to jump us by himself and by the time he could get back with some men we'll be on our way to file your claim in Durango."

I sat down and ate. When I was done I told Foster.

"Let's go on in and find out what we have."

"All right, I'm ready."

We went over to where the stone arrow pointed the way. I pulled all the brush away from the side of the mountain, and there was a large opening. We took a step inside and it was very dark; so I struck a match and I was nearly blinded by the light bouncing back at us. Foster came up beside me.

"What is it, Foster? It's so bright." He couldn't get a sound out for five minutes and his eyes were big as saucers. Then he turned to me and said, "I'se see it, but I'se don't believe it."

"What, Foster, is it silver?" In the moment before he answered me, I burned my finger and the light was gone.

"Let's get the lanterns, Buck, we'se found it, we'se found it, I so don't believe it, we'se found it."

We went out and got the lanterns lit, but I couldn't get anything out of Foster except "We'se found it."

Finally he spoke some different words as we went back in the dug-out cave.

"Look, Buck, this cave wasn't here; I'se can tell that Jeb dug it, all of it." He went on inside and I followed.

"See this, this is just about pure silver."

"What does that mean? Don't it come out like that all the time?" Now he had calmed down a lot.

"Let me explain, Buck; you'se find silver embedded in the rock and you'se have to chip the rock away to get the silver out. This here, we'se will be chippin' pure silver. If it was possible, we'se be takin' one big piece about a thousand pounds or more."

"What does that mean?"

"Don't you understand? Even with my 10 percent, I'll be rich. Think about this, you'se have 90 percent so you'se nine times richer than I'se be."

I ran out of the hole in the side of the mountain and was yelling at the top of my lungs. The horses were scared to death, trying to get themselves untied but couldn't. Foster came out of the cave.

"Calm down, Buck, calm down."

I picked him up in the air and turned around and around with him yelling.

"Put me down, put me down."

Finally I got dizzy and we fell to the ground. I just lay there and Foster got up.

"You'se all right, Buck, you'se got to get yourself together; there's lots of work to be done."

"I know, Foster, it's just that the whole thing is so unreal and excitin'."

"I'se knows, but that'll wear off; just lay there awhile and take it easy. Get that map out, Buck."

"Here you go, but why you need it? We already found the mine."

"Do you'se think if something happen to me's you'se could find your way back here without the map?"

"Sure, I think so. Why?"

"You'se have to be sure."

"Okay, I'm sure I could find my why back. Why?"

He lit a match and set the map on fire.

"Why you doin' that? The map, the map, Foster!"

"You'se said you'se could find your way back here and I'se knows my way back, so we won't need it. If we'se get kilted by those bushwhackers, I'se sure don't want them to have all of this."

"I guess you're right, but it's just that my great-grandfather wrote it, the last thing he did and I just wanted to keep it."

"I'se knows, but we'se talkin' 'bouts survival here and anyway, I'se knows Jeb and he would have burned it to keep them varmints from gettin' it. The only reason he hid it before is he was thinkin' of your mother and her family. Then again he didn't know someone was on him to kill him. Ifs they weren't so dumb, they would have found it."

"I'm sure you're right. When I found the map in his old saddlebags I thought it was crazy that no one had found it or it's just one of those things that is meant to be."

"So, let's get our packs and get our minin' tools and get some serious work done."

I unpacked Lagger and unsaddled Blacky and staked them out where some nice grass was starting to grow. We gathered up our tools and headed into the mine. We brought with us our other lanterns. That made it twice as bright in our silver mine.

"Kind of hard to tell how far this vein goes into the mountain, but I'se thinks it could go to the core. If it does, we'se goin' to have to take enough back with us so we'se can hire a fair amount of men at a good wage to keep them honest to us, to mine this here bonanza. This is goin' to be just too much work for two men. It would take many years to reach the end of this one, I'm thinkin'. We'se want to have some time to enjoy spendin' it. Don't we'se?"

"You're right on that one."

"Look at these pieces! I'se bet there's at least 80 percent pure silver. I'se never seen anything like this here."

We began working a good sixteen hours a day for two weeks. There was no sign that this vein was going to let up, but we were going to have to stop soon or we wouldn't be able to get it all back to Durango. By now Brady would have more men helping find us; no telling how many. That was a whole other problem that we had to face.

Then one night after digging in the mine all day, Foster came out with the news while we were sitting around enjoying our coffee.

"You'se knows something, Buck."

"No, what, Foster?"

"I'se thinks we'se have enough to get some men and equipment up here and start a first-class operation."

"Mean we're goin' back?"

"Yeah, I'se figure we'se leave after a day of rest."

"By the way, what you need the lumber for?"

"Well, we'se have to have cabins for's the men in the winter and beams to shore up the mine when we'se go deeper down."

"You're plannin' to mine in the winter?"

"Have to."

"Why?"

"'Cause we'se only have two to three months of good weather to get in and out of here. Remember that Lizard Head Pass? This pass is just as bad. So we'se have to have men up here by next fall or we'se wouldn't get in for a year from now!"

"Won't it be too cold up here?"

"It a be cold all right, but when the mine gets deeper it will get warmer. We'se build the cabins warm as can be done and find a spot on the south side of the mountain so when those blizzards come it won't be so bad. That's the reason to pay the men well. We'se be sure and have plenty of food and all the other supplies we'se be a needin'."

"Let's don't count our chickens before they hatch. We still have Brady and whoever he might bring back to contend with. Then when we're back in Durango we'll have trouble with that sly Walters."

"We'se figure something out by then. But one thing's for sure, we'se can't tell anybody where this thing is until we'se file a claim and get back up here with plenty of men and guns."

"Sounds like you may be expectin' a small war."

"Could be."

That night we kept the horses tied at the mouth of the mine and slept inside. We had been doing this all along, afraid someone might see the glow from the fire. Next morning we mounted up and went scouting for a place for the mining camp. We lucked out again. About an hour from the mine we found a gentle, sloping area up from a valley to the south. We had already decided that we would close off the mine entrance when we left and file two claims, one where the mine was and another around the other side in case the vein went through to the other side, one in each of our names. Then we wouldn't open the mine until all the buildings in the camp were finished. We were going to try to keep it secret as long as possible, but these things have a way of leaking out of the claim office.

There had not been a sign of anyone except the animals that would wander by to see what was going on. I had made up my mind that this mining operation was going to be different than some I had seen where they strip the land to get every ounce of substance out of the ground. This land with its mountains and the beauty of its valleys was just too precious to tear up for material things. We would just cut enough trees down for the cabins and for shoring up the mine and leave the rest for nature to take care of as it had for millions of years before man came here.

"We'se leave early in the morning so let's hit the sack early. You'se knows, Buck, I'm thinkin' we'se should take a different route back to Durango. The Animas River starts a short ways down yonder and it goes right into Durango."

"Why go a different way?"

"I'se know you'se want to see Red Bird, and this way will take us through Dancing Bear's village, but we'se can avoid any white man that might give us away."

"That makes sense, and I'm glad to be goin' to see Red Bird."

"We'se probably can't stay but overnight 'cause you know how short the summers up here is and we'se got to get everything built for the winter. You'se goin' to have to decide wither or not to marry her or leave her with her people for 'bout a year until we'se get things ' smooth up here."

"You know it a be too rough up here for her and with all the men we might have some real trouble with just one woman. I don't like the thought of leavin' her for that long, but it will be for the best."

"You'se sure are smart for your age to sort it all out like that. I'se glad you'se picked me for your partner and knows it's the right thing to do even if it is hard. Jeb be real proud of you'se right now. Buck, it's goin' to take 'bout one week to get back to Durango so I'se a thinkin' we'se only fill our saddlebags with grub and leave the rest in the mine so we'se can load more silver. We'se goin' to need all we'se can to convince the men to stay up here for least six months without women or whiskey."

"All right, your mule is goin' to carry the silver and you can ride Lagger. Think your mule is stronger for that type of load than Lagger is, don't you?"

"Sure is, as pure as this vein is he should be able to carry enough. We'se better hit the sack; dawn comes early around here."

"Good night, Foster."

In the morning we packed all the silver that the mule could carry and got the grub put away in the saddlebags. Everything else went into the mine. When it was secured, to my amazement it looked like nothing had been there except for the trampled-down grass and flowers and that was not a concern 'cause it was now late May and the grass and flowers would fight their way back up and cover the area before we come up here again. Then we headed south for Durango.

The days were now warm and long. The mountains and valleys came alive with the bright sunshine that radiated its warmth into everything that was good in the world: the deer with its fawn, the bears with their cubs, and the mountain lions with their cubs. The sunshine even brought warmth into my bones that had felt frozen for months. This was a good time to be alive.

As we worked our way down the mountain trails and came to the river, the one we would follow all the way to Durango, I couldn't help but think how different this place was now, not a cloud in the sky, compared to just a couple of months ago when there was one storm after another. I guess that's the way life is, the good and bad mixed together makes a life to be grateful for.

This was a good time to be on the trail. Foster was in the lead on Lagger, the mule was behind me and Blacky on my lead rope. We weren't in a big hurry as we went along the river, and every hour or so we would take a short spell to let the horses drink some water and nibble on the nice green grass.

This was our third day out, and like the others, it was a nice bright sun-shining day and we were enjoying our peaceful trip. Tomorrow I would be with Red Bird, at least for a while. Then out of the blue from over the next ridge came three riders. I saw them first, and as they approached us there was no doubt that one of them was Brady.

"Look, Foster, see over there?" I pointed toward the ridge. Shading his eyes to see better, Foster said, "Can you'se see who they are? My eyes not what they ought to be anymore."

"I know the one in the middle is Brady, so we better be ready in case of trouble."

Foster took his shotgun out and laid it across his saddle after making sure it was loaded. I took my Colt out, spun the cylinder, then put it back in my holster. In my thoughts I knew that I had not practiced with it enough, like with my old gun, but I just hoped it would shoot true.

"Buck."

"Yea."

"How you want to handle this?"

"Well, let's don't start anything unless they do. This might be what Brady been hoping for, to get us out with no one around. In case of trouble, you take the one on your side and I'll take Brady and the other one. That all right with you?"

"Yeah, okay by me."

As they rode up, I could see that smile that Brady had on his face. I knew what he was thinking and it didn't bother me in the least. They spread out as they got closer.

"Been lookin' for you, Buck, for weeks . . . where you been?" Brady asked.

"Around, but that's our business."

"Well, to the point, I was in Telluride after you left and got a letter from Walters. He wants to see you. Wants us to bring you back."

"We're goin' back to Durango. We'll be there when you see us in the street."

"I don't think you understand, he wants you right now."

"What if we don't want to go?"

"Don't press your luck, boy, you aimin' to get killed."

"I'm not lookin' for any trouble, but I'm not backin' away either. You other boys better move away . . . this is between Brady and me." They didn't move an inch.

"By the way, Buck, before I kill you, what you got on that mule there?"

"If you want to find that out, you're goin' to have to kill me. That's not goin' to be as easy as you think." As I finished the sentence, I heard Foster cock his shotgun. Then all three men reached to draw their guns at the same time, but none made it. All that could be heard in the still of the day was Foster's shotgun and my Colt.

I got off Blacky and tied the lead rope around the horn of the saddle, then walked over to where the three men lay; two were dead and Brady was dying. Foster came over, and looking down, said, "You'se knows you'se done kilt that one on my side before I shot him." I bent down.

"Do you know who killed my great-grandfather Jeb?" He coughed and chocked, and finally got it out.

"I did at least get one of your family."

"But did Walters put you up to it?" He just smiled and died right there.

"Foster, least we can do is bury them, it's the decent thing to do even for the likes of this kind."

After we got them buried we rode on a ways and made camp for the night. I was quiet this night, and thought about seeing Red Bird, and then the thought of the gunfight came back.

"Buck, why you'se be so quiet tonight? Not like you at all."

"It's just, well, that was my first gunfight and the first time that I ever killed someone. Even if he did kill Jeb, it still makes me feel bad inside."

"Buck, that's just 'cause of the way you'se are. You're a good man and good men always hurt some inside when they have to do what you'se had to do today. But it had to be done or we'se might be layin' back there in the dirt and there might still be more to do. But men like you'se will always do what must be done to protect yourself and other's rights." That makes me feel better, but I wish people would just leave each other alone and do things for themselves and not try to steal what others work hard to get. Look at you and Jeb, you all worked hard for thirty years, not makin' much of a living and then one day you all strike it big and then these men get greedy and want it for themselves without a lick of work. It's just not fair."

"That's why there's always men like you that will take up a gun and protect what's right even if it does hurt you inside. You'se know what, those horses we'se got would sure make a fine present for Walking Bear. You'se know they give horses as presents for a bride. Three horses are enough for a regular Indian girl but for the Chief's daughter it should be at least five or six. You'se be with her tomorrow night."

"I know, I can hardly wait. Foster, should I ask her father first or go and ask her first?"

"Well, Indian custom, you'se don't have to ask the girl first, but in your case I'se think it would be right and then offer the horses and more later to her father. I'se know he will give his permission, he knows how both of you feel."

The next afternoon we rode into Dancing Bear's village and received the same kind of welcome, if not more so, as the first time. All the yelling, dancing, and food were all there. We got off our horses in front of the chief. Dancing Bear came out and grabbed our forearms and shook them that way.

"Glad see you two, thought might be dead. Had very hard winter."

"Well, Dancing Bear, you were almost right . . . nearly got ourself buried in Lizard Head Pass. Never forget that winter."

"Was worst one in many moons."

"Where is your daughter, Red Bird? I would like to speak to her."

"You come, she go to pond."

"Excuse me, Chief, if you will."

"Go, she wait for you."

I was feelin' so nervous as I walked down to the pond, remembering it was there we had our first meeting. It was love at first sight; that beautiful woman did something to me inside that could not be explained. And then, there she was, in all her beauty, standing next to the pond, looking into the water. I walked up to her and put my arms around her waist.

"Hello, Red Bird, I'm glad to see you are all right after that hard winter we had." She turned and put her arms around my neck.

"Buck, kiss me in way you did when left last winter." So I picked her up by the waist and gave her a big kiss, and when I had put her down she said, "Miss you, Buck, my body cold without you next to me."

"It won't be a lot longer. What were you lookin' at in the water when I came up?"

"Was looking at myself to see how you could wants me. I see white women, they are beautiful and have fancy clothes and light hair fixed up to look like nice bird nest on top of head. Me so plain looking. Thought you not come back to me with my black hair and funny-looking skin."

"Red Bird, don't be silly, those are some of the reasons I do love you. Look at me, I have dark hair too and my skin is as dark as yours."

"But you man, work in sun, you should be dark but me do woman work all day and skin still not white as fancy white women."

"You can ask Foster, I refused white woman when she came to me in the room I had in town."

"Did you?"

"Yes, I did and I wouldn't lie to you any more than I could lie to my mother and father."

"Oh, Buck, I love you so much, my heart so full of happiness and joy."

"I love you too, Red Bird. It was hard being without you all winter and spring. That is the reason I stopped. We are on our way to Durango and I wanted to ask you something very important."

"What is it, you want to take me away with you this time, Buck?"

Her happiness showed all over her like a beam of sunlight was shining off of her. This was going to be harder than I thought it was going to be. But I couldn't take her with all those rough men around and no women. I hoped it could be made clear to her and she would understand. I started to tell her.

"I do love you, Red Bird, and you know it, don't you?"

"Yes."

"As I said, we stopped so I could ask you something, but I need to explain first so you'll understand why you can't go with me this time."

Her expression changed to look like a dark day in winter.

"Buck not really love me or would take me with him."

"Red Bird, let me explain please. Me and Foster are goin' to be busy and there will be lots of men with us and no women. You know what that means."

"No, Buck, I go with braves all time on hunting party to cut meat from animals. Sometimes I only woman, they not hurt me."

"No, but white men are not like Indian . . . some do not honor women as your men do. They are used to payin' money to be with women and they don't even love them."

"But me not take their money, me only love you."

"I know and I only love you, but these men sometimes take what they want when they want it, no matter what anyone says."

"You be there to protect me."

"No, I won't, there will be times I'll have to leave for a day or two at a time."

"Me no understand; me want to be with you."

"Well, would you give me a chance to ask you something?"

"Ask."

"Will you marry me when I come back in about twelve moons?"

"You do want me?"

"Of course I do, very much."

"Then you must ask Father."

"I know, but I wanted to find out if you would wait for me that long."

"Yes, I marry you and will wait even if my heart hurts for you to be in my bed."

"Red Bird." I took her in my arms and held her tight for so long that it was going to be harder to leave her. But after this time I would never leave her behind again. That I promised to myself on that spot by the pond.

"Now is time to go ask Dancing Bear."

We walked back to the village hand in hand and happy. As we entered, I saw Dancing Bear sitting on his log that was higher than anyone else's and he was sitting with his arms crossed and that beautiful headdress on. Foster must have told him what I came for. We walked on up to Dancing Bear and Red Bird bent down on her knees and bowed her head. So I started to get down, but Dancing Bear stopped me.

"Women bow, not men, you stand up straight and tall always. Hear you ask me something."

"Yes, I hope I am a friend to Dancing Bear and his people."

"You are friend."

"I love your daughter and want to marry her."

"How daughter feel? You tell me this is man talk. Woman not allowed to speak of this, just man."

"She says she loves me and I believe this to be true or I would not be here in front of you."

"Foster tells me you be gone twelve moons and cannot take her 'cause only white man, no white women. This I understand daughter does not, not important for her only me. So I give my permission to marry in twelve moons. If longer she can marry someone else. This is long to wait but allow this 'cause Jeb's blood and I believe you come back."

"I will, you see the three horses that we brought with us? These are to be yours and your people for all times. Each horse has a rifle on it and these are yours also, but you have to promise me that these rifles will only be used for huntin' and not against the white man."

"My promise to you, I give. Such a gift is honor for chief's daughter."

"But, Dancing Bear, this gift is only because your daughter has to wait for my return. When I do return I will bring you ten horses and one of these a stallion for a wedding gift for your daughter."

"This be the most ever given for a wife, even a chief's daughter. Will bring much honor among people and other tribes when hear of this. Will be honor to have as son, and you give great-grandfather much honor in afterlife."

"I thank you for your good words and it will make me happy to have your beautiful daughter for my wife for all times. I want you to know how much it hurts my heart to leave her again."

"I understand this, and wish you safety."

"Father, may I speak?"

"Yes, my daughter, you may speak now the men are done talkin'."

"I want to speak the truth, Father, I, Red Bird, love with all my heart man they call Buck Taylor. You have seen this man and know him to be good and knew his mother's father's father and he was a good man. What I say now is not to bring dishonor to my people."

"What is it, daughter? Speak up, can be truthful with father always."

"We will not see each other for twelve moons. This is a very long time to be away from each other. Father, may I share Buck's bedroll with him tonight? Not to make baby, just to be close to him before he leaves."

"This is not done, Red Bird. Do not know how things can happen and if it happened it would be wrong, would no longer be a maiden and if he was killed no other man would want."

"But, Father," she said, holding my hand in hers to her breast. "This is my man and he is good man, I know this and if he tries to make baby with me tonight I will not marry him, even though I want him so much that it hurts. This can be his test of strength and if he fails he will promise to go away forever. If he agrees to these terms, can we stay with each other tonight?"

"Buck Taylor, will you agree to these terms Red Bird set up?"

"I will agree to them. I would do nothing to endanger Red Bird's and my happiness."

"I, Dancing Bear, in front of all my people, say I trust this man with the most precious thing in the world to me, my daughter. So let it be, but if daughter is not a maiden after tonight, you will be run off of our land forever and a day. Buck, Red Bird's mother will sleep next to you two and in morning will check to be sure that Red Bird is still a maiden. Go with my blessing to my lodge, it is yours for tonight." Thank you for this time with Red Bird."

"Not thank me. Is going to be harder than you think."

Now, I didn't know what to think, all we were going to do is be with each other all night. So we went off to Dancing Bear's lodge and went inside and there was her mother sitting there watching us.

"Buck, you did not meet my mother last time you here."

"No, I saw her in the wedding but we never met."

"Mother, this is Buck; Buck, this is my mother Song in the Wind."

"Happy to meet you, I can see where Red Bird gets her beauty."

"You right, Red Bird, he says words pretty, good to meet you, Buck Taylor. Seem I know you for long time. All Red Bird talk 'bout, Buck this, Buck that, and now after tonight got to listen her for twelve more moons. I glad you came, my daughter miss you much. Think you two be happy. Do not mind me being here, just pretend I not here. But do be careful it not be easy for you tonight."

There it was again. What did this mean, "would not be easy for me tonight"? I just don't understand. Then I turned around to go to Red Bird, and I was surprised to find her takin' off her dress and nothing on underneath and then she got under the big buffalo robe.

"What are you doing, Red Bird, I'll be in trouble with your mother here."

"Not be in trouble, take off all clothes and get in buffalo robe with me. I want to be close to you. Mother tell him it all right."

"Do not worry, Buck Taylor, this is permitted just not make baby all right? Just as long she a maiden in morning when you leave."

Now I knew what they meant when they said it was going to be hard on me.

"Come to me, Buck, I all warm for you. Mother see man before got two daughters." Then she laughed.

I was embarrassed but got undressed and jumped under the buffalo robe.

"Don't worry, Mother, he turns that color all the time, he's so red, maybe he part Indian!" she laughed again.

"Now, don't mind me, going to put out fire and lay right here, no need to talk to me 'til mornin'."

It was warm under the robe and I couldn't wait to be held in Red Bird's arms. Then she moved close to me and I knew it was going to be hard to control myself. She started running her hand over my body and telling me how much this meant to her. I couldn't control myself as she reached my hardness.

"I'm sorry, Red Bird."

"Sha, it is all right."

"Now it your turn to feel me, my body is aching for your touch."

I started roaming her body with my hands and the touch of her skin was unbelievable. Her skin was like a piece of silk I had touched once. The nipples of her breast were hard to my touch. This was all so new to me, I had never been with a woman in my whole life and this was very enjoyable. As I reached down her belly, with the pretty fine little hairs on it, sticking up, she grabbed my hand and put it to her mound. This was wonderful, such enjoyment that could be enjoyed by two people. It looked like married life was going to be the most wonderful thing in my life and this was just a small sample. Then my hardness returned and that seemed to please Red Bird. There was a smile on her face, after pleasing me, then she lay back in my arms and rested.

"How do you know so much, Red Bird? Looks like you are teachin' me what to do."

"When Indian girl get her moon period, about twelve or thirteen of your years, her mother takes her out to a lodge away from the others and tell her what to do to a man to make him happy. Also teaches her how a man can make a woman happy without makin' a baby. Then she shows her daughter how a man makes baby grow in her. They stay there 'til first moon period is over."

"That's why you weren't surprised."

"I wanted you close since the first time saw your hardness at pond that first day I met you."

"You said your mother showed you how a man can make a woman happy without being inside you. Will you teach me to do this?"

"It like what I did to you." With that she told me what to do.

We went on pleasing each other all night over and over again until we were exhausted from the total pleasure that came forth from our bodies. Finally early in the morning, we fell asleep in each other's arms.

We only slept about an hour before her mother woke us. "Buck Taylor, dress and let me check my daughter."

I got out from the warmth of the buffalo robe and began to dress, this time without embarrassment, while Red Bird was checked by her mother.

"Buck Taylor," she said without a smile and then her face turned slowly to a large smile. "You have gave my daughter great pleasure but she is still a maiden. You and daughter go before Dancing Bear now, wait outside tepee now."

Then she left and Red Bird got up and put her dress on and we stepped out of the lodge, and not only was Dancing Bear there but it looked like the whole village.

"Good report from Red Bird's mother. She say you make very good husband for our daughter. When you come back, will find greater pleasure with daughter as wife. You and her be happy together always."

"Thank you, my friend, we must leave our Indian brothers now, but I will return. You can count on that, for I love Red Bird with all my heart, more now than before."

I saw Foster to my right with the horses and I turned and kissed Red Bird and shook Dancing Bear's hand then said good-bye. Foster was already on Lagger, and I mounted Blacky and headed south behind Foster with the mule behind me. I kept lookin' back, watchin'

Red Bird waving to me, until I lost sight of her as I went over the first ridge.

We were only two days away from Foster's old cabin. My mind turned to thoughts of what was goin' to take place when we hit Durango. Now the pleasure of last night was beginning to show up as the morning progressed. By the time we camped that night, I was nearly falling out of my saddle. Foster got the fire going and fixed some grub while I unsaddled the animals and staked them in a nice green patch of grass. When I came back to camp, Foster was already eating and I got my part of the food and sat down. Foster said, "What's a matter with you'se, haven't said a word all day?" As he said this, he had a big grin on his face.

"I'm just tired." I was trying to put off the question, but Foster wouldn't stop there.

"Why, I'se think that gal just too much for you."

"That's not true, we just enjoyed last night."

"I'se bet you'se did. Told you'se Indian girls not like white girls. You'se never catch a white girl doin' what she did to you'se last night."

"How you know what she did?"

"I'se know 'cause I been with Indian girl myself a few times and they'se all be taught the same . . . how to please their men."

"Foster, it was incredible. Why didn't you tell me?"

"That's something you'se have to find out by yourself. I'se knows you'se do all right 'cause those gals are good teachers."

"Well, Foster, now we have other things to get done, so I'm goin' to hit the sack and get a good night's rest. See you in the mornin'."

By morning I was feeling great. I got out of my bedroll and started some breakfast. The sun was just coming up in the east; it was going to be a bright sun-shining day. I roosted Foster out of bed. We ate a huge breakfast, then headed for Foster's cabin.

As we were riding along the trail, we came to the last peak before reaching his cabin. Foster stopped and looked out to the east sun shining.

"What you see, Foster?"

"Just look out there, Buck, look at all that beautiful land: untarnished, untamed, that land is just waitin' for someone young to tame it. If I'se were you'se, after we mine for a while, go off to the east and buy a large piece of land, get some cattle, then go back and get Red Bird and raise you all some kids on that there land. The land is something that you'se can always depend on bein' there when you'se needs it. So you'se hear me, and get some land and protect it and never let it go and that land will always take care of you'se. I'se knows that is what me and Jeb would have done if we'se hit it big when we'se be young. You'se got a head start 'cause you'se spent your young life on a ranch and know all you need to know about ranchin'."

So we traveled on, and with a good two hours of daylight left, we were in sight of the cabin that we left six months before.

"Well, Foster, look like we are goin' to have a roof over our heads tonight."

"I'se tell you'se that's the best sight I'se seen in months."

We rode up in front and got off and looked around, satisfied that no one was around, so we got everything off the animals and put them in the barn for a long-awaited rest. Tomorrow we would be heading into Durango.

Chapter Seven

We slept in a little late in the morning and got our breakfast down. After loading the silver again, we then set our sights for town and maybe a showdown with the man that had my great-grandfather killed.

"You got extra shells for that shotgun of yours?"

"Sure do, got two boxes in my saddlebags right here and got my pockets full of shells. You'se got yours?'

"Well, looks like we're ready for action, so let's get a move on, daylights a wastin'."

I was glad that I hung on to Brady's gun belt. This would show Walters that he had lost his best gun hand and show him who he was dealing with. This time he wasn't dealing with a boy from Texas but a man that had grown up in six months of hard times in the mountains of Colorado, a man to be dealt with as an equal.

As we rode into town, it could be seen that nothing had changed in the six months that had gone by. Everyone was trying to get a look at the large load on the mule. A couple of people recognized Foster, and ventured out into the street to talk to us.

"What you got there, you old devil? Where you been? Everyone thought you died, you been gone so long."

"Just been on vacation in the mountains over yonder."

"What's in the bundle? You all found gold or what?"

"None of anyone's business."

"So you did find something?"

"I'se didn't say that I'se did?"

"No, but—"

"But nothin', go on we'se got some business to take care of."

They lumbered away and we stopped in front of the assay office and got down.

"Think I should stay out here? There's quite a crowd gatherin'."

"No, come on in. We'se get it all into the office. These people we'se don't have to worry . . . they're just curious."

After five trips we got it all into the office without any trouble. The man inside looked like he was going to faint when he started unwrapping the bundles.

"What you got here, Foster, is this all of it?"

"For now, but there's a lot more where this came from."

"And where did you say you been digging?"

"We'se didn't and we'se not goin' to just get busy and weigh it, so we'se can get our money."

After he weighed the first batch, he stopped and wrote down some figures, then we put some more up on the counter, and he did the same thing. This went on for an hour until he got it all weighed and put down in the little book. Then he added up the figures.

"Well, man, how much a ton and how much we'se got here?"

"Wait a minute . . . give me time."

"We'se been shot at, been buried in the snow all winter, all you'se have to say is wait a minute."

"Okay, you always was impatient, you old scoundrel."

"Why you'se, say that."

"I got it . . . you want it or not?"

"Sure, about time."

"Well, I'd say you're rich if the rest is like this, real rich. All of this here is 99 percent pure silver. I would say if the vein stays this rich, you'll have about 1,800 pounds to the ton. Right here you have $30,145.56, to be exact. I'll give you a pay voucher to take to the bank."

"You'se hear that, Buck? We'se be rich, we'se be rich!"

"Now who's gettin' excited, Foster?"

"I'se but it finally happened for me after thirty-one years, thanks to Jeb."

"Did you say Jeb, the old miner that died while back?" the assayer asked.

"You'se bet, this here's his great-grandson Buck Taylor. You'se just make that voucher out to him; it's his mine and me, I'se got 10 percent. Buck, you'se good at figures, how much I'se get out of this load?"

"Let me see, that about $3,145.00."

"You'se don't mean that, do you'se?"

"That's right, Foster," the assayer cut in.

"Let me sit down; I'se never seen that kind of money. There must be mill . . ."

"Foster, stop it."

"I'se sorry, it's just too much for me."

"Well, take it easy, okay?"

"All right."

The man gave me the voucher, and we got our horses to go to the bank. The crowd of people was right behind us. Seems like nothin' this big ever hit this town. We stopped and tied the horses in front of the bank. I turned to the crowd and said, "I want to announce that we are goin' to be needin' about twenty men at good wages for six months in the mountains and another twenty for the next six months."

Someone in the crowd said, "You goin' to work through the winter."

"I tell you what . . . anyone interested, meet us in the saloon at eight o'clock tonight. We'll talk about it. We need men who know how to build houses also. So think about it until tonight."

Foster and I turned and walked into the bank.

"May I help you?" one of the tellers said.

"We want to talk to the president of the bank right away."

"May I ask what your business is about? he'll want to know."

"We want to open a business account."

"I can help you with that."

"No you can't, this concerns a great amount of money."

"All right, I'll be right back."

We stood there waiting and saw Walters and Jenny walk into his office across the street. There were some men still in the street, looking at the bank, I guess to see what happened next. I didn't know about Foster, but I was going to the barbers and get cleaned up. As I looked back toward the door, the teller went through. I saw the man that looked like he would be the president of the bank. He had graying hair and he was short with a potbelly, from sitting around all day and eatin' too good.

"Good day, gentlemen, I'm Mr. Winslow, the president of the bank. May I help you?"

"Yes, sir, can we discuss this in your office? I'm sorry for my appearance, but we just came in from six months in the mountains, but I wanted to get this in the bank as fast as possible."

"Why, think nothing of it. Come right this way."

He led us into his office and asked us to have a seat, and then he sat behind the biggest desk I've ever seen.

"Have a cigar, gentleman."

"No, thanks," I said, but Foster took one and put it in his pocket. "For later," he said.

"Now, how can I help you both?"

"This is John Foster and I'm Buck Taylor." He stood up and shook both our hands again.

"Glad to meet you. Go on."

"We have a small amount of money to put in your bank, but first we would care to know who is on the board of directors and anyone else that may control the funds in this bank."

"I'm sorry, that isn't done for just anybody, specially a small depositor."

"What's wrong with you'se mister, this here is no small deposit."

"I'll handle it, Foster, don't get all riled up."

"Well, Mr. Taylor you said a small amount."

"I'm sorry, it's my fault, what I meant is that this is a small amount of money compared to what we will be bringing in later."

"Well, let me see that." He took it from my hands as I passed the voucher to him, and his eyes nearly popped out.

"I see, this puts a different light on things. Give me a minute to check this out with Mr. Bower at the assayer's office. You do understand we have to make sure everything is proper."

"Yes, sir, we wouldn't have it any other way."

"Gills, come in here a minute," Winslow said. The teller that tried to help us before came in and looked at the amount. Then Mr. Winslow said, "Gills, go over and ask Mr. Bower about this. I'll just hang on to this till you get back."

"Yes, sir, be right back."

"Gentlemen, this will be the largest amount ever deposited in this bank. It said silver, where you find it?"

"Excuse me, but I can't tell anyone right now."

"I'm sorry, I understand. It's just exciting, that's all I meant."

"I know, it struck us like that at first."

Just then Gills came running in, all out of breath, and tried to say something. He kept having to stop to catch his breath.

"Calm down, take your time, Gills, it's all right."

"It's just, it's just that Mr. Bower not only okayed it, he said if it's all like that, it could run in the millions, sir."

"Thank you, Gills, now go on about your work. All right, gentleman, we got that straight, now let's get down to business. I can see why you would want to know the caretakers of the bank. But do you know anyone around here?"

"First, could I see the men's names who have anything to do with the bank, and then I'll tell you everything."

"All right, here it is."

I took the list from his hand and looked through it very carefully and then gave it back.

"The names on the list I do not know, but the one I was lookin' for is not, so I'll tell you." I went on and told him about everything including that Jeb had been killed and hadn't died of any sickness, but I left out where the mine was and left out the town of Telluride because it was close to the mine.

"Well, that's some story, but it looks like it was worth all the trouble. Now let me open an account for you."

"I want to open a separate account for my partner here. He's got 10 percent. Foster, you want any of it for spendin' money?"

"Sure do, I'se want two hundred dollars and the rest I'se keep in the bank."

"All right, we'll take care of that. How about you, Mr. Taylor?"

"No, just put the rest in a business account, 'cause we are goin' back and take some men and mine all year round. We'll be shippin' ore here and I want 10 percent placed in Foster's account each time and the rest in the business account. I think we're goin' to need someone that knows about business to handle our needs on this end. Someone we can trust. We would need things bought on this end and sent back by the wagons that bring the ore into town."

"If you would permit me to make a suggestion."

"Sure, if it would help us."

"Young Gills there, by the way his name is Bill Gills. He grew up around here and he's about your age or a little older, but anyway he was studyin' to be a lawyer, but we can't pay him too much, it's a small bank, so he had to give it up. But if you could pay him extra, he would jump at the chance to continue his education."

"We wouldn't want to take him away from you."

"Nonsense, he would still work here; he only works three days a week, and besides, he's good at working with numbers and he's honest and dependable."

"What you say, Foster? You haven't said a word."

"Before I'se met you'se, I'se didn't trust most anybody, much less a young-un, but seein' you'se work I'se say give him a chance."

"That goes for me too; he shows the same kind of excitement I did when we saw that silver."

"I'll call him in here and let him start setting up your books. I'll let you tell him the good news."

He went over to the door and called Gills in. He came over by the desk.

"Have a seat, Gills, these men would like to talk to you."

"To me, sir, what about?"

"I'll let Mr. Taylor explain."

"Can I call you, Bill?"

"Yes, sir."

"Well, you call me, Buck, 'cause I'm no older than you. How old are you, Bill?"

"Twenty-one, Buck."

"What you know, I'll be twenty-one tomorrow. Okay, now I want you to think of me and Foster here as your friends, everything we will tell you has to be kept to yourself 'cause there are people that have already tried to kill us and they did kill my great-grand father 'cause of this mine. So can you do that?"

"Yes, sir, I never discuss business except with those I do business for."

"That's fine, now Mr. Winslow has told us how hardworkin' and honest you are and you want to be a lawyer. Why haven't you tried to study with Mr. Walters?"

"Yes sir, I do want to be a lawyer, but if I may be honest with you Buck?"

"That how I want it to be."

"See, I don't like the way Mr. Walters does business; he buys up land and starts up a ranch. Then he tries to get the claims too. I mean to say, it's all right to have a little property of your own. But I think a lawyer's job is to protect men by the law, not to use the law against them to make yourself richer."

"Boy, what you think of Bill now Foster?"

"For sure he'se be our man . . . I'se like the way he thinks."

"Me to, well Bill, how would you like to be in charge of our operation here in town?"

"But, I know nothing about mining, and my job's here."

"Mr. Winslow told us you have a few extra days on your hands and you don't have to know about mining. All you would do is keep our books in order and when the silver comes in by wagon, make sure it gets to the assayer's and send supplies to us when we need them and pay our bills around town from our account. That is, oh and I want you to become a lawyer as fast as you can 'cause I don't like the way Walters operates either. Once you get things rollin', you can rent an office around town. We'll be your first client."

"That's sounds like a big job, but what I make here won't let me study law. The books cost a lot and I have to pay for the course by mail."

"Oh, that's no problem, I haven't told you. How much do you make here Bill?"

"Well, fifteen dollars a week; I only work three days."

"See, with what we're goin' to pay you, you'll be able to do all that you want to."

"You mean you're going to pay me."

"Sure, didn't expect you to do it for nothin', but you have to promise not to leave Mr. Winslow until the job gets big enough for you full-time, and I'm sure you and Mr. Winslow can find some young feller to train to take your place when the time comes and I'll pay for the trainin'. Oh yea, nearly forgot again. I'll pay you forty dollars a week, plus a bonus at the end of the year if we do good."

Bill turned white as a ghost. "What is it Bill, what's a matter with you?"

"I'se think he be in shock, the way he looks."

"Come on, Bill, snap out of it," Mr. Winslow said.

"I . . . I . . . I just don't know what to say, that's just so much money, you sure I can handle it?"

"Nonsense, tell him, Mr. Winslow, that's not much for a manger of a large company to make. He'll make more later on."

"Bill, he's right, that's not much for how big this is looking like it's going to be, and I know you can handle it. You do all the bank's books; this is just bigger. Now tomorrow is your day off from the bank, but you come in and start setting up the books for . . . oh, what you going to call your company?"

"I never gave it much of a thought, let's see."

Foster interrupted me and said "I'se got it Buck, it came like a flash of lightnin', it matches your name."

"Well, tell us, Foster, what is it?"

"Silver Buck & Co., I'se be the company."

Everyone laughed at the last part he said as he stood with his thumbs hooked under his arms and head up in the air and chin jutting out.

"I have some champagne." Mr. Winslow poured and then made a toast.

"To the newest and biggest company in Durango."

Everyone drank up and set down their glass.

"As I said, Gills you come in here and I'll get you a desk in the corner over there so you can get the company rolling. Just until you find a office. I don't know what I started here, he makes more money than I do, I'm going to have to call him Mr. Gills."

"No, you won't, I still have the upmost respect for you. Anyway, if you called me by 'Mister' I wouldn't know who you were talkin' to."

"Well, you all two work it out; we have to get down to the saloon to try to get our twenty men to take back with us. We'll be in town for about a week. We'll see you later. Thanks for all your help."

Bill Gills spoke up. "I want to thank you Buck and you too, Foster, this is a great opportunity for me and I want you to know I'll do my darnest to get the job done. Here's your money Foster, I'll put the rest in your account. So long."

As Foster and me left the bank and headed for the saloon, I had a good feeling in me about that young man. I thought we made the right choice.

"Wait a minute Foster, before we go in to talk to the men, there's one more thing I have to do."

I had noticed the light was still on in Walters's office, so I went over to Blacky and got Brady's gun belt out of my saddlebags. Then me and Foster barged right into Walters's office and walked right up to his desk.

"Hello, Buck, hear you struck it rich. Meant to come to see you at the bank, but got too busy."

"Cut out the small talk, Walters."

"It's Dan, remember?"

"Cut the bull, Walters." I threw Brady's gun belt at him and knocked him back in his chair.

"What's this, what's wrong with you, you gone crazy?"

"Don't you recognize it? You should."

"Why should I? I've never seen it."

"It belongs to one of your hired guns."

"I don't have any hired guns."

"I'se wouldn't make him any madder, mister, if I'se were you'se."

"That belonged to Brady and you know it."

"You mean you killed him?"

"Him and two others," Foster said.

"He told me you wanted to talk to me."

"Sure did, I wanted to buy the rights to your mine."

"That's funny 'cause no one knew about it except Foster and myself."

"Well, I must be mistaken."

"I would like to know why you told me that Jeb had been sick and died of that sickness. Brady told me he killed him."

"Truthfully I didn't know he did. Brady told me that he found Jeb on the trail sick and he had died on the way in. I never saw the body."

"You better be glad that I can't prove you put Brady up to it or you would be dead right now. You better stop sendin' people to follow us, or I'll get it out of them that you sent then and come back here and I won't be so gentle on you. Jeb found this silver mine and me and my family are the rightful owners, and we don't take kindly to people tryin' to take what we own away. Come on, Foster, we have business elsewhere."

We went the short ways down the street and went in the saloon. As we entered the swinging doors, my mood changed. I was now happy again. I hated it when I let a man like Walters get me so upset. Now, my happy smile was back again like when we were in the bank.

"Bartender, the drinks are on me for anyone that came to talk to me about a job."

Everyone in the place crowded up to the bar to get his drink even if he didn't want a job. Some just came to hear about the silver we had brought into town. I got up on the bar and tried to get their attention.

"Can I have everyone's attention please? Everyone quiet please." They were too involved with their drinks to pay any mind. Foster broke in with a shot from his shotgun. This caused everyone to stop in their tracks and shut up.

"My friend and partner here, Buck Taylor, wants to talk. Now be quiets a minute. This will put Durango on the map. Okay, Buck, the floor's all you'se."

"Thank you, Mr. Vice President." He looked at me like I was crazy.

"First of all, those of you who decide to go to work for us . . . when I'm not around, Mr. John Foster will take my place and orders will come from him only. I am goin' to tell you what we intend doin' and what you are expected to do and how much you will be paid.

"First, we need miners to work in the mine. But before we can mine, we have to cut down trees and build cabins for you all and one road for wagons to take loads in and out.

"Secondly, twenty men are needed for the first six months and then twenty more for the next six months. The second six months will be the hardest 'cause of the cold.

"Third, no women, no liquor for six months while you're up there. For this you will be paid twenty dollars a week for six months for the work in the summer, and if we get through before winter crew gets in, there will be a fifty-dollar bonus for each man. Now the winter crew will be paid thirty dollars a week for six months. I know there will be times we can't get to the mines, but you'll still get your pay. The extra ten dollars is because of the hard times that comes in the winter and there will be only a thirty-five dollar bonus after the six months 'cause you will be gettin' paid for days you won't be workin'. Every Sunday will be a day of rest for everyone. Oh yea, no one will get paid until his six months is up. You won't need it 'cause we are goin' to provide everything you will need.

Another thing, you may have to fight, 'cause there has already been some attempts on us. No one knows where the mine is except Foster and myself, and it's goin' to stay that way until we get up to where cabins and the road are to be built. So now if you have any questions, you can ask."

"Yea, can we have some more beer since we're not goin' to have any for six months?"

"Sure, bartender give them all they want to drink."

I noticed Foster was the first to get a refill, and had to laugh to myself about that. "Any more questions?"

"Can you tell us how far we will be away from town?"

"It's a good week's ride in good weather, but with wagons it may take a week and a half or two weeks."

"How many men to a cabin? I mean we won't be all crowded together, will we?"

"The ones that sign up can talk about this on the way to the area we are goin' to build the cabins. I thought maybe four or five men in each and Foster and me will have one together. By the time we get up there you should find three or four men you can get along with. I'm glad you brought this up because the first group that goes we really need at least ten that know something about buildin', and it will be to your advantage to find someone good 'cause you'll have to live in the same cabin and it will be gettin' cold before the winter crew comes in. I want the cabins as winter proof as possible for everyone's safety.

"Can we sign on for the whole year? Like me, I don't have any family, and the extra money would be good."

"The reason I set up six month terms is 'cause of families and also I thought after six months in the mountains with just each other you would be goin' crazy."

Everyone laughed at the thought of twenty men coming out of the mountains all crazy.

"Tell you what I'll do, after six months if you want to sign up again, we'll let you if we think you did your job well and been loyal to us and not a troublemaker. Is that fair?"

Everyone in the room was saying, "Yes, that sounds fair enough."

"When will we leave, and can we take our own horses?"

"We'll start signing up men tomorrow in the bank. Then we'll all leave Monday mornin' in two wagons. No one will be allowed to take any horses. They are too hard to feed in the fall and winter. We were trapped up there last winter and our animals nearly starved to death. There will be at least one wagon with a team of horses in camp in case someone gets hurt. They can be taken to the docs. Like I said before, 'cause there may be trouble with claim jumpers, everyone will be required to have a rifle and side arm. If you don't have either, we will give you one."

"After we work the first term will we be hired back the first term of next year?"

"Again, that will depend on you, if you like the work and if we like your work, and how you work with the other men. Then if you stay out of trouble while you are back here. I'll be able to find out what every man is doin' because Mr. Gills at the bank is goin' to be takin' care of our business in town. He's the business manager."

"You gave young Billy a job?"

"Yes, a very important job."

"Good for you; he's a nice young man, he deserves a break. He's a hardworkin' man."

"I'm glad to hear some respect for him 'cause he's the man that's goin' to pay you. I think the smart men will leave some, if not most, of their pay with Mr. Gills to watch over and only take out what you need to live on. 'Cause I'm payin' you very good, and the smart men will save every year and buy some property for their family. But that's up to you. That's all for now, we'll be back in the mornin' to start signin' up men. Think about it and come back in the mornin'. It's goin' to be hard work, so be prepared. I'll be workin' right beside you. I'm a workin' boss as you'll find out; I don't like lazy men. So good night and good luck."

I paid the bill and we headed for Foster's cabin. As we rode north to the cabin, I had a good feelin' about everything that had happened tonight, except Walters. How was I going to prove he was the force behind Jeb's death? I could just gun him down, 'cause I knew deep down he was guilty, but that's not my way of doing things.

In the mornin' we got up, ate early, and got started on back to town.

"Foster, I think we should get rooms in the hotel 'cause we have a lot to do before we leave, and this is a long ride every mornin' and every night."

"I'se been meanin' to ask you'se why you'se made me vice president. I'se don't knows nothin' about bein' vice president. What do I'se do?"

"You're my trusted friend, and all you have to do is what you been doin' for thirty-one years. You know more about minin' than anyone I know, and I sure don't know nothin', so you will be in charge of minin' operations."

"That all, I'se can do that I'se thought you'se coop me in an office all day. Couldn't stand that for a day, much less a year."

When we started up the next ridge we heard shots coming from up the road a ways. I spurred Blacky into a run and Foster was right behind me on Lagger. As we came on top of the rise, I saw two men pinned down by gunfire from the next ridge.

"Foster, go around to the west and I'll come around from the east and try to get behind those on that ridge."

"All right."

He took off and I went the other way. I worked my way through the trees and met Foster back behind the bushwhackers.

"Let's surprise them by rushin' right in and maybe they'll take off. You see their horses anywhere."

"Yea, right over there to the left."

"Look close, as we go in for any markin', so maybe we can find who they belong to later."

"Okay."

"Let's go."

We took off in a gallop; I could feel Blacky's excitement under me as he took off. We started firing at the three men, not really intending to hit anyone, just scare them off. When the three saw us coming with our guns a-blasting, they jumped up and headed for their horses. As they jumped on their horses, I noticed a large circle with a W in the middle on the hind flank of a big bay. They headed for town as fast as their horses would carry them. Foster started out after them.

"Let them go, Foster. Let's see if those two men are hurt down there."

"Shucks, I'se want to get those three. I'se be gettin' tired of all this trouble."

As we rode down, the two men came out to greet us.

"Glad to see you, those guys really had us penned."

"Anyone hurt?"

"No, not really, just some scrapes from falling off my horse and hitting the ground."

"Where you headin'?"

"To Durango, heard there's two men discovered a silver mine and need some carpenters."

"You all know about those things, do you?"

"Might say that," he said as they gathered their horses up and then came a third horse packed full of tools.

"I see what you mean."

"Yea, just got into the area yesterday from Denver where we were workin' on a hotel-saloon."

"What is that?"

"That's a hotel and saloon built in one building. We thought we'd try our luck in California, then we heard about this silver mine and knew they would need good carpenters." The second man, who had been quiet until now said.

"And we're two of the best in the west."

"Don't mind him, he's always doing that to me."

"Well, we are and that's our motto."

"By the way, I'm Jim Burke, and this here, the one with the fancy words, is Tim O'Kelly. You have to excuse him, his family came from Scotland."

"So, that's better than coming from South England, fancy pants."

Me and Foster sat and were getting a bellyache laughing at these two.

"Okay, Tim, that's enough. What are these fellows who saved our lives going to think? By the way, have you heard of a man called Silver Buck? Wasn't that it, Tim?"

"Sure was, Jim, it fits what he does. I still wonder why those three were shooting at us anyway. We didn't do nothing."

"I'se say it's what you'se be goin' to do in town. Would you'se say so, Buck?"

"Buck? Are you Silver Buck we heard about?"

"Well I'm Buck Taylor, but my old partner here thought the name of our company should be Silver Buck & Co. and the bank president and my business manager was all for it, so I agreed. But how did you find out that was just yesterday afternoon?"

"It came over the telegraph in the town we were in, that's all we know."

"We better get goin'. We should have already been in town. They're startin' to hire this mornin'."

We rode on into town and told Jim and Tim to give their names to Mr. Gills at the bank. We would be there later.

"Foster, let's go on over and file those two claims we talked about. I'm kind of afraid to, 'cause everyone will know then and be rushin' up and destroy all the beautiful country around there. And I'm afraid if we don't, Walters will get his hands on what Jeb worked for, and that would make me mad as a dog. What do you think?"

"Only way I'se see to do it, 'cause everything you'se been sayin' is true, is pay large amount of money to the claims office and pray he's honest and won't tell anyone."

We walked into the claims office, as I was thinking of what to do. Then the man at the counter spoke up.

"Been wonderin' if you'd come in or not, I've looked over the map and sure couldn't figure where you found it. Far as I know, there's no silver around here."

"It's some distance away. But before we file, can this be kept between us three or not?"

"Well, that's hard to do; you know how things get around."

"Don't get me wrong, it's not that I want to keep honest people away. It's just the claim jumpers around here, if they know, they'll try to get up there before we can and try to keep us off our claim. We also don't want the people that will just go and tear up the land."

"How long do you need? See these records are for public use, anyone can demand to see them."

"Altogether about three weeks would do it."

"See, you can file today and then if anyone asks I can tell them before it becomes public record it has to go to Denver to be okayed. That should give you time. You were talkin' about people going up and tearing up the land, weren't you?"

"NO, I plan to just put up five or six cabins and one road, and not to disturb the land too much. It's so beautiful up there."

"I like you, heard about the high paying jobs you are giving out. So I'm going to tell you about a new law, it's called Homestead."

"What that about?" Foster said.

"It works like this, you pick some land, build on it and make it productive and in three years it's yours. If it's in a homestead area, I'll have to know where it is to see. But I don't know, you have to be twenty-one, are you?"

"I'm twenty."

"No, you'se not, you'se told us yesterday that today is your birthday."

"Is it?"

"I forgot all about it. How much land?"

"One hundred and sixty acres for each of you. That's three hundred you can control around your mine. Now where is it? Here's the map."

"It's right here, on the east side of Red Cloud Peak. Isn't that right, Foster?"

"Sure, that's it all right, I'se never forget seein' that."

"So both of you together will control. Let me see if I got this right, the west side down to here and the north and south down to here where the level spot is shown and let's see, this creek way down into the valley will be on your east side. Someone must be on your side, all right?"

"Why?"

"'Cause this piece is on the very corner of the homestead section. If it would have been half a mile farther down the west side, you couldn't have gotten it."

"Thanks a lot, you sure been a help . . . here's a hundred dollars for your trouble."

"Thanks, but it's no trouble for a man of your caliber."

"Take it anyway, I feel good."

"All right."

"Let's go, Foster, got to get to the bank. Oh, here's a note and ten dollars, would you go and send this to Denver from the telegraph office and then go eat and have a beer? I'm just goin' to be standin' around the bank seein' who all shows up. Tell the man to bring me the answer at the bank, if you don't mind."

"Why no, sure, you'se the boss."

"See you later, Foster, be careful."

I walked on over to the bank just before opening time, Tim and Jim were waiting outside. I said hi and knocked on the door. That's when Bill came and let me in.

"How you comin', Bill?"

"Just fine."

"I didn't mention, really I didn't think about it until the meetin' last night, if it's all right with Mr. Winslow I told the men applyin' for jobs to come in here today."

"With all that money you're bringing in, I'm sure he won't mind. I'll be right back."

Mr. Winslow came out of his office and came over to me. "Why, Buck, I'll be happy to let you interview men here over by Gills there, he'll have to put their names in the payroll book anyway. Be real handy over there."

"That a be fine, Mr. Winslow. May I ask who was the one that told you that my great-grandfather died?"

"Why, it was that lawyer, Mr. Walters. Never liked the man myself. Most people around here feel that way. Come to think, aren't you the fella that spent so much time with him and his daughter a few months back?"

"Yes, that was me. The reason I was with them is he's the one that contacted my mother about Jeb. Now, I have learned a lot about them I don't like. Don't let this out, but his man Brady tried to gun me down on the trail comin' back and he's the one that killed Jeb, he told me before he died, but he wouldn't tell me who put him up to it."

"You killed him?"

"Well, I'm here, aren't I?"

"Yes, you are, and I'm glad of it. That man was a terror around this town. I wondered where he went. That man Walters might be behind it but it will be hard to prove."

"That's why I started lookin' for this mine to draw him out, but he keeps sendin' his men after me. So I don't know. Well, I better get over there. I need to talk to Bill."

"If you need some kind of help, come see me."

I said so long and went over to where Bill was sitting. Then I saw Jim, and Tim was out standing in the small line that had formed. Knocking on the window and finally getting their attention, I waved for them to come in. They got out of line and came on in, and it was then, as I shook their hands, that I noticed what a firm handshake they had. To me that was a sign of a strong and honest man.

"Mr. Gills, this is Tim O'Kelly and this is Jim Burke." They all shook hands and then I said, "Bill put these two on the payroll as of today. These two are carpenters."

"What's with this company, is everyone as young as you two?"

"No, Foster is the vice president. You all weren't here for the meetin' last night, so if you'll be at the diner at noon I'll buy you dinner and explain the rules when we go up to the mine. Now I need eighteen more men."

"Thank you, Silver Buck."

As they walked away, Bill asked, "Why they call you that?"

"Oh, it's got to do with the name of the company. They were in a town somewhere when a telegram came and it said Silver Buck was hirin' so that's what those two call me now. That Foster, with that name. Be all over town before the day's out."

Ten men came in the morning about the jobs, but I only hired four. Five were too young, only sixteen or seventeen, and didn't look strong enough to handle a pick and shovel all day long. Then about eleven-thirty a man came with the telegram I was expecting from Denver. I gave him a tip for getting it here before noon. I told everyone to come back tomorrow, then headed for the diner.

As I sat down at a table, someone caught my eye. It was that devil of a woman, Jenny Walters. She was coming over to the table where I was sitting.

"Hello, Buck, nice to see you. Heard about your big strike. Where is it?"

"Jenny, that's not for people like you to know. By the way, how many gentlemen have you got their pants off before Brady came bargin' in?"

"How dare you talk to me like that? Haven't seen him anyway."

"You won't either. He's lyin' in a grave down the trail."

"You killed Brady? You couldn't have in a fair fight, he's too fast for the likes of you."

"Sorry, but he wasn't fast enough to keep himself above ground. Now if you'll excuse me, I see my men coming to talk with me."

Silver Buck

With that, she didn't say another word and stormed out of the diner like a tornado in a spring rain.

"Who was that? She looked mad as a wet hen," Jim said.

"It's a long story, but just stay away from that one. She's nothin' but bad news. How you all been doin'?"

"Just looking the town over."

The waitress came over to take our order. After we ordered, I asked her to have the owner come over when he had time. While I was waiting, I read the telegram from Denver:

> Mr. Buck Taylor of Silver Buck & Co.*stop concerning a
> Jim Burke and a Tim O'Kelly*stop
> Did work here, three months 'til job finished*stop
> Boss says excellence work and no trouble*stop
> Never had trouble with me *stop
> Hope this helps *stop
>
>   Sheriff of Denver
>   Sam Dunn

"What is that you're reading, Silver?" Jim said.

"Wish you wouldn't call me that, it's embarrassin'."

"We like it, boss, and so does others in town."

"All right, guess I'm stuck with it. See this boys? This is a telegram from the sheriff in Denver."

Just then the owner of the place came over.

"May I help you, Silver Buck, I'm the owner, John Russell."

"Glad to meet you," I got up and shook his hand then sat back down. "Have a sit for a minute if you have time."

"Just a minute, that's about all."

"Well, Mr. Russell, seems like you already heard what I'm doin'."

"Yes, sir, and it's a great thing to happen to this town."

"We are goin' to be leavin' Monday and these men that don't have families around here that I'm hirin' need to be fed. So if it's all right with you, I would like to have them eat here and Mr. Gills will settle up with you after we leave."

"That's fine with me, oh, I'm going to have to hire some help."

"Thank you very much."

He walked away with a jump in his step and a smile on his face.

"Why did you check up on us, didn't you believe us."

"Yes, I did, but for what I been thinkin' it needed to be confirmed, that's all."

"What you talkin' about?"

"After this telegram, there's no doubt in my mind. If you two want it, you can have it."

"Have what?" Tim said in his accent.

"You two are my new construction supervisors at forty dollars a week apiece."

The waitress brought our food, nice and hot. I looked over at my new construction supervisors and couldn't help but laugh out loud for they hadn't moved an inch since the news of their new title and pay.

"What you all got to say . . . yes or no?"

Getting their mouths back together, they both spoke at the same time.

"Yes, sure. Thanks, Silver Buck."

"We never thought or expected that."

"Haven't seen anyone around with your qualifications. Just sit back and eat while I explain what I want you two to do. There is to be five or six cabins, which will be made out of the trees around the mine. One will be a lot larger 'cause it will be headquarters, with rooms for me and Foster, then one for an office and a large space for, I don't know, I guess just some place the men can get together and talk or whatever. You know what I mean. And a kitchen."

"Yes, I think so."

"Well, the other cabins will be just one room with four or five bunks with enough space for the men to have, like a place of their own. We need stoves for heat and beddin', but we can build the bunks. Can't we?"

"Sure, no problem, how many men will we have?"

"At first, everyone will help, all twenty, but after the trees are felled and the cabins are underway, Foster will take about ten men to start on the mine."

"That will sure be enough to do a fine job."

"Can it be done before we get snowed in? And they have to be weather tight."

"Sure, no problem, if we have good hard workers."

"Okay now, between now and Monday you two design the camp and get all the tools you all need together, and I'll tell the owner of the store to put it on my bill. Be sure to get extra of anything you might need. I don't want to run out. Another thing that just came to mind: I would like both of you to stay all year long if you can. They'll be a hundred dollar bonus for each. And I want you to design the timbers to be used in the mine. I don't want anyone hurt. You'll work for your money."

"It sounds like it, but we don't mind, never had a title like that. I'll be glad to stay."

"Me to, boss, sound good."

"Well, finish your meal and get busy, I have to go find Foster."

"We saw him going in the saloon."

"That makes sense. Oh yea, there will be rooms at the hotel for you. See you all later."

Going over to the saloon, now I had time to look around. I'd been too busy to notice the bright warm sunlight and how hot it was getting to be durin' the day. Going on in the saloon, I find Foster in the corner.

"How you doin', Foster? I've been lookin for you."

"I'se doin' all right."

"Foster, before tonight, would you go to the hotel and get us each a room and two more for our new construction supervisors?"

"Who?"

"Tim and Jim, that telegram from Denver said they were good, so I hired them to be in charge of the buildin' of the camp. I sure couldn't do it as fast as someone who knows what they're doin'. You're in charge of the mine, so we needed someone to build the camp."

"They'se seem to be all right, at least they will make us laugh."

"I'm goin' to the stable and get the horses settled. Don't forget the rooms."

Walking over to the horses and Foster's mule, I noticed they were sweating. "Sorry, boys, didn't know it was this hot." I took off my coat and put it in my saddlebags. As I led the animals into the stable there was a noticeable change in the temperature, at least fifteen degrees. "This is better, isn't it, boys?" I got them unsaddled and brushed out their coats, then took my rifle and went to the back of the barn looking for someone to make arrangements with.

"Hello there, anyone here?"

"Here I am, over here."

"Howdy, just put two horses and a mule in the stalls over yonder. Want to buy two wagons and rent some more. I'm not for sure how many yet. Can you get them by Monday?"

"Think so, but have to check around to make sure."

"All right, I'll check back with you tomorrow, and would you feed the animals later for me?"

"Sure."

As I was walking down the street toward the bank, I noticed, tied back behind Walters's office, a horse. Going back to the alley, there was the big bay tied to the back rail, and sure enough, there was that circle W brand. They were the same horses, the horse that belonged to one of the men that attacked Jim and Tim on the trail outside of town. Just when I was about to turn and leave there was a click, and a man spoke.

"Mister, what you doin' around my horse, and while you're at it, put your hands over your head."

"Two of my friends were attacked on the trail and I saw this horse leavin' as we chased the bushwhacker off."

"That was me all right, but I'm no bushwhacker. There's been some cattle missin' from the ranch and we been lookin' and saw those two strangers."

I heard another clicking sound and then I recognized Foster's voice.

"Now you'se mister, can drop that there six-shooter and put your hands high, and I'se mean now. You'se all right, Buck?"

I put down my hands and turned around to see the man that belonged to the bay. He was a tall man with black hair and a big black bushy beard.

"Sure, I'm all right. This here is one of the men that jumped Jim and Tim on the trail; I noticed the horse."

"Yea, so did I'se. That's the one all right."

"Let's take him to the sheriff." I picked up my rifle that I had dropped when he got the drop on me, and then picked up his gun.

"Let's go boy, you'se heard the man," Foster said.

We walked over to the sheriff's office and went on inside. He was sitting behind his desk looking at Wanted posters. Looking up when we slammed the door, he asked, "What can I do for you boys?"

"Well, Sheriff, this hombre tried to bushwhack two of my men this mornin'."

Just then the door of the office broke open and Walters came in.

"What's going on, Buck? I saw you with a gun in Peter's back." This time the sheriff spoke up.

"Take it easy, Dan, it's just that they say old Peter here's a bushwhacker."

"What?"

"Yea, him and two others, but I saw that big bay of his back of your office and it was one of the horses this mornin'."

"What about that, Peter?"

"Like I tried to tell him, John, me and two other hands were lookin' for cattle rustlers and saw those two strangers and was about to ask them some questions when they started shootin' at us."

"That's the truth, John, that's what he reported to me, and we had some cattle missing this mornin'."

"Sheriff, that's a lie! My men didn't fire at them first, they already told me that."

"Well, I'm sorry, but I can't do anything about it, even if you bring your men in. It's just their word against his. You can go, Peter."

"But, Sheriff."

"I'm sorry, that's the law."

Walters and his man turned around and left the office laughing. I heard Walters as he went out.

"Peter better get back to the ranch and look for rustlers." And they both were laughing. When they were out of sight, the sheriff turned to us.

"Look, Buck, I believe you. There's just no proof. By the way, my name's John Cameron. We didn't get to meet, your last time in town."

I shook his hand, then told him.

"That man's no good nor his daughter, why don't you do something about them."

"There's a lot of wrong things goin' on around here and I think he's behind most, if not all of it, but there's no proof and a sheriff needs that before anything can be done. He'll slip up one day and I'll catch him. Wait and see."

"Do you know Brady that worked for Walters?"

"Sure I do, bad man, real bad."

"Well, let me tell you that the six months we were gone that fella was followin' us all the time. But back up the trail him and two others tried to out draw us. They didn't make it."

"I'm glad to be rid of that kind, but you see there's no proof that Walters sent them after you. Sorry."

"Me too." I walked out mad, with Foster right behind me.

"What I'se tells you'se before? He won't do anything but sit in that office and get paid. By the way I'se got rooms for six people at the hotel. That's when I'se seen you go in the alley, then that man went in after you'se."

"Good, I'm glad you did. I'm goin' to the bank."

I was in no mood; I was still mad.

"I'se goin' back to the saloon, if you'se need me."

"All right."

By the time I went into the bank the anger was nearly gone, but the frustration was still on the inside.

"Bill," he looked up at me.

"Yes, sir, what can I do?"

"I just stopped in to let you know that I set up accounts at the diner, and hotel, and the stable man is goin' to try to locate five wagons, two to buy and the others to rent, to take the supplies up to camp. And I need to set up an account at the general store for our supplies. So after we leave, you can settle all the bills."

"Sure thing, Buck."

"Better be gettin' over to the general store, I told Jim and Tim to start gettin' things together."

I went across to the general store, and sure enough, they were there piling up things. As I was walking to the counter, they spotted me and came over.

"Glad to see you, Silver, what took you? We been stallin' 'cause the man said you didn't talk to him yet."

"About to right now . . . just ran into a little trouble." The man came up to me at the counter; the same man that fixed me up before.

"Hello, young man, so it is you found all that silver?"

"Yeah, think Jeb did find those big ones that only one can be carried by a mule. I just followed the map he left me that's all, but that's no matter now. I burned it after we found the mine."

"Those fellows say they buying for someone name Silver Buck."

"Well, that's me, but it's a long story how I got that name. But if you would fill the order of whatever they need for construction . . . These two are my construction supervisors. Later we'll be in to order foodstuffs. Do you have a place to keep all this? We're tryin' to get wagons to put all this in."

"I can keep it in the back; got plenty of room back there; just hope I got everything you need."

"Me too, 'cause we'll be leavin' Monday. The bill will be paid by Mr. Gills at the bank; he's my business manager now. So keep in contact with him, 'cause we'll be sendin' for things with the wagons when they come back from the mine from time to time."

"Sure thing, glad for the business, looks like you going to make another boom town. By the way, my name is Ed Themes."

"You boys get everything you need. Glad to see you again, Mr. Themes, but got to be goin', see you later."

It was already suppertime by the time I left the general store. I hadn't had time to think about anything, but now my stomach told me it was time to eat. So I grabbed a bite to eat, then went to the hotel and ordered up a hot bath to be brought to my room. I asked what room Foster had gotten for himself and which for me.

"Let me see, here you go, yours is 202 and his is right across the hall. That bath be up in about ten minutes."

"Thanks, I sure can use it, feels like I been out on the trail for a week."

"Know what you mean, been like that a time or two myself."

"By the way, did he get you squared on the rooms for my men and for you to collect from Mr. Gills at the bank?"

"Sure did, it's all taken care of. I talked to Mr. Gills at my dinner break, and he filled me in on the details."

"I'll be in my room waitin' for my bathwater. Oh, make sure the girl that brings it up knows it's just a bath I'm wantin'."

"No, problem, it's my wife be bringing it."

"That's good, last hotel I stayed the girl wanted to stay all night."

"Won't have any of that here."

As I reached the top of the stairs, I noticed this was the same room I had before. I stopped off at Foster's room and could hear he was up to his old tricks. I knocked on his door.

"Foster, it's me, Buck . . . just let you know I'm still in one piece as if you could care right now."

"That's good, Buck, see you'se in the mornin'."

"Yea."

I went over to my room, went in, and put down my rifle and took my gun belt off. Then I lit the lantern and took out my Colt and sat on the bed to clean it. I was about finished when someone knocked on the door.

"Hello, it's me with your bath."

"Just a minute." I went over and let her in. She rolled in the tub and the water and filled the tub up. I asked her, "Do you have someone who washes clothes? These are dirty."

"Sure do, me. That is an extra four bits though. Aren't you that man who found silver?"

"Sure thing, that's me."

"Well, why don't you buy some more clothes? These are threadbare."

"You know, I never thought. Look, ah-ah—."

"Just call me Glory."

"Look, Glory, is the general store still open?"

"'Bout another twenty minutes or so."

"Would you take my old clothes and match them as close as you can? There will be five dollars for you; just tell Ed to put it on my bill."

"Well, what you waiting for? Get out of them there clothes so I can get."

She left with my clothes, all but my hat and boots; I wouldn't give them up. It felt so good to get in the hot water and get clean and shave. I finished up and got in bed to get warm and wait for Glory to bring back my new clothes. She got back, and there was no difference in the clothes, they were just brighter in color.

"Here's your five, thanks."

"What you want to do with these old things?"

"Oh, just burn them or give them to someone."

"All right, I'll take the tub out in the mornin'."

She shut the door and I got up and locked the door and put on my long-handles and climbed back in bed. By the time my head hit the pillow, sleep was on me, and my dream world came like a whirlwind bringing the dust. There before me was my beautiful Red Bird, with her shining black hair and her eyes full of stars like a clear night on a Texas prairie. There I was again riding up on Blacky, and there she was on the front porch of a ranch house with two children, one boy, one girl. I woke up like a shot had hit me. I couldn't believe it was already morning, but it was. Then I remembered havin' that dream before, but could not think of when. It seems so real, then fades away so fast.

I got up out of bed and went over to put on my new store bought clothes. They fit all right, but they felt strange in a different kind of way. Anyway, they fit and that's what counts. I strapped on my gun and put on my old hat and boots, picked up my rifle, and felt much better. I headed down to breakfast, not bothering to look in on Foster because I knew he was still busy. When my feet hit the dirt on the street it struck me like a bolt of lightning. We needed a cook! What was wrong with me? The cook was one of the most important men in any kind of camp, cattle ranch, sheep ranch, or mining camp men were men and had to be fed.

As I went in the diner I looked around for Mr. Russell, but didn't see him. I had a seat and ordered my breakfast, just then Jim and Tim came over.

"Mind if we join you, boss?"

"No, have a seat. How's your room last night."

"There fine. I haven't slept in a bed for almost a month."

"Yeah, I couldn't hardly sleep on that soft bed."

"Well, boys, you better get used to it . . . goin' to have a bed under you for a spell."

Then I saw Mr. Russell out the corner of my eye.

"Mr. Russell, can I talk to you, over here?"

"Sure, be right there, Silver."

After a minute he came over and sat down at the table.

"It just dawned on me, we need a cook for our minin' camp."

"Well, you can't have mine, it took me over a year to teach him all I know." Then he let out a laugh.

"You got me wrong, just want to see if he knows anyone that fits the bill."

"All I ask is, don't tell how much your paying. I've heard all those high wages you're paying. They're outrageous."

"Well, it's hard work and lonely up there and I want good men that can take it."

"Let's go back and ask him."

I followed him to the kitchen and there was a short, skinny man, looked like he was doing the work of two men.

"Juan, Mr. Taylor wants to talk to you a minute."

"Si, señor, may I help you?"

"This sure is a small world."

"Si, como, I mean, what?"

"It's that I understand some Spanish, I come from down in South Texas. I rode with some good Mexicans down on the ranch my father works on. Oh well, to the point, I need a cook to take up to my mine, to cook for about twenty-five men."

"But, señor, I'm happy here."

"I know, but I thought you might know someone who could cook as good as you."

"I'm glad you like my cookin' but I know of no one that I can think of. Sorry, señor.

"I'll let you get back to work, but if you think of someone I'll be at the hotel or the bank. Thanks."

I went back and finished my breakfast, and headed for the bank. I spent all day there and ended up with six more men, which made ten so far with only two more days before we left. I still needed a real good cook; if anything would keep the men together, good food would, or at least make it easier. I stopped in at the saloon and had a beer and as I raised my glass, there in the corner of the saloon was Foster playing poker with four other men. I walked over to see how he was doing.

"Winnin' anything, Foster?"

"Nope; just stayin' even, thought I'se do all the devil's work I'se could before we'se get stuck up in those mountains all winter."

"Sounds good to me; just don't lose your shirt, if you know what I mean. I need your experience up there this winter."

"They'se never get that from me'se."

"Good, see you tomorrow, I'm goin' to bed."

I walked out of the saloon and started for the hotel, when I noticed a light in the stable. I thought I'd go over and brush out Blacky. He'd never been neglected like this; usually I was around him all day long. My life was changing and he would have to get used to it. Just as I pushed the barn door open, there inside were my five wagons. Beside them I saw two men piling up some hay around them and one of them was striking a match, when I let out a yell.

"Hey, you two! What you doin' to my wagons?" As I spoke, the match fell to the dry hay and the two men ran out the back. I didn't have time to chase them, because the fire was already spreading and I had to get my wagons and horses out and fast.

I ran to let Blacky and Lagger and the mule loose and chased them out of the barn door. Then getting two horses, I hitched up and got one wagon out in the street. That's when I noticed the fire bell outside the barn door. I ran to it and started ringing it as hard as I could and yelling as loud as my lungs would let me.

"Fire! Fire! Fire!" Several people ran out into the street, and I waved them over to the barn as I ran back in and got another team hooked up. As I got the second wagon out, half the town was outside bringing water in buckets and throwing it on the flames. Then I saw Tim and Jim.

"Tim, hurry, go in from the back and try to find the man that runs the stable, I haven't seen him." He took off running. "Jim come to help me, we got to save the wagon." As we ran in the barn it was already blazing around us. We managed to get four more horses and two wagons out. Then as I rushed in, I saw it was too late, the fifth wagon was on fire, so I ran over and let the rest of the horses out. They were very frightened and ran out like there was no tomorrow. When I came out of the barn, everyone was just standing there looking, and as I turned around, I saw that the stable was gone, the flames were reaching up, way up, into the night sky. That's when I saw Tim dragging a body around the corral. Everyone went over to Tim.

"You all right, Tim?"

"I am, but he was already dead when I got to him."

The sheriff came over and looked at the body.

"Why, that's old Gus, the stable man."

Tim said, "Look on his head, he was dead before the fire started, you can bet your boots on it."

The sheriff turned to me. "How'd it get started, Buck?"

"I was on my way to the hotel and dropped by to see my horses and to see if Gus found any wagons yet. Well, when I opened the door, I saw two men in the dark, lighting a match and yelled at them and one of the men dropped it and ran out the back."

"Did you see who it was?"

"No, Sheriff, I didn't, too dark. But I can tell you who put them up to it."

Just then Walters and Jenny came up in their robes, from the direction of the hotel.

"What happened here?" Walters said.

"The stable burned down."

"That's too bad. How you goin' to get your things to the mine?"

"Your men didn't get to burn all the wagons, see Walters."

I pointed to the four wagons in the street.

"What are you saying? I was asleep in the hotel. Did you catch one of the men or what?"

"No, Dan, we didn't, but Buck here saw two men running out of the barn."

"They weren't my men."

"There's no proof, but, Dan, if I find you had anything to do with this, you'll hang, and I mean it."

"Why do you say that? It's just an old barn?"

"It's strikes me funny, since Buck came back to town too many things have been happening and tonight it went a step too far."

"What you mean, Sheriff?" Walters said.

"Gus was killed before the fire started."

I looked over and Jenny was falling to the ground, and she hit hard for nobody was there to catch her. Dan went over and asked one of the men to help him take her over to their room. As they left, I wondered what would make a man go as far as this for money. That was beyond my understanding. I directed two of my new men to take the body over to the undertakers.

"Comin', Foster? Got to get the stock rounded up."

"Sure."

After two or three hours we had all the animals in the corral, which was all that was left of the stables, and the wagons we pulled up on the outside of the corral.

"Well, Foster, I'm goin to stay and keep watch. You go on to bed, and get some rest. Tim, would you or Jim relieve me in about five hours. We leave day after tomorrow and can't afford to let anything else happen."

Tim spoke up, "I will, boss, after finding that man dead like that, want sleep all night anyway."

"Thanks."

They went off, and everyone had gone back home to bed. The night went without anything happening, and Tim relieved me about two in the morning and I went and stumbled into bed and went to sleep without even taking off my boots or hat.

The next morning I went first thing to the corral and found Tim leaning up against the gate to the corral.

"Howdy, boss, things been quiet around here."

"That's good, how about goin' and gettin' Jim up and you get some sleep? Tell him to get the rest of the supplies we need. I have to find ten more men today and a cook. If you would, after you get up, get our men together and drive the wagons behind the general store and get the supplies loaded. We'll pull out first light tomorrow."

"You got it, boss."

By the time I got to the bank, I thought my eyes were playing tricks on me. There was a line of no less than twenty-five men waiting at the front door.

"How come so many of you showed up today?"

This one man stepped out of the line; he had a big guitar around on his back.

"I can't speak for these others, but after what happened last night, I mean old Gus dying, nobody goin' to be tellin' me I better not work for you or I'm in trouble."

And everyone in the crowd seemed to be of the same mind.

"Come on in, you with that there guitar. You know how to play or you just carry it for show?"

Well, he let go with the likes I hadn't heard since I left the ranch.

"Come in and sign up! That might come in handy on those lonesome mountain nights. If you ain't afraid of work."

"No, sir, these here hands seen plenty of that."

We walked into the bank, and he signed the book "Sam Ganger."

"Good havin' you with us; we leave in the mornin'. By the way, who was tellin' men not to sign up?'

"It was that Miss Walters, she always had this here big guy with her."

By noon I had all the men we needed this trip and told the rest to give their names to Mr. Gills if they wanted to come up to the mine for the winter months. Not a man got out of line to leave. They all signed up for the second hitch. After everyone was gone, I went over to Bill and shook his hand.

"Thanks, Bill, for all your help. This is good-bye if I don't see you before we leave in the mornin'. Pay all the bills and find a buildin' for an office. I don't think we'll be able to get another shipment in here for three or four months. I'll let you know how many men to send up by November first. I'll send a map of how to get up there. By then most everyone will know where the mine is. Don't think I don't trust you, but if I was to give you a map now, after last night, I'd be afraid that it would endanger your life."

"Don't give it a second thought. I understand."

"Can you find out who owned those wagons and pay them even for the burned one?"

"Sure thing, Buck."

I was about to walk away when Juan came over to me with another man.

"Señor Silver, can I speak?'

"Sure, Juan, what is it?"

"This my cousin, I forgot about him, he's a good cook, not as good as me, of course."

"Of course not," I agreed just to show him I knew he was a fine cook.

"But he's nearly as good. You hire, he does his best."

"If you say so, I will hire him. What's your name?"

"Manuel Salazar, señor."

"Mr. Gills, please put him down on the books at the same pay as the regular workers."

"Will do. Manuel Salazar, right?"

"I need to be getting back to the diner . . . it's lunchtime."

"Thanks, Juan, follow me, Manuel."

I took off for the general store with Manuel right behind me all the way. When we got inside I called Ed Thames over.

"Ed, have my men been by?"

"Yes, sir, they're out back loading the wagons; we got nearly everything they wanted except some minor things."

"That's swell, now Manuel you tell Mr. Thames what all you'll need to cook for twenty-five men for six months. Order all the extras you think you'll need and pots and pans. He'll fix you up. Manuel, we leave tomorrow mornin' early, so pronto, Manuel, pronto."

"Mr. Thames, can I go through the shelves and get what is needed and you write it down? This way will be faster."

"It's fine with me."

I watched as Manuel rushed through the store getting things and stacking them on the counter as Ed entered the prices in his book.

"By the time you leave here, Silver, I'm going to need a small wagon train to get the store back into shape."

"Not complainin', are you, Ed?" I said laughing.

"Oh no, not me!"

I went to the back to see how the loading was coming along and was satisfied with the progress, so I went to look for Walters. They weren't in his office, and no one had seen them since last night's fire. At the last minute my mind turned to my mother and father, so I headed over to send a telegram. In it, I explained all that had happened and said I wanted them to move up to Colorado and retire to a life of leisure. That was short, but I could write later and explain more in detail.

Just when I was coming out of the telegraph office, there was a man staggering out of the land office. The sheriff and myself and two others ran over to him and he fell into the dirt. I picked his head up. It was the man that helped us homestead around the mine.

"What happened, Bob?" the sheriff asked.

"They jumped me."

"Who?" I asked.

"That Walters and his daughter and four more men."

"What they want?"

"They wanted to know where Silver Buck had his mine. Silver?"

"Yes, Bob."

"I didn't tell them, they held me and beat me, but I didn't tell. They went through the files and found the Homestead papers that told where the homestead is, but not the mine. But, I didn't tell, I'm sorry."

"It doesn't matter; let's get him to Doc's."

"Just a minute here, Silver, I had this in my shirt, they didn't find it. This is the proof you need that the land up there belongs to you two. Get them for me, will you?"

"Sure will, Bob."

I took the papers out of his shirt and showed the sheriff and as we carried Bob to the doc's, he died.

"What a fool I've been. You were right."

"That doesn't matter now, you had no way of knowin', I'm a stranger. But I want your permission to go after him, and whatever happens I'm in the right. This is me and Foster's claim."

"You have it, Buck, need any men?"

"No, I'll have my whole crew with me, and I know where he's headin'. He'll have trouble findin' that mine. We have three hundred and twenty acres up there, and it a take some time to find it and we're on our way tomorrow anyway. It a take about two to two and a half weeks to get up there. There's no hurry, they'll still be there. It's not lying around on the ground."

"All right, Buck, but be careful. You're an honest man and we want you to stay alive."

I left and found that the men had finished loading and told them what had happened and to be prepared to fight when we got there. "Right now," I told them, "get some sleep, we'd be leavin' early."

"Ed, put ten rifles in there and five or six cases of shells."

"You got it. Hope you get those sons of bitches for all of us."

"Sure goin' to try. Thanks for all your help."

I went off to the hotel and went to bed after tellin' Foster what had happened." Be ready to ride early,' I said.

"Sure thing, we'se get them!"

I didn't get much sleep and morning came too fast. I got up and dressed and went and got Foster up and we headed for the wagons. When we turned the corner to go behind the general store, all the men were there and ready to go. Foster and I got our horses, and I tied Lagger behind one of the wagons and mounted up on Blacky and our small wagon train headed north. It was rough country to take wagons over, but we were determined to do it. It was going to be done, and no claim jumper like the Walters were going to stop us.

Chapter Eight

We were on our way to the new Silver Buck & Co. mine. It had been seven months since my arrival in this wild, untamed country, but even in that short time I had found one old man that was my best friend and would trust my life to him. Just in the past week, the men that have come into my life as only workers, but I could already feel a friendship building between a few of them. Then there was Red Bird, my lovely wife-to-be. Meeting and falling in love with her was one of life's few unexpected pleasures that happen up here in this country. These things were making a bond that was too hard to break. Just because of one man and his evil daughter, two good men had died and four bad men—if they were all bad, for sometimes even a good man can turn bad for money.

Foster came up beside me a few miles out of town. "Buck, think I'se ride over to my cabin and make sure everything is all right and then ride ahead to spot any trouble that might be comin' your way."

'Good idea, Foster, you know the country better than any of us and we should have a scout."

"I'se come back every night and check in. If I'se see anything wrong I'se shoot in the air three times. Then you'se know to get ready for trouble."

"All right, three shots."

We stopped for dinner at noon and Manuel outdid himself. I'll keep it to myself, but to me he's better than Juan in town.

"Jim, Foster went ahead to scout. Would you like to saddle up my other horse, Lagger, and help me keep an eye on the trail ahead a little ways in case there's something that the wagons can't see in time to stop? Don't want any broken wheels."

"Sure I'll be glad, gettin' kind of stiff sittin' in that wagon."

Then Sam lit into a tune on his guitar that put everyone in a better mood than they had been in that morning 'cause most of us had known Bob and Gus and liked them. But we had to get on and let their passing go out of our minds, but not of our thoughts.

We were getting back on the trail again to try to make as many miles a day as we could. Everything went good the first day out, and Foster came in to report that there was no sign of anyone as far as he went, but to be on the safe side I posted two men on lookout and two more every four hours. I decided to rotate the guards; the four that guard at night would sleep during the day and the other would take turns driving. The men that guarded didn't complain because sleep would take away some of the boring day that riding in the wagon brought on. The night passed without any trouble, and in the morning we hit the trail after a good down-to-earth Mexican breakfast. It was so tasty. I never heard a complaint from anyone even if not one of them had ever eaten a Mexican meal before. Being from South Texas I had eaten them all the time when we were out checking the herd. I had nearly forgotten how tasty they could be.

I rode up beside the wagon that Manuel was riding in.

"Say, Manuel."

"Si, señor."

"Where you come from, I was just thinking I hadn't eaten food like that since I came up from South Texas."

"That is where I come from also."

"What town?"

"I should not say for you were good to give me a job, but I want to be honest with you. I was accused of stealin' a horse that was not taken by me."

"That's all right, I don't think you, a man that cooks like you do, would steal a horse. So now, where you come from?"

"I come from a village named Alice, Texas. That is what we call it, but it does not have an official name yet."

"That's funny. You came all this way to get lost from people looking for you and here I am from Kingsville, Texas. We were like neighbors, I've heard of Alice; it's north of the ranch my father works on."

"That must be the Backo Rancho."

"That's right, glad to have you with me, neighbor. I better get now, we'll have plenty of time to talk in months to come."

I left and scouted out to the east and north to be sure everything was still going all right ahead of us. As I cut back toward the wagons, I came to a creek that was over its normal banks. Couldn't figure out why it was overflowing; it hadn't rained in days or weeks. Then riding to a high ridge to the east I saw it some ways in the distance with snow still on top. That's what it was; the snow was melting. As I rode back to the wagons I felt a sadness come into my heart because to the west of where I was riding was Sunlight Peak and at the base of that peak was Dancing Bear's village and the woman that was in my thoughts and my heart. I wished my thoughts could travel to her village and find her thinking of me.

When I came to the wagons I told them about the creek but I thought with everyone's help we could get across with little trouble. We reached the creek but it had risen even higher in the short time since I was there an hour ago. I rode across the creek on Blacky, and Jim rode across on Lagger, and the water rose up to their bellies by the time we got to the middle of the creek. Tossing my rope to the driver of the first wagon, he tied it to the axle, and Jim threw his rope to the driver and he tied it also.

All the men got out and started to push as the driver drove the team into the creek, which was now raging like a river, and Jim and I started pulling. About half in the creek the wagon stopped and rocked a little, then the team moved on until the front wheels were on the dry part of the bank. We did this three more times, and when the last wagon was safe across the creek, everyone fell in a heap from exhaustion. We set up camp for the night about a mile from the creek. By the time we had eaten we found out why the creek was rising so fast as the rains hit us as hard as a cowboy hits the dust thrown off a mustang. It was like someone was up there pouring buckets of water right on top of us. We were under the wagons when Foster came riding in on his mule. He jumped off and came under the wagon with his slicker dripping water all over.

"I'se tried to get back to warn you'se this was comin' but it outran me. Glad to see you'se learned to get across the creek and then set up camp."

"Yeah, we came across that creek when I was out scoutin' and noticed how it was swollen and went back and hurried the men along. We got all the wagons across when this downpour hit."

"It's a good thing you'se got across or we'se be stuck here a week or more."

By morning the rains had stopped and we were underway again. It was harder going now 'cause of all the mud. It was everywhere, I even found some in my teeth. Then there was the mudholes. These are holes that fill in with water and lay in wait for a wagon wheel to roll into it, then it tries to pull it deeper. But with all the men out pushing and the horse up front pulling, we got through them all right. By nightfall everyone was covered with mud from head to toe, and we were laughing at each other 'cause of the way we looked. Then Manuel came running into camp with a bucket full of fresh water and clean as could be.

"Everyone go and have a bath before we eat, there's a nice clean stream over yonder."

No one was left in camp but Manuel. As I passed him, I said. "Keep a close watch and your rifle handy, all right?"

"You all just better make a lot of noise when you come back or you might be eatin' one of my bullets for supper." I laughed at that remark and headed for the stream. When I got there everybody was in the water with their clothes on trying to get them clean. One of the men said:

"Wish we had some soap."

So I rousted around the woods until I came across what was in front of me, the soap plant that I had used when I was with Red Bird. When I got back they were happy to have the soap. Getting in the water felt good and when I was clean, I felt better.

After that miserable, muddy day the ground dried out, and the sunlight glowed on the leaves and everything went smooth. Then a whole week went by and we were getting nearer to the men that had come to take what was ours away. Foster didn't come back that night, and it worried me a little, but just a little, because I knew Foster and he knew these mountains and the forest. About midday of the next day he came riding up to me as I was riding along side one of the wagons.

"Where you been, you old reprobate?" I started laughing.

"Here, I'se been out all night tryin' to save our mine and you'se be callin' me names."

"You been up to the mine?"

"Well, as close as I'se wanted to get, they'se up there all right, but as I'se thought they haven't found it yet and the wagons are just two days away."

"Good to hear they haven't found it, but I'm sorry they're still there. I hate to put these good men into our fight."

"Then give them a choose."

"What?"

"Give them a choose, and I'se bet they'se stick with you'se all the way."

"You think so? That would make me feel better."

That night when we stopped I explained things to them. "You have two days to make up your minds, but if you don't want to fight, you'll still have a job if you want it."

As we ate nobody said a word, and after a while I walked out a ways to think, away from the fire. When I came back to the campfire everyone was close around. Then Jim came up to me. I looked him straight in the eyes and saw a friend and hope.

"Buck, while you were out there we talked and the men want me to tell you we are with you all the way."

Around the fire could be heard all the agreements among the rest of the men.

"You gave us a chance to make a real good living and we're not going to let those thugs take it away from us without a fight."

"Thank you, all of you. I think with all your help we can win."

That night sleep came to me much more easily.

The next morning Foster was heading out again. Before he left, he stopped by to talk.

"If I'se don't get back tonight, don't worry I'se just be keepin' a eye on them. From now on don't let anyone start a fire, they might see it. I'se try to get back 'cause I'se think we'se should leave the wagons with one man to guard them, about two or three hours away from the mine so we'se can sneak in and surprise them and hopefully that will be enough for us to win. I'se better get goin' now."

"Be careful."

The men hooked up the teams, and we headed north again. In the saddle I could tell Blacky knew something was going on for he was a little skittish, but not enough for anyone to tell but me. I rode west and made a circle to the north and told Jim to ride east and come in from the south. I was trying to keep from us being surprised by someone. That night we made no fires and everyone kept to their self to keep the noise level down. The teams of horses were also quiet, content with the grass where we had staked them out. We ate dried beef jerky that night and the next morning I told the men Jim and I were going to ride north and if we weren't back by noon to stop until we came back.

"Keep your rifles handy and you all in the back wagon keep an eye peeled toward the back, just in case, let's not get careless this close."

Me and Jim left going north and about two hours out we rode into Foster.

"What you doing out this far?"

"I didn't want to get too close to their camp, and you didn't come in last night, so we decided to find out how far their camp was."

"The boss here told them to stop at noon and camp until we came back."

"We'se about four hours from their camp. How far you come?"

"About two hours."

"Me and Buck will stay here and you'se go back and get them movin' toward us. Maybe we'se can attack early in the mornin'."

"Jim, see this piece of cloth? I'm goin' to put it in this tree right here, if we're not here, keep goin' no more than two hours and stop and wait."

"Sure thing, boss."

Jim took off at a fast pace heading for the wagons.

"Foster, let's go back, I want to see the situation at first hand and maybe we can plan an attack while it's daylight." We took off for the mine.

After about three and a half hours, Foster said, "We'se leave the horses here; it's only about a mile and a half. We won't have any trouble gettin' in close to see 'cause they aren't keepin' guards."

We got in close, and from where we were I could see Walters and Jenny around outside a tent and only two other men.

"Is that all there is?"

"No, the rest are out lookin' for the mine; there's about ten men altogether. We have twenty-four countin' us; we shouldn't have any problems."

"You'se forget those are gunmen; some of our boys probably couldn't hit the side of a barn, but we'se do have the odds in our favor."

"We sure don't want to lose anyone if we can help it. Let's see, their camp is in a clearin' and trees all around, if we can spread out and surround the camp and rush them before sunup, just maybe we can capture them alive."

"Sounds good to me, we'se better get back to the men and set your plan into motion."

We took off on foot and made it back to the horses and worked our way back to the wagons. We were about three hours back, and there were the wagons waiting for us.

"Get the wagons movin', we got about two hours before we leave the wagons. We're not goin' to get any sleep tonight but tomorrow we'll be settin' up our own camp in place of theirs. I'll explain our plan when we leave the wagons."

It was already dark, but we had to be set to hit them by morning. So we took off down the trail and me and Foster and Jim went out around the wagons about half a mile to keep a lookout just in case Walters got smart and sent out scouts. As we came near to where we would stop, me and Jim rode up to the wagons and rode alongside while Foster went to check how many were in camp. While we waited, I explained what we would do and told Manuel he would stay with the wagons and animals.

"Why me? I want to come and fight."

"We need someone here in case anyone gets past us, and you are the most important to us."

"Me, why?"

"'Cause you're the one that's goin' to keep our bellies full every day. If we lost you, we couldn't get another cook as good as you and that's the truth. Right, boys?" Everyone said "Yes" at the same time.

"So, Manuel, we're not thinkin' of your safety, we're thinkin' of our bellies. I sure don't want to cook, I wouldn't have a man still workin' after a week."

Everyone was laughin', including Manuel.

About midnight Foster came back to camp and let us in on the situation.

"All the men are in camp and they'se have a big campfire goin' so we'se do have an advantage. We'se goin' to have them right where we'se wants to have them."

"Okay, men, let's spread out and surround the camp, and at sunrise we attack. Let me get this straight, we're not like them. We don't go in shootin', but if they shoot at you, return fire and make it count."

So we all surrounded their camp and waited for sunrise. Me and Foster went along the circle of men reassuring them. No one was falling asleep for there was too much anticipation in the air. When I stopped by Jim, he asked.

"Is the mine up that mountain?"

"Yes, sir, right behind them, they been walkin' by it for days, but it is very well hidden. My great-grandfather was a smart man. I'm just sorry he worked up here for thirty-one years and didn't get to spend any of the money that's goin' to come out of this mine."

"That's too bad."

"Well, just keep your head down and hope for the best."

I went from man to man waiting for sunup.

As the sun rose over the mountains to the east, I gave the signal to rush in slowly with no noise. We were within fifty feet when Walters came out of his tent. He spotted us tightening up the belt around his camp. I heard him in the stillness of the morning.

"Attack, boys, get up! We're under attack!"

I signaled for everyone to speed in and take control; we were now within thirty feet, and at this range we couldn't miss and someone would be killed. But it was too late. Walters's men started firing as Walters rushed back in the tent. Everyone of us hit the ground and I yelled, "Fire, boys, fire! And don't let up till they give up!"

It was then that I saw Walters run from the tent with Jenny carryin' two rifles and a gun belt around his waist. He was heading up the mountain, the only side we couldn't surround. I kept my eyes on them as the firing went on around me. There were already five of his men lying dead on the ground. I yelled.

"Is everyone all right?" I heard the replies as they came back.

"All right over here."

"Over here, too."

Then I asked the five men of Walters to give up.

"Your boss has ran away and we have twenty men out here, so give up."

They threw down their guns and got up off the ground and held their hands in the air.

"Foster, you and Jim check and make sure the men on the ground are dead and we'll keep an eye on the live ones." Foster and Jim got up carefully and went over to the bodies.

"Yea, Buck, they'se all dead, come on in."

All the rest of us got up and walked slowly in.

"Tim, Sam."

"Yes, sir."

"Yes, sir."

"You two round up all their guns and pile them."

As they went round and gathered up the guns, I ordered three other men to go back and tell Manuel to bring up the wagons and our horses. As they left I turned to the prisoners.

"Have a seat, boys, they'll be back with the rope to tie you up. Tim, you and Jim take charge. Foster, come on, let's go. I saw Walters and Jenny go up the mountain that way."

"I'se be ready. I'se had my eyes on them, too."

We took off up the mountain side. The sun was already up in the sky but the shadows among the trees and rocks still lingered. We kept going up but had not spotted them yet. It was hard to imagine them going too far because they weren't used to this type of terrain and would get tried easily. Then I saw it—a flash of light, like a reflection off metal. I motioned to Foster without making a sound, indicating the direction to go, and he followed quietly, not letting our presence known. As we went on they came into view, and as I thought they were stopped, resting on a ledge high above us. We kept on, each of us going in an opposite direction to come in on them at both ends of the ledge. Getting closer, I knew there was no escape for them, as Foster was at one end and I at the other. I spoke to Walters.

"Walters, you better give up before one of you gets hurt." I surprised him, and he turned and started firing at me and backing toward Foster. But I just ducked behind a large rock and the bullets missed. Then Foster spoke.

"I'se give up if I'se be you'se."

As Walters turned toward Foster, you could see the fear in his eyes. He must have bumped Jenny as he turned 'cause she went flying off the ledge and she was yelling all the way down. It was a good hundred feet, and as she lay among the rocks below there was no movement. We knew she was dead, and Walters put down the rifles and sat down and just stared at her body below. He didn't say a word as Foster led him back to camp.

"I'm goin' to go down and bury her body, Foster."

"Right, see you back in camp."

Working my way down to Jenny's body, I thought to myself, what a waste of such a beautiful girl. Her father led her down the wrong path of life and she followed. So I buried her down there among the rocks, high in the mountains where no one would see the grave except the birds and animals of the wild.

When I returned to camp the men had the five prisoners and Walters all tied up and in the wagon that the men had drove in. I walked over to Walters, who was staring into space.

"Walters, I buried her in the rocks where she fell. Sam, you and the men unload another wagon and then pick two men, one to drive the empty wagon and you and a guard for the prisoners. Take them back to Durango and turn them in and then tell Mr. Gills at the bank to sell those two wagons and teams. Then tell him to see if he can buy Walters's office for our mining office, buy, not rent if he can. I'm countin' on you, this is an important job."

"Yes, sir, I'll do as you say."

They took off the next morning after a good night's sleep and a good breakfast.

I set all the men getting the remaining wagons unloaded and then put them to cutting down the trees around the sight where the main camp was going to stand.

"Don't cut down any trees toward the mountain side of the camp. Those trees will help stop mud and snow slides." Then I called Foster, Jim, and Tim off to the side to discuss the campsite.

"Foster, this is where we decided the camp was to be, isn't it?"

"Sure is, Buck."

Jim took out their plans and rolled them out on the ground in front of us.

"See, Silver, the main building is in the middle with five bunkhouses around them," Tim said. Then Jim came in.

"See, the main building here will have Foster's and your room over here and then the office area here, then at the opposite end is the kitchen and Manuel's room. We thought since he had to be up earlier than anyone he should have his own room next to the kitchen."

"Good idea."

"Then, see this large space between the office and the kitchen will be tables for the men to eat or play cards, you know just a place to gather and relax on our off time. If someone wants to be alone he can go to his bunkhouse which will have four beds with enough room for each man to have his own private space."

"This is a good plan, don't you think so, Foster?"

"Looks mighty fine to me, like a small town."

"Glad you said that, Foster," Tim said, then continued. "We thought since Manuel was in charge of the foodstuffs, that right here could be a small general store for the men to buy things they will need in their bunks. This could be deducted from their final pay."

"That sounds fine so you all get to stakin' out the camp and instructin' the men on what to do."

"We'll have it all leveled and staked out today and in the morning will start laying timbers."

"Good."

After only a week it was starting to look like a mining camp. I'd seen men work but not as hard as these men. Here it was the middle of June and things were looking bright. About the middle of the second week Sam and the two men rode in on some fine horses. Sam got off his horse:

"This place is lookin' up."

'It's comin' along, where you get the horses? Did everything go all right?'

"Sure did, why we got them back without a hitch, old Walters, he just sat there lookin' out in space like he's crazy.

Anyway, Mr. Gills sold the wagons and rented these horses to come back on. He thought you could send them back with the first load."

"You all three go and get some grub. Tell Manuel to rustle you up something and then get some rest. You all can start work tomorrow. Sam I'm goin' to have a special job for you. We'll talk about it later."

Going over to where Foster was sitting down on one of the logs that had been cut down earlier.

"Foster, have a seat, I need to talk to you." He sat down beside me and picked up a stick and took out his knife and started whittling on the stick.

"Been up to the mine yet?"

"Nope, you'se said, wait till camp is done."

"How would you like to get started tomorrow?"

I could see his eyes brighten up like a clear night sky full of stars, mining was in his blood, and without it he was nothing and with it he was in heaven. The mine was his domain. I saw Sam walking with a plate of food.

"Sam, over here. Sit down, we want to talk to you. Go ahead and get to eatin', Sam. Well, in the mornin' you get those two that came back with you and go with Foster up to the mine and get started."

"If it's all right with you'se, Buck, I'se make Sam here my assistant."

Sam started choking on his food. I hit him on the back.

"Take it easy, Sam. Foster, that's a fine choice."

"But I never been anything like that before."

"Well, I never owned a Silver mine either. And look at Tim and Jim, they're goin' about their job like a duck goes to water and they never been in charge of anyone either. You can do it."

"I'll try to, that's for sure."

The next morning Foster took the three men up to the mine about half a mile up the east side of the mountain. They didn't come back at noon. So I packed some food and took it up to the mine on Blacky. When I got there, I didn't see anyone, so I got off and went inside. As I entered, there was a light.

"Anyone there, Foster? Sam, where are you?"

"Over here, Buck."

"What you all up to? Didn't come back at noon."

Bob came over to me. "We just got carried away, this is some place . . . look." He handed me a large piece of rock and I held it up to the lamp. It was nearly pure silver. We walked back to where Foster and Sam and the other man were hammering away. They had silver stacked up all around them.

"Foster, can you stop to talk to me a minute? Have your dinner here."

He stopped and turned, and I saw he was covered with silver dust. "Well, boys, we'se can take a break and eat."

We all went outside and they started eating.

"Buck, you'se know this mine is richer than either of us thought."

"You mean it, Foster."

"Think we'se goin' to have two wagons full by July."

"Why, that will put us two months ahead of what we planned."

"Jo, you'se and Bob go after we'se eat and hitch up the wagon and bring it up here and start loadin'. Me and Sam will keep diggin'."

"You need more men up here?"

"No, not now, maybe in a month or so. There's not much room in there right now. We'se four will make it larger where more can get in there at once. Anyways, the others have to get the camp finished so we'se have a roof over our heads before winter."

"I'll get back now. Goin' to start helpin' them with the camp."

I got back just in time to help finish the outer wall of the first cabin. We kept working day after day, and then another two weeks went by. We had three cabins finished with roofs and beds, so twelve men drew sticks each time a cabin was finished and the winners got the cabin with no hard feeling between anyone. Right now the nights were warm, so it didn't matter. I called a meeting the night of July third.

"I don't know how many of you are from states back east, but I'm from Texas, and even though Colorado isn't a state yet I still celebrate Independence day. Tomorrow is the Fourth of July and you all have done a good job, so everyone has tomorrow off."

They were so happy, they were jumping around and hugging each other and yelling loud as they could.

"Wait a minute, calm yourself. I got some more good news. Sam and Joe are leavin' the day after tomorrow with the first two loads of silver. This is at least a month early, so everyone will get a bigger bonus than I first told you. The amount depends on how rich the ore is, but Foster thinks it's richer than the first we brought in."

Well, they let go again, this time throwing their hats in the air and dancing round the campfire. After a while the pre-Fourth party broke up and everyone went to bed.

The next day everyone had a big breakfast and then most sat around writing letters for Sam to take the next day into Durango for their families. Then Sam got his guitar out and started playing the old Western tunes, and this got all the men in a dancing mood. No women, but still they danced with each other in a big circle and yelling with all their might. Me and Foster were sitting around enjoying the men having fun. Then in the middle of the afternoon Manuel brought out food and everyone ate until their bellies were bulging like a balloon. In the evening they sat around playing cards or mending socks or whatever they thought to do.

The next day was another big event. Nobody went to work; they all came to see the first shipment off. We covered the wagons with canvas and tied it down tight.

"Sam, try to go along the same trail there and back. We have to make a solid road by the time the fall rains come."

"All right, will do."

"You both got your rifles?"

"Right here, don't worry. We'll be back in no time."

They started out when Manuel came running out.

"Wait, here Sam . . . a list of things we need."

He looked at me and I nodded 'yes' and the wagons took off down the road after he tucked the list in his pocket.

Everyone went back to work, even me. I would get out there and split a few logs and just do anything that needed doing. The weeks passed fast, working as hard as we were.

It was now the middle of August and Sam and Joe had taken two more loads to town and were now back in camp. Sam brought news of the trial of Dan Walters and his five men, they were found guilty of two murders and sent to Denver to hang. I knew it was right, but it made me a little sad that anyone could go that wrong.

By this time we had finished all the cabins and the main headquarters. To me, being from South Texas they looked very odd, but Foster, Jim and Tim assured me, they would be warm in the winter, as they took me on a tour to show me why this was so. The cabins sat flat on the ground but you had to go upstairs that went about twelve feet up to the door. This was so we wouldn't have to be pushing snow away from the front door. In the winter the snow would easily reach the top of the stairs. Inside when we went down the inside stairs, there was a large fireplace made out of large stones found around the area. Foster explained that when the snow was deep it would block the wind off the bottom half of the cabins where the men were. He reminded me how the cave we spent last winter in was warmer when the snow covered up the opening to the cave. I asked Jim to put two men to work cutting trees along the road that had formed coming into camp and stocking up each cabin and the main buildin' with firewood inside, enough for the winter.

The next morning I talked to Manuel.

"You know how to smoke meat, Manuel?"

"Si, señor you put me in the kitchen and I do anything."

"Well then, I'm goin' to have Jim plan and build a smoke house on the back of the kitchen. Now, me and you are goin' to go out and hunt up some deer or even a moose and then you can smoke and store it so we'll have meat all winter."

"That's a fine thing to do, Señor Silver."

"Next day or two another wagon is goin' to town, if you need any extra things for smokin', meat make a list."

"Señor, may I ask for something that you may not have thought of?"

"Ask away."

"A helper for when I smoke meat. It has to be watched and I can't cook all the meals and clean the kitchen and watch the meat."

"You're right, that does sound like a lot of work. Would you like for Sam to try to find someone in town, maybe a fellow Mexican so you can talk in your own tongue to them."

"That would be fine, you understand me?"

"Manuel you know, that down on the ranch all the cooks and most of the cowboys I worked with were of your people and they were a good lot. It was just those bandits from Mexico that stole our cattle, even our Mexican cowboys didn't like them."

"This I understand, it was those type of bandits that got me in trouble for stealing horses. I guess one of them looked like me. But you know, to some Americanos we all look alike." He let out a big laugh and so did I.

I took off and rode Blacky up to the mine. We now had ten men working and loading. When I went inside, how different it looked now. Instead of only going back about fifteen feet, it now went about thirty feet back. As Foster saw me, he came over.

"You'se knows Buck we'se back pretty far now. It's goin' to take more men to carry and load the wagons. But we'se can save if we send Sam to get some sections of rail steel and two minin' carts and we can just load and unload and not have to crowd in more men. They'se get in each other's way."

"We will have to order them from Denver. I'll have Sam send a telegram. Anything else we might need before winter sets in?"

"Let me'se think, not for sure."

So the next day Sam and Joe pulled out again and me and Manuel went off hunting. He had left supper on the stove in case we didn't get back that night. Jim said they would have the smoke house finished by tomorrow. It wasn't much to it. Making it varmint tight was the most important thing about it.

We were heading northeast. This was all new to me never been this far to the north. With every new rise came a new excitement within me. I had to ask Manuel.

"You know Manuel, this country is so much different than where we come from. I don't know how to tell you about what I feel inside."

"Si, know what you mean, I feel it also. Everything is so green and down under all these trees, it is so damp and smells so fresh."

We rode on, but only saw old bucks. Manuel said 'no', he wanted younger ones, cause the meat would be most tender and he was the cook, so I listened to him.

While we camped that night I made a far reaching decision. Mining was not in my blood. My place was on a ranch with cattle roaming all round me. By spring everything should be running smooth at the mine. I was going to take a big hunk of money out of the bank, then marry Red Bird and go find ourselves a beautiful valley somewhere east of here and rise our kids right alongside our cattle.

We rose early, and by noon we had two young deer and one young, but huge moose. Foster's mule could barely carry the load but we was only a day's ride from camp so we spent another night out in the mountains.

"The men are goin' to be mad at me."

"They been livin' too good off your cookin'; do them good to go without it awhile. Make them appreciate you more."

We got back the next morning and sure enough the men were complaining about not getting a good breakfast and supper the day before.

"But look, men when these are smoked and the winter is all around, you all will be glad we went out and got this. I know, ask Foster about last winter, what we went through." That stopped all the complaints.

Sam and Joe rode in about September first and he said: "They said we could have the rail and coal carts by October first, but we'll have to pick it up in Grand Junction. That's where the nearest railroad is right now."

"Foster, you know how far that is?"

"You'se goes north a few miles, you'se hit a plateau that will take you'se right up there, no big mountains after this Red Mountain we'se be by. I'se say about seventy miles. There and back about seven weeks, if the weather holds good they'se make it. After October first it be anyone's guess about that."

"Well, Sam I hate to do this to you but give the horses a couple days rest and head out. Foster can make you a map. Oh, take one man and three or four rifles and lots of ammo. That's Indian country. Pick someone to go except Joe, he already knows the trail back to town and we need him to take some more ore in."

"You know, when you gave me this job I thought it would be easy sitting all day long. But you know my ass is sore and I got blisters too." Everyone started laughing and making fun of Sam. Then I spoke up.

"Well, Sam you better stand up for these two days cause you're on the move again." I started laughing and everyone roared with laughter, even Sam.

"I guess that's what I get for leaving all of you with the hard work. I thought I'd put something over on everyone, but if you could see my butt you'd see I put one over on myself." The men were rolling on the floor. They were saying "Stop it, we're going to bust."

After a while things calmed down and men started drifting off to bed and as they left for their own cabins, you would hear a deep bubbling laugh once in a while and tears of joy and friendship in their eyes. Before Sam left he came over and handed me two letters.

"I forget about these. One from Mr. Gills and the other from Texas."

"Thanks, Sam, it's from my folks. Good night."

I sat there looking at the letter and hoped no bad news was in it. It had been almost a year since I left the ranch. A lot could happen in that time. Opening the letter, I could tell it was written by my mother. She had a beautiful way of writing that I hadn't seen before.

Dear Son,   June 16, 1872

Everything is fine with us, we are well. I was glad to hear from you and that you are well. I was sorry to hear about Jeb, he was a fine old man and I did love him dearly.

Buck, Jim Backo was killed in a stampede on that drive they were on when you left. His son has taken over and he will not listen to your father. Your father is always upset because young Tom is breaking up the ranch by selling to land spectators. I won't go into all the details now. But your father is thinking about what you said about coming to Colorado. But by the time this letter gets to you it will be late in the year. So maybe next summer. If we do come let us know, and we can bring some of the hands with us. They are starting to lose their jobs because of young Tom selling.

Well I hope this letter finds you well.

Bye now.

Your loving Mother

I put the letter down on my lap and wiped a tear from my eyes thinking about my mother and all she had done for me. And my father, he had always been good, teaching me everything he knew. He deserved better than he was getting. Now I knew what had to be done. I would talk to Foster in the morning. Then remembering the other letter from Bill, I tore it open. It was a statement.

Dear Silver Buck:

As of the shipment of ore that was delivered today and minus all debts are up to date. Minus the purchase of Walters's law office which was seven hundred dollars. Your account stands at $155,698.82. Tell Foster his share is $23,354.77.

I have started on my law degree and should be a lawyer before spring, I hope. All thanks to you. Come to town to visit some time.

Your Friend and Assoc.
Bill Gills

In the morning I went to Foster's room next to mine and set down and showed the letter to him. After he read the bank statement, he turned to me.

"Doin' pretty good, ain't we'se."

"Sure are, but read the other letter from my mother."

"Should I'se, it's to you'se?"

"Go ahead, I want you to. After you read I want to discuss something with you."

He leaned back on his bed against the wall and started reading. When he got through, he looked at me.

"Sounds like they're unhappy for sure."

"That's what I think."

"Well, now I'se knows you'se have something on your mind so let's have it."

"I've learned a lot from you up here in these mountains and I've come to love them. You, why you I consider my best friend in the world next to my parents. Jeb and you are miners and now he's dead, but, Foster, I'm a rancher and I love being around cattle."

"What you'se tryin' to say you'se be leavin'?"

"No, not yet, let me finish. It's hard to say 'cause I will miss you. I'm goin' to town with the next shipment and wire my folks money to bring cattle up here next spring and start a big ranch. You remember we talked about the land east of here? Well, I want to look over there after I marry Red Bird in the spring. What do you think about it?"

"What about the mine? I'se can't run it by myself. It's too much, I'se gettin' to be an old man."

"Oh, Foster, you know you couldn't live without this, and anyways I thought Jim and Tim would be good around here. Everything is finished except the rails, and they will be here and in place before spring. Don't you like Jim and Tim?"

"Sure do, I'se think they'se be hardworkin' and honest for you'se."

"Let me tell you the rest; you can become the manager of the mine and teach one of them the mine, the other can learn the office and you just set back and relax or you can still help in the mine if you want to. Also, when I get to town I'm goin' to arrange with Bill to give you; startin' with the spring shipments 25 percent and Jim and Tim 5 percent each and Sam 4 percent. My family and me will keep 61 percent. Will you do it? You can come stay with us any time you want, you're like family."

"Sure, Buck, I'se do it. You're right, these mountains and that mine is my life."

"I'll go and talk to the others."

I left Foster with the feeling of joy and sadness. I walked over to the table where the three, now all friends among themselves, sat.

"Jim, Tim, and Sam, come over here, I want to talk to you." They came over and sat down by me.

"What is it, boss?"

"Just talked to Foster, and startin' next spring he's takin' over. Got a letter from home, and my folks are comin' up and we're goin' to start a ranch over east of here next spring. If you all stay up here all winter, and you and Tim learn all you can from Foster about minin' and, Jim, I'll teach you the office work. Sam, you get off that wagon seat and watch over the supplies and keep everything in top shape. Come spring, all three of you will have nearly one thousand dollars each. That's a lot of money. But as you know we have become friends, and I trust you with anything of mine, so I'm goin' to do just that. But you three, Foster, and me will all have shares in the mine."

"Buck, you mean we will own part of all this?"

"Sure do, if you want it. The shares will be 61 percent is mine, Foster are 25 percent, 5 percent is Jim's, 5 percent is Tim's, and 4 percent for Sam here. Let me show you what kind of money we're talkin' about. Look already this year and we haven't even been up here four months. Foster had 10 percent before and he has $23,000 in the bank. That means you two could have $30,000 apiece this time next year and you, Sam, could have about $14,000. That should take care of those blisters on your butt."

"Don't laugh, it's not funny," Sam said.

We all started laughing anyways.

"Well how about it? Is it a deal?"

They all said sure, and I shook each one's hand and told them I was going to town and Mr. Gills would draw up the papers. "Silver, you beat all I've ever seen; you go to all that trouble then you just give half of it away."

"It's just I'm a rancher, not a miner and anyway 61 percent should keep me happy."

"It should at that, shouldn't it?" Sam said.

Sam headed for Grand Junction the next day with the understanding to wire me in Durango for the money to buy the mining rails and cars for the ore. In another two days the wagon was ready to leave, and as we left I noticed how the trail had turned into a road. It had been three months since I've been down this trail. Blacky was tied behind the wagon cause I was going to be in town longer than a day or two and they needed the wagon. I was also going to scout around for some fine horses as a wedding present to Dancing Bear for the hand of his lovely daughter Red Bird. I saw her standing before me with her beautiful body exposed to my view. What a wonderful thought to carry me through the long hard winter months.

We stopped every night and camped under the late summer skies filled with twinkling stars. I would be glad when we reached town tomorrow, because being alone except for Joe's company was hard on the mind. The loneliness brought on thoughts of Red Bird. And when my thoughts turned to Red Bird, I could be standing in the middle of a crowd and still be lonely. This was how much in love I was.

The next afternoon we pulled up in front of our new mining office. Somehow the town of Durango had changed. I could see there were a few new stores in town. Then I noticed it, the large sign above our mining office. SILVER BUCK & CO. is all it said, but a lot of meaning was behind that name. I felt a little ache come into my heart as I thought of the men I would be leaving behind after this winter. They were good and honest men that could and would build this land into a place to be proud of.

When I walked into the office with Joe beside me, it was apparent that Bill had made changes so that no one would have known it had ever belonged to a different type of man. Joe sat down in a chair close to the front door to keep an eye on the wagon. I walked up to the desk.

"Howdy, Bill." He looked up, and with surprise in his face showing he stood up and grabbed my hand and shook it.

"Well I'll be, never expected to see you till after winter. Nothing wrong, is there?"

"Oh no, just wanted to come in and take care of some business. Everything is goin' fine up at the mine."

"Can I help you, Silver?"

"Joe, take the wagon over to the assay office and check in. Hire a man to help you, here's ten dollars to pay him. Tie Blacky outside in front here. Then have a couple of drinks on me."

"Yes, sir boss, I'll take you up on that one."

"Now, Bill, by the way I like what you've done to the office, looks fine. You remember the letter from my mother you sent out to me."

"Sure do, hope no bad news was in it."

"Oh no, just that the owner of the ranch where my father works died and his son is ruining it and my family might be comin' up here next spring."

"That's fine."

"I'm a rancher, not a miner, so I want to start a ranch up here, and me and my father will run it and leave the minin' to Foster, Jim, Tim, and Sam. I'm givin' Foster a bigger share and the three others smaller shares." I told Bill how many shares went to whom and then completely surprised him.

"And you, Bill, will have ten percent also. You're a fine young man and deserve a break, and I consider you a friend."

I thought he was going to fall out of his chair right in front of me. Then after he recovered, he spoke up.

"Silver Buck, what a name for a man, for you are a gem. I'm just at a loss for words what to say."

"Just say yes."

"All right, yes."

"By spring you will be a lawyer and will already have two clients, Silver Buck & Co., and my new ranch."

"Will you draw up the papers for me to sign? The startin' date is the first day of spring next year. And if you ever get too fancy like Walters, I'll come over and whip up on you." Then I let out a big laugh.

"Speaking of Walters, did you know his ranch south of town is for sale? With the right person handling it, it could be a fine ranch."

"I don't think I want anything to do with whatever that man had his hands on. Anyways, I was thinkin' of eastern Colorado. Heard of some ranches startin' over there."

"Now, I'm talking to you as your financial adviser as well as a friend. Listen to me closely. Walters only owned about one hundred acres; there's a lot more to be bought and not one rancher has found out about it, yet. But they will. I want us to ride out there in the morning."

"Oh all right, I'll look."

"You said we are your friends and you like it around here, it would be perfect for you and you could keep your hand in minin' if you had a mind to."

"All right, all right, I said I'd look."

"Okay, it just excites me 'cause if you're a rancher you'll love it."

"Right now the only thing you said I like is bein' closer to my friends. I'll see tomorrow. Well, I have to get a room now, see you in the mornin'."

"Bye now."

I left and went to the hotel and got a room, then went to the saloon for a cold beer with Joe. He had already had two or three, so I got a beer and sat down with him.

"Got a room yet, Joe?"

"They always have one for me and Sam ready and waitin'. They come to expect our arrival every month."

"Are you from around here, before you hired on with us?"

"Sure am, been all my life."

"Mr. Gills—."

"You mean Billy? We went to school together a few years back."

"Bill told me about the land south of here, Walters's ranch and more. Do you know anything about it?"

"Sure do, it's good land, not much for farming, too uneven, but for cattle or horses it's fine, plenty of grass and water if you have the right part."

"Any trouble with Indians?"

"Not too much, just the Utes and they're pretty friendly. They might take a cow or two if they can't find any buffalo around. That's not much to pay since it really was their land first. Walters had a gold mine if he would had put in as much time workin' that ranch and not stealin' from other people."

"Thanks, Joe, I'm goin' to eat and go to bed."

I drank the rest of my beer and got a bite to eat. Everyone was very friendly everywhere I went. I took Blacky to the new stable and fed and brushed him, then headed to my room for a good night's sleep.

I got up early and found out from the hotel clerk where Bill lived. I walked over to his house and knocked on the door. Bill came to the door.

"Ready, Bill? Want some breakfast at the diner?"

"Sure, let me get my coat and hat."

We walked down to the diner and ate a nice hot breakfast. While we were there Juan came out to see me.

"Hello there, Juan, how are you?"

"Fine, how Manuel doin'?"

"Well he's fine, I'll tell you only your cookin' could match his. One day me and him went huntin' for fresh meat for two days and when we got back I thought we were goin' to have a hangin' and it was me they wanted to hang for taking their cook." I let out a laugh.

"Told you, didn't I?"

"You did, well, we better get over and get our horses, Bill. Good to see you, Juan."

"Si, for me also."

Chapter Nine

We got our horses and headed south out of town.

"Bill, I've been talkin' to Joe, and he said it is good land for cattle."

"That's what I been tellin' you. Just 'cause I spend my time in a office all day doesn't mean I don't know a good thing when I see it."

We were about a half mile outside of town along the river when Bill drew up and got off his horse, and I did the same.

"Over here, Buck, see that small house, that's Walters's old place. This is the beginning of the ranch all along this river. After you left yesterday, I figured out how many acres I'm thinking of. From here North to the border of New Mexico it's seventeen miles and thirteen miles east of here is the Los Pinos River, you'll have two rivers for water all the way to the border."

I stood there looking out over the country and back to town.

"That's a big hunk, how many acres and how much?"

"There's 141,440 acres and you can get it for seventy-five cents an acre. That makes it $106,080.00. You have that right now, and by spring that will double."

"It's as big as I ever dreamed of, but let's take a ride out a ways and have a look-see."

We mounted up heading south for the New Mexico border. The plateau was high above the river bottom, which was good for in spring the river would be flooded by the snow melting from the high country. The plateau continued for a few miles, then there was a gulch about five to ten feet deep, then up again on another plateau. We rode till noon not seeing anything except grass. We then turned east and rode about five miles, then turned north back to Durango with ten or twelve gulches in our path. The rest was just plenty of grass with a tree or two here or there where the snow melted in the spring and would last into the summer months.

It was past dark when we rode up to the stable and left our horses. We ate at the diner and discussed my plans. After I ate I sat back and relaxed.

"You know, I think you're right; that could be a fine ranch. I haven't seen so much unbroken land since leavin' South Texas. This is fall and the river still had enough water for cattle."

"I'm not going to lie to you, Buck, we had a lot of snow-fall last winter and that's where the rivers get most of their water. So if we don't have much snow, the river will be much lower than now. It's a chance, but I think it's worth the chance."

"There's a risk in any type of business where you depend on the weather. You should see South Texas when we don't get rain for four months."

"Do you think you want to do it, Buck? You'll still have over fifty thousand dollars to bring cattle in and hire hands and build a find home."

"Before I say yes, there's something that needs to be said. I need a honest answer from you if you're really my friend. Bill, I'm in love and goin' to be married in the spring."

"That's great."

"Wait, let me finish. The girl is the daughter of an Indian chief, Dancing Bear. They are Utes and they live a little north of here."

"That does surprise me, to say the least, and there are some people that will look down on you. But your true friends will stand by you and I think most people around here know how generous you are and have brought a lot to this town. They will overlook their resentment toward you. But there will be a few that will try to make trouble for you, no matter what."

"That's just what I was thinkin', and if you and my other friends will stand by me, I say go ahead and buy all that can be had between the two rivers down to the border and be damn to those others."

"I'll get started first thing in the morning. It's a good investment. You won't be sorry, Buck. What is your bride-to-be's name?"

"Red Bird. We met last fall when me and Foster were searchin' for the mine. It was love at first sight and her father agreed. He knew my great-grandfather Jeb and liked him very much. After only two days he knew I was cut from the same cloth as Jeb."

"That's fine, Silver."

"Can you have it bought by spring?"

"Sure, the Walterses' place will be yours tomorrow. The other might take a month or two."

"Then I'm goin' to wire my parents tomorrow. What would be a good date to tell them, so the cattle can get up here without worryin' about snow?"

"They come through the southern route to Santa Fe, I think they could start by the end of February. They should take about three months to get here."

"Thanks for everything, Bill, I'm goin' to hit the sack. I want to talk some more in the mornin'."

"I'll be at the bank all day, so long."

In the morning I got an early start, at sunup, and rode out to the ranch house of Walters's old place to have a look. As I looked around it was plain to see that Walters didn't care about ranching. The place was all run down. As I walked up the front porch a step broke from dry rot. The inside wasn't in any better shape; there were rats running around, and the back of the fireplace had a crack from top to bottom. It wasn't very large, just one big room with two bedrooms and a kitchen. I couldn't see moving Red Bird into this. It all had to come down. The barn was in worse shape, and the corral also. It would all have to come down and start from scratch.

As I mounted up, there was a flash of light from the darkness of the barn. But I knew it was too late to do anything about it when a sharp pain went through my head and I fell off Blacky into the dirt. The next thing that came to me was the bright sun as I tried to open my eyes. The pain was worse than anything I had ever felt. It must had been hours since the shot was fired which had put me in the dirt, because the sun was in my eyes as I lay flat on my back. It was at least noon. That meant I'd been there four to five hours. As I was tryin to get up by holding on to Blacky's leg, my head felt about two sizes bigger than usual, and I became dizzy and fell back into the dirt. Then there was the sound of a horse's hoofs. It wasn't Blacky; he was still standing over me blocking out some of the sun. Then a voice came to me like from a distant echoing out of a rain barrel.

"Buck! What happened?"

Then someone was helping me get on Blacky, but I could not tell who it was, everything was so fuzzy looking.

"Let's get you to the doc's . . . you've been shot. What happened?"

I could not respond, but I understood what was said.

"Hold on to Blacky, Buck, tight, okay?"

I felt like the next moment my eyes were trying to open and I was lying on a table with someone over me. But it was impossible to tell who it was. I could not speak, but I could hear someone talking.

"Come back tomorrow, he'll be better."

Then everything went black again.

My eyes opened and it took a minute for them to adjust to the light, but I could see, except there was two of everything I looked at. Then the short baldheaded man with a fat belly came into view.

"Well, you're awake . . . about time," he said.

"Where am I? My head is splittin' in two. What happened to me?"

"Take it easy, you'll be all right."

He went to the door and yelled for someone, then he said something to this person and the man left. As I tried to get up, he came over and pushed me back down. I was helpless to resist, and fell back onto the table.

"Just lay there, son, you've been shot, but you'll recover fast enough when my wife gets her broth in you."

So I lay there barely aware of anything going on around me. Then the door opened and someone came in that looked familiar. He came over to the table.

"Good to see you awake, Buck, how you feeling?"

"My head hurts, where's Blacky? . . . my gun?" as I reached for my head, "and my hat?"

"Don't worry, Buck, I took Blacky to the stable. You know he stood over you for hours out there."

"My gun and hat?"

"They're here, you won't need them. Doc here says you'll be in bed two or three more days."

"Okay, you two, that's enough for now. He needs his rest. You can talk again tomorrow, now get Billy."

Then my eyes closed and it was dark again, but this time more peaceful.

I would wake up every now and again during the day and the doc's wife would be there with some beef broth. It was difficult at first to get it down, but feeling as weak as I was, it was necessary to keep my strength up. By the second day my sight was returning to normal and I could stay awake for four or five hours at a time. This is when Bill came in to see how I was.

"How are you, Buck? Another half inch and you might not be here talking to me."

"I feel much better, but I'm still a little hazy."

"What happened out there anyway?"

"I went out to check the condition of the buildings and had decided to have them torn down. I was headin' back to meet you when there was a flash of some sort, guess it was the blast, then I was lyin' on the ground. How you know where I was?"

"When you didn't show at the bank like you said, I thought you may have forgotten, so I went to the hotel about ten and the clerk said you left early. Then after going to the stable and finding Blacky gone, I figured you had second thoughts, and rode out to check it again before you signed any papers. You know, when I got there, Blacky had been standin' over you blocking the sun for hours. He's sure loyal, isn't he?"

"Yep. Wouldn't give anything for that animal. He's really a friend and companion. You have any thoughts on who might have done it?"

"Funny, I was about to ask you the same thing. I haven't seen any strangers around town lately."

"Do you know if Walters had any other kids or kin?"

"No, but it was known around town that he came from St. Louis. I know, we'll send a wire there and see what turns up."

"Sounds good to me. I'm gettin' out of here tomorrow. Did you have the papers on that ranch deal?"

"Got the Walters ranch, but the other's going to take some time. I'm waiting for some information on it from Denver. But you come in the morning and sign the papers and you'll have a start on your ranch anyway. Can I expect you in the morning?"

"Sure thing, soon as Doc lets me go."

As Bill left, I felt a little worn out by the whole conversation and lay back and rested for the remainder of the day.

Doc came to me the next morning and said, "You can go about your business, but don't ride a horse for a week and rest as much as possible. Eat good meals, and no drinking."

"Thanks, Doc, and thank your wife for me, will you?"

"Sure will, Silver Buck."

I headed for the diner and ate a good breakfast, then went to our office. I met with Bill and signed the papers for the ranch. I then went to send a telegram to my father and mother:

> Sending five thousand dollars. Hire as many of the old hands from Backo's ranch and buy as many longhorns as you can for a cattle drive up here by February. Bought ranch with over hundred thousand acres. Old timers know way to come up. Details to follow in letter. Send reply.
>
> Love,
Your son Buck

Then I thought about Walters and sent another telegram, this time to St. Louis:

> To Sheriff of St. Louis:
>
> Would like to know of any information on any kin of a Mr. Dan Walters hung here for murder and daughter died in fall while trying to escape.
>
> Silver Buck
Durango, Colorado

I told the man at the telegraph office to bring the reply to either telegram to me at the hotel, room 201. I would be there all day.

I went to my room and lay down a couple of hours, then got up to write to my folks about the route I wanted them to come with the cattle in the spring.

September 25, 1872

Dear Folks:

I am writing this letter before I receive a reply from the telegram, for I am sure you will come. Hope this letter finds you both well. It has been a long time since I left home. I want to tell you in a letter before you come up, so you won't be surprised. I am getting married in the spring. She is very beautiful and I love her very much. But she is an Indian, a Ute princess, her name is Red Bird and her father is Chief Dancing Bear. She is smart, kind, gentle, and very open and honest. She is only seventeen but loves me very much.

Now to the cattle drive. Some old timers have told me how the cattle can get here through a southern route. That is why you have to start from South Texas in the middle of February. By the time you get to New Mexico the winter snows will be melting off the mountains and the rivers and creek will have water until June or July.

The first leg of the drive will be familiar to you. From Kingsville, head northwest until you reach the Nueces River, then follow it until it ends. Then head straight west, there should be five or six rivers and creeks until you reach the Rio Grande River. This should have plenty of water by the time you reach it in March, it starts in the foothills north of here.

Just follow the Rio Grande all the way to Santa Fe. I'll be waiting for you in Santa Fe about May Fifteenth. If you can't make it by then, send a rider to get me and I will come meet you with some extra hands if need be. From Santa Fe it's only about two hundred miles to the ranch. If any more money is needed, send a telegram for it.

Love you all,
Silver Buck

P.S. Silver is the name the men up here gave me when me and Foster discovered the silver mine, and it's the name of the mine also.

There was a knock on my door that afternoon. It was the telegram from my folks.

Buck Taylor:

Plenty of men and cattle, waiting to come with me and your mother, awaiting letter for money and instructions. See you in spring.

Gratefully yours,
Father

I had to get out of my room. I'd been coupled up too long, so I walked to the general store and talked to Ed Thames.

"Well, you a bit sore? I heard you got shot. Glad to see you up and around. How you feeling?"

"Doc had me laid up too long. Just had to get out. I need a couple of apples to give my horse. He helped save my life and he loves apples. Looks like you got your store back in shape from all the supplies we took."

"Sure have, took a while, but I did it."

"Come next spring you better be prepared again, 'cause see this letter, I'm sendin' for my parents down in South Texas and they're a comin' with four to five thousand heads of cattle and twenty cowboys."

"What's this?"

"Yeah, I just signed papers for the old Walters place and land south of there. About the end of May they should be here, and we'll need a lot of things, so be ready."

"Glad you told me, I can order extra come spring."

"Well, better be gettin'. Thanks, he'll enjoy these apples."

I was walking toward the new stable when Ted came up to me with a telegram from St. Louis. Putting it in my pocket to read later, I entered the stable. Blacky was there with his ears all back. I knew something was wrong with him, and he looked skinnier than before. When he spotted me his ears perked up straight. I cut up his apples and he nearly swallowed them whole, and started neighing at me. I knew that he was happy to see me. Then I noticed a man coming over from one of the other stales.

"You Silver Buck, the one got shot?"

"That's me. This here is Blacky."

"I know, they brought him to me the day you got shot. By the way, my name's Gabby."

We shook hands. "Glad to meet you, Gabby."

"I know horses and you must have raised that one from a colt."

"How you know that? By the way, I did."

"Just knew it, see that bucket of grain and that hay. Well, since they brought him in he hasn't ate a lick and it was beginning to worry me. But now you're out of bed he'll be fine. See, look, he's eatin'."

"Gabby, he likes to be rubbed down. Would you mind doin' it for me? Doc told me to take it easy for a week."

"Sure thing, Silver."

"Blacky, now Gabby here is goin' to rub you down. You be good and let him. You better eat, 'cause we got to get back to camp."

Blacky shook his head up and down like sayin' he would.

"Sure we're partners. Here's ten dollars for your understandin', Gabby."

"Thanks, never got a tip like this before."

I left and went and got some of Juan's good cooking and headed for my room. Being out sure tuckered me. I lay down in my room, then remembered the telegram and took it from my pocket to read it.

Dear Mr. Taylor:

I made inquiry as requested and have found out that a Mr. Walters had a daughter about twenty years of age named Jenny and also he had a son that has been in prison for murder. He escaped the day his father hung. Name is Jack Walters. Please show this to your Sheriff in case he comes your way. If he does, contact me.

Sheriff of St. Louis
Jeff P. Jones

In the morning I would show this to John, but now it was just too much to handle. I fell off to sleep.

Getting up in the morning, I went straight to the sheriff's office and showed him the telegram.

"Sheriff Jones in St. Louis wanted me to show you this in case Walters's son shows up here."

"Buck, I want to say I'm sorry for not believing you about your men being ambushed, but I have to try to be fair to everyone. How did you know to wire St. Louis?"

"That's already forgotten. I sent a telegram to St. Louis cause that's where Bill told me Walters was from, Since he died I didn't know anyone around here that wanted me dead."

"I don't think anyone around here even knew he had a son. You better be careful; it's a possibility that he's the one that shot you. He had time enough to get here from the time he escaped."

"I'm sendin' a man down from camp to hire men to tear down the old Walters place. I bought it, and I hope they don't run into trouble if he's still around by then."

"I'll have my men looking for him, to send him back, but until then you and your men keep a sharp lookout. I don't want any more good people hurt or killed by that family."

"Sheriff, you mind if I take this? I want to show it to Bill. I'm worried that anyone connected with me might be a target."

"That may just well be. Go on and take it."

Walking over to the bank, I became aware of myself, the way I was looking around. That wasn't like me. Guess it's just being self-conscience because of my wound.

"Bill, read this. I thought I'd let you know that anyone connected with me might be in danger. So be careful."

"Well I'll be, no one in this town knew about a son. Guess he didn't tell anyone because they might not trust him then."

"Could be, well I'm goin' to go rest. Gettin' shot sure tuckers one out fast."

I went to my room and rested all day. I fell asleep and slept through supper and breakfast the next day. It was about noon when I woke up. I felt so much stronger and my mental attitude was better. My head felt like my old self, and now I wished Jack Walters would come out in the open and show himself but I guess he's like his father, doing things behind people's back. That seemed to be their way.

There wasn't anything more to do in town, so I got my things together and went to the stable and saddled up Blacky. Then I rode down to the bank and told Bill to send the papers back with one of the wagons when he got all the land together and I would sign them and send them back.

"Also, Bill, I'm sendin' Jim or Tim to hire some men to tear down the old buildings and build Red Bird and me a real fine house on the SILVER BUCK RANCH. From now on anyone calls it the Walters place, you correct them right fast. You see that, when my men get here they get anything they need. Sam's goin' to be needin' some money. When you get his telegram from Grand Junction, sent it to him."

"Will do, Silver Buck."

I headed north once again with my partner Blacky and my trusty Colt 45 and my .44-40 at my side. My black wide-brimmed hat had been through a lot, but it was still on my head. I didn't get far that first afternoon, but it was good to be out on the trail again. The evenings were getting downright cold out here in the clear, starless nights of fall.

The next morning was cold and crisp, and the sky was clear and full of bright morning sunlight. As I mounted and went up the trail, I began to notice the trees. Aspens, I believe I was told, how their leaves were of a bright golden color. It's funny this had taken place during the ten days I had been in town. It was now on to a year since stepping foot in this land. These trees brought to mind how life and the country keep changing even if we don't have time to stop and enjoy or notice it. This thought stayed with me for days as me and old Blacky wandered down the trail. What would I be doing if I had never left Texas? If I had married a girl like Jenny, never to know a girl as lovely and as open and giving as Red Bird?

I knew it had been my intention to own a ranch, but down in South Texas, and not even 1 percent as large as was going to be mine up in this beautiful and dangerous country. Stopping by a mountain stream to let Blacky have a drink, I stepped down to have myself one too. When getting up, I saw a figure come over the ridge. I mounted and got Blacky back into the brush and waited. It wasn't too long of a wait, because he rode right up to where I had gotten a drink. He looked to be around my age and he resembled Jenny, so this was Jack Walters, this I was sure of. I rode up to him off to the side so he would be off balance if he tried to draw on me.

"How you doin', Jack? You followin' me or not?"

He turned with a shock of surprise on his face, and took a minute to recover. Then he spoke.

"How you know me? I'm just riding along minding my own business. Who are you anyway? I don't know you."

"You know me, and I know you tried to kill me. You are wanted for escaping from prison where you were 'cause of a murder."

"You sure did your homework. Now what?"

"As I see it, you can give me your gun and let me take you back, or you can draw and I will bury you next to this stream."

You're sure of yourself, aren't you?"

"More sure than you are. I'd rather face you now than get shot in the back."

"Well, I'll tell you I'm not goin' back to prison. So if we can get off our horses, I'll face you right here and now."

I didn't trust this man, knowing his father as I did, so I turned Blacky so when I got off Jack's line of fire would be hampered. As I got off it was plain to see he wasn't getting off. As my foot touched the ground, he drew his gun, so I whipped at Blacky so he would move out of the line of fire and at the same time drew my Colt and let the lead fly. His shot was unsure and hit the ground behind me, but my two shots were true. Jack caught both slugs square in the chest. He fell off his horse, facedown in the stream. As I turned him over he said.

"Told you I wouldn't go back to prison. At least this here's a pretty spot to buy the farm."

Then his head fell to the side, and he was dead. I buried him a few feet away from the stream as I had promised. I put a board at the head of the grave and on it I wrote.

> Jack Walters Sept. 30, 1872
> To be right is not always good,
> But to be wrong is always deadly.
> This man was wrong.

I left that spot with only one regret, that the whole Walters family was a bad lot that always went looking for trouble. They always found it.

By October fifth I was back among my friends at the mine. Foster was surprised to learn about me being shot and of Walters son. He was not surprised to learn about the ranch, but was glad it was that close.

"I'se can come visit more and Red Bird can see her family more often. It's good you bought around here cause it's Ute territory. No problem as long you'se be married to one of the chief's daughter. Over where you'se were thinkin' of is Comanche country and they'se be enemies of the Ute's and wouldn't be so kind to you'se bringin' a princess into their territory."

"Never thought of that. Guess it's common for a white man to think that all Indians are friends to each other."

"That's could be a deadly mistake."

"Yeah, and I nearly made it. I need to talk to Tim and Jim, want to come with me?"

"No, got to get up to the mine."

I walked out of the office and went to find my two construction friends. I found them supervising the cutting of the trees to make braces for the mine.

"I need to talk to you two, if I can."

"Sure."

They both came over to me under the big Evergreen that was standing so stately on the side of Red Mountain.

"I know both of you are good workers and the men work good for you, but I need one of you to go back to Durango. I bought a ranch and need you to hire some men and tear down all the buildings and build a new house. Also barn and bunkhouse for some twenty or so cowboys. The more you get done before winter, the better."

"What should it look like?"

"I'll leave that up to you. Whatever you think, but big enough for me, my wife and a few kids and my folks. They're comin' from Texas in the spring after I marry Red Bird."

"That's the gal Foster was tellin' us about," Tim said.

"Now look here, Silver, after we get done with these timbers, Foster will have enough to last all winter and all these remaining men will be working in the mine. This winter Tim and I won't have anything to do. All the buildings are done and if any minor things happen the men can take care of it. What I'm getting at is, if we both go, we can put our heads together and come up with a well-planned house."

"If it's all right with Foster, it's all right with me. You both can leave tomorrow with Joe. Bill at our office or at the bank knows about it and will give you money to pay for everything you need. Hire as many men as are needed to finish it by at least the last of April."

"Do you want it built in the same place?"

"No, but you look at the lay of the land and decide. Bill will show you a map of the ranch, it's goin' to be over one hundred thousand acres when we buy it all. Don't put it too close or too far from town."

"We'll go and ask Foster."

I went back to the office and noticed how happy Lagger looked now that Blacky was back. It was strange how two stallions got along so well together. It was like we were thrown together in this world for a purpose and Foster and all these good men were part of it.

That night Jim and Tim told me Foster had agreed, and I looked over at Foster and he nodded his head. The next morning I handed them a note for the sheriff to explain what had happened on the trail so they could stop looking for Jack Walters. Then they headed down the road with Joe.

It was now the middle of October and starting to get cold. The nights were well below freezing and days in the middle forties. Winter usually came early up here for we were high in the mountains. In fact, the top of Red Mountain had snow on its top. This would not have worried me except Sam was still gone. He wasn't due back until early November, but if the snow hit him, he would be stuck because of the weight of the rails he would be coming back with. Another week went by and no sign of Sam. Now all the men were working in the mine, and that left me with little to do, so I told Foster that night:

"You see the snow is comin' closer down the mountain to us. The trail is gettin' muddy from all the light rain."

"I'se saw that; does look like snow in a few days."

"I'm worried about Sam, he may be stuck somewhere and if the snow hits before he can get here, we may not see those rail or Sam 'till spring and we need them now. I think it would be wise for me and two men to take off and find Sam and make sure he gets back."

"Sounds good to me'se. One man can take my mule and you'se two horses will be able to help if he'se caught up somewheres. I'se tell two of the men to be ready to leave in the mornin'."

"That's fine, I'll sleep better tonight."

We went off in the morning to the northwest. We didn't see any trouble for two days, and then it started snowing. It was a light snow, so it wasn't bad on us because in this mountain region one always carries his slicker and coat, even in the early fall.

"Men, let's head down until we get out of this."

"All right, boss, he wouldn't have that wagon in this stuff."

So we went down for about one and a half thousand feet, and that's where the snow stopped. Going quicker now, we were off the mountain and into a nice green valley, for this was evergreen country and the trees stayed green all year. It had been raining off and on since the snow had been left behind. Seemed like the farther north we got, the wetter it became.

The third day out we came out of the valley and on to a plateau. It was here that we spotted the wagon, and there was Sam sitting on the seat driving and singing away at the top of his lungs.

We rode up to Sam, who was grinning by now, because he knew who it was.

"Glad to see you, what you boys doin' this far away from home? You not worried about old Sam, are you?"

"Nope, just out for a little ride," Slim said.

I said, "You might be glad we're along when you get up ahead. It's muddy and it's snowin' up a ways. That's why we came to meet you."

"Well, in that case, glad to have your company. Why not camp here and take on the bad stuff with fresh horses tomorrow? See you're up and walking upright. Heard about you gettin' shot."

As we set up camp, something clicked in my head. How did he know I was shot?

"Sam, how you know I was shot?"

"Mr. Gills when he sent me the money for the rail he told me about you bein' shot."

"Oh, I see. I was a little out of it."

"Where you get shot? Don't look damaged to me."

"Just a head wound, but it gave me a concussion and I was laid up for a while."

"Well, glad to see you're all right now. Thought you might be dead and I'd be drivin' this wagon for nothin'." He started laughing so hard that it started the other two and then me. All the laughing wore us out and we collapsed in bed that night, but in the morning we weren't laughing. During the night it had snowed and the white stuff was everywhere, about five inches.

We didn't even eat, just hitched up the team trying to get down into the valley and hoped it hadn't snowed down there yet. We reached the bottom of the valley by noon, and there was no snow as of yet. Stopping just to eat and give the horses a break, we headed on, skirting the edge of the snow line. When night fell we did not stop. We kept on until we had to stop right before dawn so the animals could water and eat and rest for a few hours.

Let's get goin', I don't like the look of those low-hangin' gray clouds to the north there. If a blizzard hits now, we won't move this wagon 'til spring."

There was no stopping for us now. We were dead tried, and the horses looked worse, but we kept on going. By the next morning those gray clouds were past us, but with their passing came the lightened rain clouds and the rain followed. It reminded me of the first time I went to Foster's cabin. That meant snow was not too far behind. It was raining so hard we could not see too far ahead of us and then the wagon hit a mud hole and bogged down. We tied the horses and mule to the team, and with us pushing from the back the wagon moved, but didn't come out. Then I spotted a branch off a tree and used it as a wedge under the front wheel that was stuck. We tried it again, but nothing. To make things worse it now started to snow. But now, through the trees there was the camp not a half mile away.

"Look, the camp, I'll be right back with some help."

I unhooked Blacky and went to get some more men. When I came back, there were ten men coming up behind me. Putting Blacky back on the line, we all pushed and the wagon came out.

"Don't stop, Sam, 'til you get to camp, we'll walk. Pull, Blacky, pull, Lagger, pull!"

As we came up I saw they had made it. Sam and me unhitched the horses and put them in the barn and fed them, then headed for the warmth of the office.

Foster was sitting in the chair he now claimed as his own even though it was for me to do the paper work in. But I didn't mind because there wasn't much paper work to be done. Most of it was done by Bill in town.

"Good of you to drop in like this," Foster said as I walked over to the fireplace to get warm.

"That's not funny, Foster, it's cold and wet out there."

"Wasn't my idea to go out in this weather." He laughed again.

"I know, I know. Good thing I went anyways, or you wouldn't have your rails until next summer."

"I'se knows, I'se just havin' a little fun with you. First thing in the mornin' snow or no snow those rails are goin' into that mine even if I'se have to stop production until they're installed. I'se been sittin' here thinkin' while you'se out freezin' your balls off. As soon as the rails and cars are put in place, I'se goin' to start rotatin' the men, ten one day while the other rest, 'cause these hard winters takes lots out of a man. We'se be minin' the same amount and everyone will be happier, I'se hope."

"How many new men a comin' back with Joe?"

"I'se ask all the men and only four are leavin', so I'se sure Bill will send them up on the wagon if Joe can get through this snow."

True to his word, Foster had all the men. Even I pitched in a hand, unloading the rails off the wagon. Everyone had to wear gloves because it was well below freezing and that steel would stick to your bare hands in this climate. I drove the wagon back to camp after it was unloaded. After getting the horses into the warmer barn, I walked back to the mine and helped Foster put the rails cars together while the men made a bed for the rails. Sam had brought back enough for about hundred and fifty feet of track and the mine was only seventy feet deep. We should have enough to make it until spring when someone could be sent for more. I just hoped Joe could make one more trip to town so the four men that wanted to go home could do so.

The next week went well; the snow melted and the sun came out with the temperature on the rise. We had half the seventy-five feet of track laid. The next day Joe pulled in with the new men.

"What kept you? Been shacked up with those gals in the saloon?"

"No, boss, just couldn't get through with that snow. Had to let it dry up a little."

"I know, just funnin' with you. How's the road? Think you can make one more trip to take the men to town?"

"Don't know, but me and Sam can try. Don't we have enough ore for two wagon loads?

Foster spoke up. "We'se sure do, think ought to get as much in this time as can be got. Maybe the last load 'til the thaw. You're all get goin' in the mornin'. Horses just have to make it one more time. They'se get a long rest after that. They'se be fine."

So Joe and Sam and the four men going back left with two wagons full of silver. We did no more mining until the tracks were finished by the end of November. Would have gotten through a day early, but we took off Thanksgiving Day to give thanks for all our good fortune. Manuel had gone out in the cold morning and killed a turkey, and by noon we had us a feast if I've ever seen one. The men were in good spirits. They were thankful for they had food, a place to sleep, a fireplace and blankets to keep warm and a job and the best of friends. As one of the men said to me:

"What else could a man want except maybe a woman?" Everyone laughed and laughed until late that night.

December first saw a return to mining silver, but with one difference, the rail cars. This eased the work load on the men. It gave them more time to rest or whatever they wanted. By December fifteenth we had our second snow fall, although more snow fell, it was not as heavy. The thought accede to me that Joe and Sam were holed up in town all winter. We were sitting around one night when Foster came over to me and sat down to talk.

"Say, Buck, you remember last year about this time, where we'se were?"

"Oh yeah, in that cave above Lizard Pass freezin' and nearly starvin' to death."

"But remember we'se forgot all about Christmas until in January. We'se laughed at ourselves about that one."

"Been meanin' to ask you, Foster, you goin' to be at my weddin' come spring, aren't you?"

"Sure am, and I'se goin' to close down the mine and bring the men and some of the town folks."

"You think they'll come?'

"Not all, but friends like Bill, Juan, Ed and a few others will and that's what counts. And I'se thinks it a do both sides good to get together and see the good side of one another for a change. One of each side are gettin' together to form a bond that cannot be broken or both sides will be hurt."

"Foster, when did you become a diplomat?"

"There too many white folks comin' in here and I'se don't want to see Indians get pushed out."

"I don't either."

Everyone worked hard the next week. Since the wagons were still gone the men were making a pile of silver outside the mine and at night if the moon was out, it shone like a thousand little stars. The next day, when the men were through with their day's work, and were sitting down eating. I got up on a chair and announced that tomorrow was Christmas and everybody had the day off. I looked over at Foster and smiled, then said with a bigger smile.

"See that man over there. If he wants the work done tomorrow he's goin' to have to whip hisself." Everyone broke up laughing and Foster turned red, which was hard to tell under all that hair on his face.

"Hold it down fellows, listen do you hear what I hear?"

Everyone yelled "Bells!"

Everybody was trying to get up the stairs and out the door at the same time. Finally everyone got out. There coming down, where the road was, were some lanterns. Lo' and behold Sam and Joe drove up and stopped in front of the office.

"How you all get here? We thought Santa was comin' down on us with his reindeer."

Sam spoke up, "Well, it's like this, the town folks are so happy at what this mine is bringin' to the town they just couldn't see all of you up here with no presents or a party, so the blacksmith built special skis for the wagons, see. Now, who wants to get their presents and have a party? Everyone grab something and head inside, me and Joe been out here long enough."

The men jumped in the wagons and started giving out gifts and then the cakes and pies and cookies.

"Manuel,"

"Si, señor."

"The womenfolks said to tell you not to get mad about the goodies, but they thought the men would enjoy Christmas more knowing a woman baked these just for them," Joe said.

"Si, señor, I understand and I enjoy the food too," Joe laughed "that you will, there's plenty for everyone, and more."

We got everything inside and I took the horses to the barn and unhitched them and fed them. Then I went over and put my head against Blacky and cried. For the first in a long time tears rolled down my face. It's not that I was mad, but I missed Red Bird so much that my heart ached for her.

Then the barn door opened and Sam came inside.

"Buck, you all right?"

"Sure," I said, wiping my eyes.

"Come on inside, we have your present."

"All right, I'll be there in a minute."

Sam left, for I think he knew what was wrong. I really didn't want to go inside, afraid I would spoil everyone's fun and they needed this party more than anything to make it through the long, hard winter. But as I walked up the outside stairs, it came to me that it was so quiet inside that I wondered what was wrong, so pushing open the door and rushing in I saw everyone staring at me. I looked down on everyone.

"What's wrong?"

"Just waiting for you, Silver Buck," Sam said.

"What for?"

"Here, open your present."

"No, you go ahead."

"Come on, nobody's going to open anything or eat 'til you do. Here it is." Coming down the stairs I took it out of Sam's hand.

"All right."

"Go ahead, it a make you happy. I know what it is."

I started opening it and when I got it opened it puzzled me, it was a shirt of white buckskin with silver trinkets hanging from fringed buckskin all down both sleeves. There were pants to match, also moccasins of the same white buckskin. I was speechless.

'Well, Silver what you think? They're beautiful, aren't they?" Everyone in the room agreed with Sam.

"Where they come from? Who sent them?" I finally got out.

"It's like this Silver, this Indian come riding down the street of Durango. He stopped in front of the saloon where me and Joe happened to be. We came out and he asked "Know where Buck Taylor is please? Me friend of Buck Taylor." I spoke to him.

"I work for him. I am goin' to see him in a few days, he's up in the far-off mountains."

He took a blanket from in back of him and unwrapped it and this was inside. Then he said:

"Please tell Buck Taylor this from my daughter Red Bird. She makes for him to wear when he takes daughter for his own for all times. This Chief Dancing Bear says, when trees first come out with leaves, all friends of Buck Taylor come to village to have big feast for happy couple." "That's just what he said and then left town. You should have seen everyone, including me, with our mouths hanging open at the beauty of this and to think a Chief would bring it to town. That's when we all thought of the party and what a special man we had as a friend."

"This my Red Bird made." I held it to my chest and hugged it. "Thank you, Sam for bringin' some sunshine into my Christmas. Now everyone, let's have a real party!"

"Buck, Bill sent something, but he wanted me to ask you first. He knows your rule against liquor. But he thought on this special day you wouldn't mind. He send beer for everybody."

"Go ahead, you all work hard for me so you deserve it . . . have fun."

The men started drinking until the beer was all gone and it was way into the night. Christmas Day they were paying for their fun the night before. I saw men outside sick as a dog. But if they had more, they would do it again. That's the kind of men they were. Work hard, play hard, and drink hard, and don't worry about tomorrow until it comes.

The men went back to work the day after Christmas and everything was back to normal except now I had a new set of clothes to wear on my wedding day.

On New Year's eve we got our first full blown blizzard, and we got to find out what these cabins were made of as the wind whirled outside. We were nice and warm inside the cabins and our bellies were full. The storm raged for three days and no one worked during the storm. When it was over, we didn't have to use the stairs; the snow had piled up to the top of the outside stairs and we walked around looking for damage but found none. These cabins were very well built.

Now the men could go back to work, this time filling the wagons up and then adding to the piles. The work went on and on through January with two storms that gave everyone a nice rest, for the mines were cold but the hard work of digging out the silver kept them from feeling it. Manuel kept the men happy by cooking cookies, cakes or pies. You always saw a smile on their faces when they came from the mine to find the goodies on the stove because they knew after supper they would get their sweets. Every night they went to bed full and content.

It was February now and the storms abated for a while and the sun came out bright and shiny. After each storm before, when we got to the mine in the morning, we had to dig snow out of the mouth of the mine. But now the sun was out and this made everyone feel a lot better. The warmth of the sun did miracles for the coldness that lingered in the bones.

I made it my job to see to the animals every day. Of course Blacky, Lagger, and the mule got special attention. This winter was different for them. They had a warm barn and plenty of food.

Now at the start of March all that had to be done, was wait for the snow to thaw. It was that morning that I told Sam and Joe they had better hook up the teams and get the wagons to town and get the wheels put back on before the snow was gone and the wagons couldn't be moved. Two extra men in each wagon, with shovels in case they got bogged down. The trip back would be harder with wheels, so the four extra men could shovel down the high parts of snow to allow the wheels to pass. In other words, make a road down to the old road under the snow.

It was the first official day of spring and the snow was meltin'. It was later in the same day that the wagons came rolling up the side of the mountain.

"Sam, how is it down there?"

"Well, in town the snow's gone, but about half way up here we ran into about two feet of snow all the way, and it's kind of muddy. Before we hit the snow, we got stuck four or five times."

"Think you can start takin' loads in?"

"If we keep this sunshine, and can take four men again, it should be about a week for things to dry out."

The week passed fast and the men were getting ready to head for town. I was talking to Foster.

"You know, Foster, I promised Dancing Bear ten horses, but I feel the wedding is getting close and I want them to be fine horses."

"Yeah, from what Dancing Bear said when he brought the present, it would be 'bout April the twelfth, about three weeks." Sam came up and interrupted us.

"Heard you talking Silver, when I was coming back from Grand Junction, up on that plateau, there was some mighty fine-looking horses."

"Would they still be there and is there a stallion?"

Foster spoke up, "Wild horses always stay in their own territory. Might have to look awhile, but they'se be there, and you'se be a rancher Buck if there's a bunch of horses you'se know they'se be mares and there's always a stallion where there are mares."

"Guess it's gettin' too close to the weddin' I'm losin' my mind."

"Boss?"

"Yes, Sam."

"Can someone take my place on the wagon? I want to go with you. Only I know where they were."

"Well, I don't have much time to look around so I guess you're needed all right."

"Go get Blacky and Lagger saddled, and get some food from Manuel. We'll leave in an hour."

"Yes, sir, thanks."

"Might be gone a few days Foster, can you handle it?"

"Son, I'se was handlin' it before you'se been born."

I laughed and turned toward the barn. As I reached the barn I saw the wagons loaded with silver heading down the now muddy road. Sam came out of the barn with the horses.

"What's wrong with these horses, they're sure acting strange?"

"They're just happy to be gettin' out just like we are in the spring. Come on, I want to tell Joe something before they get too far."

We rode out and caught up to the wagons. As I pulled up beside, "Joe wait." He stopped "yeah boss?"

"When you get to town, would you go out to the ranch and see how the house is comin' along? Tell Jim or Tim if they need more men, hire them and start on another house for my parents. Just tell them to find a nice spot to put it up."

"Will do, see you about three weeks, want to see you get married."

He turned and headed on down the road. Sam and I headed northwest to find the horses.

Chapter Ten

Riding down the mountain was still a chore for the snow was still piled up in places where the sun didn't get to shine on it all day. In the same afternoon we were down in the valley where the wagon with the rails had been caught in a downpour last fall. You could tell that the winter wasn't too hard down in this valley, protected by the mountain on one side and the plateau rising up on the other. The birds were out and some of the animals. We saw a wolf, but did not bother it for it was eating a large rabbit. Wolves wouldn't attack humans if they had other game to eat.

By nightfall we were near the plateau but decided to set up camp in the protection of the valley because it was still chilly during the day and downright cold at night, and up on the plateau there was no protection, just open land. We were sitting there eating and Sam said:

"You know, this plateau up ahead, they call Uncompahgre Plateau? There's lots of gullies and canyons where those horses could be."

"Where do you think we should start? You're from around here."

"There's a place up the Uncompahgre River called the Delta and this time of year the river will start rising from the snow melt and the grass starts growing best and sweet near the river. You get too far west and it's more dry. So I think if we work our way up the river toward Delta we'll have a good chance of finding them. But got to stay away from the river itself cause this time of year it's dangerous with flash floods coming off the mountains. Camp too close and we may drown during the night."

"Let's get an early start, I want to get back as early as possible, only three weeks 'til my wedding. Can't hardly stand the waiting. You know it's been going on a year since we even seen each other."

We got to sleep, but my dream now came back during the night. There I was riding up to a handsome ranch house after a hard day's work. There was Red Bird standing on the wide porch with two children: one boy, who looked like me, and one girl that looked like her mother. This dream always makes me sleep peacefully and I woke up refreshed.

We were now up on the plateau. Blacky and Lagger were feeling fit and raring to go.

"Sam, they want to run, they been barned up all winter. Let's give them their head and get it out of their system."

"All right by me."

So I told Blacky it was all right and loosened the reins and he knew what this meant and took off. Then Lagger saw what was happening and let loose and flew with the wind. They ran and ran and ran some more until they were tired out. So we stopped by a swollen creek and let them water and graze while we ate.

"I'll tell you those two got the get up and go."

"Yeah, their muscles need stretching out."

"You know Buck, I'm like you, I mean that I'm not a mining man, I was a ranch hand. I know it's a lot to ask but when you get your ranch goin' can I work there instead of the mine?" "I didn't know you ever worked on a ranch."

"Only took the mining job 'cause I was out of work."

"Where you work before?"

"That's why I never brought it up before. Used to work for Walters."

"What, Walters?"

"Let me explain, that's why I was out of work, it just didn't cut me the right way all the things he was doing around Durango, so I up and quit. Anyways, that was before you came to town."

"Wish you'd told me sooner."

"Well, I needed a job and thought you'd think I was just spying for him. I think now you know you can trust me and I am your friend. Anyway I feel better now I got that off my chest."

"Tell you what, you come with me to Santa Fe when I meet my folks with the cattle and if my dad agrees you can be the assistant Forman. My dad and me are goin' to run it but when we're gone you'll be in charge. Anyways I can't ask a rich man like you to be just an everyday cowhand, can I now?"

"What you mean by that?"

"You don't remember with that load of silver that took off yesterday you get 4 percent."

"I plumb forgot about it, but it won't be too much, will it?"

"Look here I'll show you, last year we didn't mine but five months and the total was about $170,000 and this year we'll be mining twelve months. So you double that amount and 4 percent is around $13,000."

"You sure?"

"Sure, I'm sure, I'm the boss."

"Then yo ho, yo ho I'm rich."

"Well, by this time next year you will be a partner."

"That I am, am I?"

"You sure are, let's move on now."

We mounted up and headed up to the Delta. We rode all the next day with no luck. But then on the fourth day out, early in the morning, Blacky started acting funny, pawing at the ground and snorting in the air and as we came to the top of a canyon we saw why. There below us was the most handsome white stallion I had ever seen, and about fifteen mares.

"Sam, if we can go around and get in front of the canyon and rope the stallion, the mares will follow him."

"I'm game."

As we made our ascent to the floor of the canyon, I kept an eye on the big white and so did Blacky.

"That's it, Blacky, keep an eye on him; we catch him and five of those mares will be yours."

Hearin' that his ears perked up and he was stepping more lively than ever. As I reached the floor on this side I saw Sam on the floor on the opposite side. We headed in and met in the middle and then moved toward the big white stallion. Me and Sam both had our ropes out and were ready. The stallion would spot us any minute now and take off.

Then he spotted us and let loose with his warning signal to his mares. They took off with the white in the lead.

"Sam, let's get the white; Blacky don't let him get away." I could feel Blacky respond to my signal, but the white went by us and I turned Blacky around and he took off like the wind. Sam was coming up behind us.

"Come on boy, now let's get him." We had caught up to him now and I let the lasso whirl around my head until we were very close and then I let go of the loop in the lasso. I never threw so sure, for it was on his neck and Blacky was slowing him up by pulling back on the rope that I had tied to the saddle horn. Then we all three came to a stop. Then here comes Sam and he put his loop around the white's head.

The stallion didn't want to give up; he kept tossing his head trying to throw the rope, but Blacky would just back up to tighten it back up. Then the white would throw his front hoofs in the air, where he would be standing just on his back hoofs, then come down hard.

The mares of his came around and watched. They were confused; the stallion would snort out a command but then Blacky would snort out and they just stood looking not knowing what to do. The white stallion finally saw it was no use and gave up.

Sam and I mounted up and shortened up the rope so we were but fifteen feet apart with the white stallion between us and the mares following a short distant behind.

At night he put up a fight as we would tie him between two trees. This went on for four days and as we were about to reach the mine camp he made one last ditch effort to break away. He got away from Sam and tried to go around in a circle, but this failed because the trees were too close together and my rope just went around the trees and he was brought in tight against them. By the time we got him untangled he had worn himself out and gave us no more problems.

We came into camp in the early evening and all the men came out to see what we had. I led the white stallion into the corral that had been built for our horses for warm days during the winter. It would be a little crowded but it was only for ten days or so. Then all fifteen mares followed him in.

"Sam, tie him to the post in the center."

"You'se out done yours self this time Buck, that's a handsome stallion." Foster told me. Tell me, Foster, do you think I should break him or give him to Dancing Bear and let him break him?"

"I'se thinks you'se should let him. Just tell him that the honor of breakin' such a fine animal should only be done by a great and honorable man. That will make him happy to know you'se think so much of him."

"Then I'll do it that way; thanks, Foster. Joe's not back yet. I need to find out about the house."

"Should be back any day now. You'se not gettin' nervous are you'se."

"Well, just some."

The two wagons came up the next day and I went out to get the news.

"Hello, Joe."

"Hi, boss."

"What about the house. Did anything go wrong?'

"No, sir, that's the most handsome house I've seen since I was in New Orleans one year."

"Really?"

"Right, handsome, and nice new barn and bunk house is near being finished. They said your folks would have their house by the first part of June. Oh, here's a letter and package all the way from Texas, came in on the first run after the thaw begun."

"Thanks, Joe, you did a good job; go get fed, Manuel got some good grub."

"You know when I go to town I sure do miss that Mex. Think I'll work here forever just for the grub."

"You might have to change jobs; I'm goin to ask him to cook at the ranch."

"Carlos, his helper, is nearly as good; he's got a good teacher. I'm going to eat."

I went to the office and sat down to relax while I read the letter.

February 12, 1873

Dear Son,

> We are leaving in the morning. We had a mild winter so your father says we should get on the trail. You know how he likes the trail. He says he has around two-thousand head of cattle. He hired fifteen men, all of whom you know, with a promise of a job and five more men with no promise of a job unless you think you need them and I am

stuck with feeding them all. He told me we don't need a cook, you can cook, ha, ha how you like that.

We're sorry we can't be at your wedding but we wish you luck and we know if you picked her, she must be special and that's all we need to know. We told your friends that are coming with us and they think the same. and anyway I always wanted to be a princess, so now I have one for a daughter.

Open the box, this is for your bride I hope it gets there before the wedding. By the way, you know your father he went away, about a month, said it's a good trail if we stay along the Rio Grande.

See you and your bride in Santa Fe.

Love from your
Mother and father

I put down the letter and started opening the package. I couldn't believe my eyes; there in front of me was my mother's wedding band, the one that was her mother's and her mother's before. It had been in our family almost a hundred years and now my Red Bird would be wearing it and she would pass it on to our daughter when she got married. My mother really did understand my love for this Indian princess. I went to Foster.

"Foster, will you do something for me?"

"Sure, you'se just names it."

"Would you go to Dancing Bear and make sure of the day? I don't want to be late, and don't tell him about the white stallion. I want it to be a surprise."

"Think I'se can do that for my partner."

He took off that day on Blacky, because he was the fastest. While Foster was gone the work went on as usual. The last of the rails that had been brought from Grand Junction were laid. It was now April eighth and the snow was gone except in patches where the sun didn't reach all day. That was good, because the rivers south would all be full or overflowing. This would give the cattle plenty of water all the way to Colorado. After supper I went to the kitchen to talk to Manuel.

"How's Carlos doin'? Does he learn what you teach him?"

"Si, señor, he learns well; he is also very good cook. I think sometimes when he cooks, the men they know no different."

"That's fine, 'cause you know I'm startin' a ranch south of town and I would like it if you came to cook for the men on the ranch. I'll even pay you the same as you get up here. You also will be able to go into town and see your cousin when you buy the food for the ranch and you'll have a helper."

"Señor, I will do it, you are so kind. I never met a man like you."

"Well, you're goin' to meet another one like me when my folks get here from Texas. They're comin' in with cattle and cowhands."

"You know of my trouble near where you lived; do you think this is wise?"

"Sure, you are my friend and you have worked here for nine months and never caused any trouble. No one's goin' to bother you as long as I'm around."

"Thank you, señor I will always do my best for you."

"There's one thing a cowboy enjoys and that's good food and the way you cook, if someone was to hurt you, he'd probably be hanged from the nearest tree." I smiled at him.

I walked over to the corral to look at the horses Sam & I had brought in and there stood the big white stallion. He still looked ready to put up a good fight if given half a chance. Five of the mares were going to be left here for Blacky, as I had promised him. Later I would take them to the ranch to be broken for cow ponies. As I was leaning against the rails of the corral looking at the big white, I heard someone coming up the trail. As the rider came closer, I recognized Blacky and there was old Foster in the saddle grinning down at me.

"Well?" I said.

"Got to leave in the mornin'. I'se was right, it is the twelfth. That gives us three days to make it."

"All right, I'll tell the men."

I rung the alarm bell we had in case of trouble. All the men rushed out trying to get into their pants.

"Look Foster, what a funny weddin' procession they're goin' to make." We both started laughing. The men came up.

"What's wrong, you crazy or what? Silver ringing that alarm and then laughing at us in our drawers."

"Don't worry men, there's no trouble, I just wanted to let you know in the mornin' we leave for my weddin' and everyone gets a holiday with pay."

Everyone threw up their hands and yelled loud enough to wake the bears in the woods.

"All right, now get to sleep; we'll start early. Sam and Joe, you all, if you will help me with the stallion and mares."

"Right, Buck; see you early."

I could hardly sleep that night and was wide awake when I saw the sunlight come over the mountains in the east. I got up and packed some of my things, including my wedding clothes that Red Bird made me, along with my razor and soap. Foster didn't know it, but I had a bath planned for him in the pond at the village.

We all ate, then Manuel closed up the kitchen and put out the fires. The men got the teams hooked up to the wagons. I let Sam ride Lagger and Joe rode Foster's mule and we got the stallion out with a whole lot of trouble. We lead him as before with ropes that we kept tight with him between us and Joe just making sure the mares stayed and didn't wander. Then the men and Foster rode in the wagons behind us so as not to scare the wild horses too much. Foster had agreed to let Joe ride his mule because he said, "I'se not much good handlin' horses."

We went along very well for two days, then the night before the wedding I called the men together for a talk.

"You all listen to me. Tomorrow I am gettin' married and we are goin to be in an Indian village as their guests. I know you are good men, but I also know some of you don't care for Indians; maybe you have a good reason, I don't know. But tomorrow you are goin' to get along with them cause if there's any trouble, the man that starts it will be fired. Right Foster?'

"That's what we'se decided, boys," Foster spoke up.

"If everything goes off well, me and Foster have agreed, you all after the weddin' can go to town and collect your money from Mr. Gills and go see your families or whatever you want for one week. That's if there's no trouble, remember?"

Everyone started howling and yelling and throwing their hats in the air.

"Wait a minute, I want to address something that I think is important." Everyone got quite again.

"I don't know if you realize how much money you all have comin' but it is a lot for you to get all at once. Most of you have nearly two thousand dollars in the bank. You would be smart, if you are goin' back to the mine to only take what you need and leave the rest to draw interest. I gave you a chance to become well-off men, so don't take all of it out and blow it away. That's all I have to say." Foster stepped up and said, "Wait Buck."

I stood there as Foster came up to me.

"That last trip Joe made into town we'se all signed papers to let Joe take money out of our accounts to buy you'se and Red Bird a present."

The men brought out of the wagon a big box with ribbons around it and wrapped up in brown paper.

"Why you do this? You didn't have to."

Joe got up and came over to me and put his hand on my shoulder and said.

"I speak for all the men when I tell you this. You are by far the best and most generous boss we had ever had and Foster too. That goes without saying. But we would all follow you to hell to fight the devil if you asked us to. We know you are leaving the mine and going to be a rancher but we want you to know if you ever need any help just send for us and we'll be there at your side."

"Well thank you all, but, Joe, I never knew you had that many words in you." All the men laughed and pulled Joe around joking with him and he turned all red.

"I better open this now, before I shame myself by bawling." I torn into it and couldn't believe my eyes; it was a portrait painting of Red Bird the way she looked the first time I saw her at her sister's wedding with the same dress. I just stood there and stared at it with my mouth open wide.

"But, how did you know what she looked like?"

"Foster wrote a description on paper and I gave it to an artist that was in town. That's why I took so long that time; we paid him extra to do it fast. I was worried, but when I got back and showed it to Foster he said it looked just like her. I was worried cause I never seen any women that handsome, white or Indian, but I relaxed after he said it was fine. It's to put above your huge fireplace in your new house, and before you ask, how I know, that artist went out and measured above it."

"I don't know what to say; it looks just like her, I know she'll love it. So thanks to all of you. I'll never forget this. The same thing goes as Joe said if any of you need any kind of help just come and ask, I'll be there. Let's get to bed now, we have a weddin' to go to tomorrow. Should get there midmornin' so we have to get goin' early so we'll have time to clean all this trail dust off us."

Chapter Eleven

Sam and I had the white stallion tied between us as we entered the village. We stopped, and I had Joe come up to hold the stallion. I then asked Foster to come with me to see Dancing Bear. All the people of the village were outside and looking at the beautiful horses we had brought.

We stood on the outside of Dancing Bear's teepee while one of the braves went inside. Then in a few minutes Dancing Bear stepped out to greet us. He took my hand and shook it.

"Happy see you all right, Buck Taylor, daughter worried, worried after Foster say been shot."

"It wasn't bad, but I am happy to be here with you again. I have brought you a weddin' present as I had said. They are over there. Too big to bring over here. Would you like to see what I bring?"

"Me like to see, go."

We walked over to where the horses were. Indians don't show much excitement, but when he saw the white stallion he just looked in amazement.

"How catch this one?"

"On my horses there, Blacky, the red one."

"Must be good speed to catch this one. You give me much honor with this one. These his mares?"

"Yes."

"You say bring ten horses, but you did not."

"There are ten there."

"Yes here, but stallion already make more, see five mares are ready with colts, so you bring fifteen, no ten. Why not white stallion ride?"

"Such a handsome horse should be broken by an equal. You are his equal. He is yours to break."

"This will be done. After wedding I, Chief Dancing Bear, will break in front of all."

"Dancing Bear, I'm grateful that you allowed my friends to come. Some more may come from town."

He signaled for a group of braves to take the horses away and prepare for the ride later. All my men got down from the wagon.

"Chief, can you ask two of your women to help us? We are goin' to all bathe. I have the handsome clothes that Red Bird made, but my men need their clothes washed while they bathe."

"Yes, Buck Taylor, this is your day . . . anything you want."

I went over to Sam and Joe, and got two other men and went over to Dancing Bear and whispered to him.

"Yes, Buck Taylor agree with you he does need a bath on your day."

"Grab him, boys, he's not goin' to my weddin' without a bath."

We all grabbed Foster, and I saw two women coming with soap root. We carried him down to the pond as he was kicking.

"Buck, you'se can't do this, I'se thought you'se be my friend."

"I am, but friend or no friend, you ain't goin' to my weddin' dirty."

All the people were laughing, for they had never seen anyone not wanting to bathe as much as Foster. We were out of sight of the village, so we undressed him and threw him in and then we all got out of our dirty clothes and jumped in the pond. The Indian women came over and got all the clothes and started washing them as we bathed Foster and then ourselves. Foster was yelling.

"You'se are fired . . . I'se don't wants you'se around me!" We dunked him under the water to shut him up. That got him quiet. I now washed and shaved real close, as did everyone except Foster who wouldn't let anyone touch his beard. But at least he was clean.

After I was finished, I dressed in my handsome white wedding buckskins and went to talk to Dancing Bear. As I reached the teepee, I was told to go in.

"Where is Red Bird?" I asked Dancing Bear.

"Cannot see her till wedding in afternoon."

"Dancing Bear, I have something to tell you."

"Anyone that can give Foster bath, I will listen to." We both laughed.

"I have bought a ranch of many acres south of Durango. This is where your daughter and I will live. I will raise cattle and children there. You come anytime to see us, you and your people will be my guests."

"Is expected my daughter go anywhere husband goes. This is way of my people."

"Anytime your people are hungry, you come and live on ranch and can have cattle to feed your people. My father and mother are comin' with many cattle from Texas, when they get here I want you to come and meet them."

"I will come on white stallion."

A brave came in and said something I didn't understand and Dancing Bear got up and said.

"People here from town; we must get ready, wedding soon." We went out and sure enough there were about twenty people. I took the chief to meet some of them.

"Chief Dancing Bear, this is Bill Gills and this is Mr. Winslow and Mr. Thames and these are their wives,"

"Glad you come, you welcome. We have wedding, then eat. Who this man with white backward collar?"

"Foster, come here."

Foster came over, "Will you help me explain what the preacher is here for."

"After what you'se done to me?"

"Foster, that was all in fun and you know I wouldn't want to hurt you, but you stunk and it's my weddin'."

He smiled, "I'se guess you'se do have the right. I'se help you'se out of this."

We walked over to where the preacher and Chief were standin'. Foster started talking.

"See Dancing Bear, this man marries white folks and you marry Indians folks, so since Buck is white this man will marry them in the white man's way and you'se marry them in the Indian way."

"Mean we have two weddings. Yes, I like that, show Buck and Red Bird in love more and will be part of both people and their marriage last forever. Let's begin."

Everyone stood around and the preacher stood beside Dancing Bear and Foster was beside me as we waited for Red Bird to come out.

Then the drums started beating and out of the teepee came Red Bird's mother, then Red Bird and, last her sister. I was so nervous as she walked toward me, she was so beautiful, just as I remembered. She had on a white buckskin dress decorated just like my buckskins were. As she stood beside me, I could not believe that she was so lovely. I knew nothing of this woman or her people, but I loved her honesty and her touch set me on fire. Even if I hadn't seen her for a year, when she touched my hand, I knew this was right and we loved each other so deep. That touch said it all. We would be together all our lives.

Then Chief Dancing Bear did what he had to do. He said words I didn't understand and then he put a branch in front of Red Bird and she stepped on it and broke it in two. Foster said, "Buck, you have to pick it up and mend it. Here I'se know about this." He handed me a leather patch and a strip of leather. "This means she breaks her ties with her family and takes you'se, when you'se mend it, that means you accept her as your wife to start a new branch of your own."

I picked up the two halves and put them together and wrapped the leather around them and then tied it together with the strips of leather. When I finished, Red Bird smiled at me and Dancing Bear said, "You are now married, my son."

All the Indians yelled in their way and the town folks clapped. Then Dancing Bear stepped aside and spoke.

"Quiet, they be married in the white man's way now."

The preacher stepped before us and said his little speech, and I said "I do," then he asked Red Bird the same thing and she said "I do."

The preacher said, "Put the ring on her finger," and I took out my mother's ring and placed it on her finger.

"You are now married, forever man and wife. You can kiss the bride." As I kissed her, all the miners yelled with the Indians and the town's people clapped nicely.

Dancing Bear stepped up "Now time to eat and enjoy, I will ride white stallion after eat."

Everyone came up and shook our hands and then went to eat and watch the Indian dancers. We just stood there looking at each other and then I said, "I love you," and as I kissed her, her eyes were looking into mine, then she said "You do love me very deeply, I can see it in your eyes. And I love you, Buck Taylor, you are forever my man."

We made our way to the dancers and then sat down to watch. We were at the head of the circle that had formed around the dancers.

"Buck, I have never been this happy. You remember the first time we met and I told you that maybe one day we go to the marriage teepee? Well tonight we go. This time my mother not be there and we have to stay inside whole week or will not be happy."

"I know Red Bird, and I am happy also. It is a night that I have wanted for over a year."

I called Jim over to talk to him. "Jim, this is Red Bird."

"Howdy, ma'am, happy to meet you. Me and Tim over there been building your house and it's finished for you."

"Me a house? I never thought I live in house."

"Jim, will you bring that large package in back of one of the wagons. I want to show it to everyone after the dancers are finished."

"Why, sure, Silver Buck."

Jim left, and soon as he was gone Red Bird asked.

"Buck, why he call you Silver?"

"Oh, just because me and Foster went up in the mountains and found some silver."

"What silver?"

"It's a metal, see here like your ring."

"Yes, is pretty."

"White men like it very much and trade it for things they want, or give in love like I gave this ring."

Red Bird tried to understand about this ring. "It is very important to me for you to always wear it."

"Why, Buck?"

"To white men that see it on you, they know you are married and will not bother you. This ring is very special; my mother sent it from Texas. She got it from her mother and her mother got it from hers. Do you understand?"

"I think I do. It like my mother, mothers, mother gave something to me. That many moons."

"Yes, and my mother gave it to me for you, 'cause she now has a daughter, and when our daughter gets married you can give it to her."

Right then Jim walked up with the painting, and the dancing stopped. So I got up and went to the middle of the circle with the painting.

"Can I have everyone's attention? I want you all to see this before it goes above the fireplace in our house. All the men in my company bought this for our weddin' present. Come on, Red Bird, you're goin' to open it."

She came out to me and looked so shy.

"Come on, for me? It's for you too."

"All right, for you."

She tore the paper away, and the surprise on her face was of amazement.

"That's me, how?"

Dancing Bear came over and touched it.

"How did it get on there? It's Red Bird."

"An artist in town did it from how Foster described her."

"I never seen such beauty," Red Bird said.

"It's just you, my love."

"Quit teasing me; you know what I meant."

"I'm sorry, I know what you meant."

"Jim take this to town with you and hang it."

"All right, boss, will do."

"Is time me break white stallion," Walking Bear said.

Two braves took hold of the ropes tied to the white stallion and guided him down to the pond. Dancing Bear followed and then everyone else, even the town folks. Four more braves pulled the stallion into the pond. He just stood there belly deep in the water, while two braves took off the ropes and the other two grabbed a hold of the stallion's neck and ears. Then Dancing Bear waded into the pond and jumped on the back of the stallion. He sat there and rubbed him behind the ears for a while. Then he waved the braves away. The stallion just stood there, wide-eyed, not knowing what to do. Then with no warning he started trying to buck, but could not jump up too high because of the water pressure around his legs and belly. That didn't work, so he tried to go forward, but Dancing Bear pulled back on the rope around his neck. So he tried backing up, but again the rope was pulled tight and he stopped. It was the stallion's move again, but he just stood there with Dancing Bear rubbing between his ears for about ten minutes. Everyone backed away from the pond as Dancing Bear came out of the water on the white stallion's back. Dancing Bear just rode him off into the distance and everybody gave out hoops and hollers and clapped at the sight of the wild stallion being ridden.

"Is this how your people break horses?"

"Yes, it has always been the easiest to do."

"Sure is; I never expected that horse to be ridden so soon."

About twenty minutes later here came Dancing Bear riding high and mighty, still on the horse's back.

"What think of white stallion now, Buck Taylor my son?"

"I'm amazed at how fast and with no one gettin' hurt, you rode that wild, and I mean wild horse!"

"The water takes the wild spirit out of wild animal. Look you, you come first time here and took bath in pond's water, now you married man. See, it takes wild spirit out of you."

All the crowd started roaring with laughter and I turned red. I looked over at Red Bird and she was smiling at me.

"Well, have to admit that I meant Red Bird when I was in the water, but if it's the water that made me love her so much, I thank the pond."

I took my hat off and bowed in the direction of the pond. Everyone laughed some more.

"Let us eat now," Dancing Bear said.

He led the way to the center of the village, and sat down. Then me and Red Bird sat, one on each side of him. He reached out and took our hands in each of his and looked up to the sky.

"Here I sit with the old part of me, my daughter, on my right and the new part of me, my son, on my left and I pray to the mighty one in the sky that this bond be blessed forever. This why we gather here, white man and Indian together and eat this food, so my daughter and son can and will be part of both worlds. Now we eat. Everyone sit and eat."

Everyone sat down and dug in and devoured the whole meal. The pastor came over to Dancing Bear and said, "That was a real nice thing you said for these two young people. But I didn't think Indians believed in God."

"We do not call him God, but he is of the same spirit as you call God."

"I'm glad I came here, it has been a learning experience that I will try to show the other white men. I see from today we can all live together."

"Yes, think we can. I want peace more than anything."

The pastor put his hand on Dancing Bear's shoulder.

"You are a very wise man; I am glad you invited us, but we must go now."

"You stay in village tonight . . . leave with new sun. Tonight is the most important part of the celebration."

"What is that?"

"Everyone walks the young couple to wedding lodge and wait."

"For what."

"For Buck Taylor to take daughter as wife for all times."

"I am sorry, but I have to be back by midday tomorrow to marry another young couple. I'm sorry, Dancing Bear."

"To marry is great, so I understand why must leave."

Everyone rose, and all the town's people gathered their things and left for town. Jim and Tim had the picture to hang. As we stood there waving good-bye, Red Bird reached up and whispered in my ear with a smile on her face, "Nearly time us go to wedding lodge; can't wait have you inside me."

I could feel myself rise a little at the word she spoke. Then Dancing Bear spoke. "Time take young couple to wedding lodge."

With all the miners and all the Indians around us, we walked the half mile to the wedding lodge. There Dancing Bear blessed the lodge where his daughter would become my wife in the eyes of God.

"This to be a good marriage; have to stay whole week. Women of village bring food every new day, leave outside lodge. Not go more than ten feet away from front of lodge. Go now, this is your night."

Red Bird and I entered the lodge. The moon was out bright this night so I could make out a little of the interior. There were drawings on the side of the lodge of different events of the past and on the floor, there was a colorful decorated blanket with, what looked like a white fox skin on the top of it.

I looked over at Red Bird, and she came to me in the dark of the lodge.

"Let us take our clothes off, it is hot to me."

She pulled her dress over her head and as the times before had nothing under it. Her body was more beautiful than I remembered. She started getting me out of my clothes.

"What's the hurry, Red Bird? We got all night to enjoy each other."

"Buck, Dancing Bear, my father, has to stand guard outside until you make me yours."

"But how will he know?"

"This," she said, picking up the white fox, "will be under me when you enter and it will have blood spot. After first time I wrap up and put on outside of lodge and father make sure I am your wife."

As she spoke my clothes had come off with a little persistence on the part of my new wife. We were there in each other's arms, then I kissed her and started to rise. She left my arms and lay on top of the white fox and opened her legs to me. She said to me as my fingertips ran over her now-erect nipples of her large supple breasts, "Buck, my husband, enter me now, I am ready for your hardness. Do not be gentle the first time, enter me with force, for there has to be blood on the white skin, so enter my opening hard, I can stand the pain. It will be a pain of joy that's been in my body since we met."

I rose up and kissed her on the mouth with our tongues finding each other as I pushed my rigid shaft into the delicate opening between her legs. She wrapped her legs around my butt as she put her hands on my butt and pulled my shaft all the way in until my belly touched hers. As this happened, she cried out in pain of joy, for only this way the first time would she be mine forever. I pulled back and entered again and again. I could tell by the look on her face it was more enjoyable now that she was opened all the way up like a morning flower in the spring and my shaft entered now with ease.

She was now bucking up and down trying to get it in deeper. She was yelling out loud, with sweat pouring out of our bodies. She told me, "I love you, Buck Taylor, let your juices flow into me now."

"I love you forever, Red Bird." As my juices flowed deep into her body, she grabbed me and held on tight and yelled as loud as she could. Then about thirty seconds the tension left our bodies and we were relaxed once more in each other's arms. She rose up and took the white fox from under us to inspect it. Sure enough, there was a large bloodstain on the pure white surface.

"This is good; more blood more and better love," she said as she rolled the white fur up and placed on the outside of the lodge. We heard Dancing Bear come up and stand there, then we heard him say, "These two show great love, protect them always." Then we heard him leave back to the village.

That night was like I had gone to heaven and back. After two more intense fulfillments of our love, we fell asleep in each other's arms.

I didn't wake up until about midday, and it felt like, a dream came true as I sat there looking at my beautiful wife in all her lovely nakedness as she slept. I opened the flap of the lodge and stepped outside to let the sun bathe my bare body, then I remembered the ten-feet boundary; so I stood in front of the lodge. That's when I noticed the food left by the women. After about ten minutes, I went back in with the food and closed the flap. This is when I saw the pictures on the side of the lodge. Now I could see better what they were depicting. This was the lodge for first married couples, and the pictures showed men and women making love on their first night.

I looked over and noticed Red Bird's mound had little hair and the lips of her opening were swollen and looked so delectable, so I couldn't help myself, I bent and kissed them. This awoke Red Bird and she smiled and pulled me to her.

"I am ready for you any time, day or night." This is when I entered her again, this time more gently. This went on for six more days. We took pleasure in each other's body. On the last day she said, "Now have to paint our picture on the wall, what should I show?"

"I don't know, honey."

"What you say honey for?"

"That's what a man sometimes calls his wife to show love. It's like sayin' sweet as bee's honey."

"I like that, honey. Now what I put in picture on wall? Look, here is my sister when she came here that night we met. I do not think Walking Moose that big; you much bigger." She covered her eyes and laughed. "I do not see a picture like the way we did it two nights ago. I put that."

Silver Buck

She took out the colors, out of the bag she had brought with her. Then she drew a picture of her on her hands and knees, with her legs apart, and me on my knees entering her from behind while massaging her large breasts with my hands as my finger and thumb worked on her nipples. "That's a good one all right."

"You pleasure me so much during week. Must have made baby. Hope looks just like you."

That night we walked back the half mile to the village of Dancing Bear. The week had been so great. It had gone so fast we had made this walk just a week before.

"You must stay a while, and enjoy your new life."

"Father, we leave in the morning, I want to see my new white man's house. See how I like it."

'Me understand, but sad to see daughter and Buck Taylor go. Buck Taylor good to you, and is Dancing Bear's good friend."

The next morning we got ready to leave, still dressed in our wedding clothes. After all, they hadn't been used for a week.

"Red Bird, you can ride Lagger until we can find you a nice mare for your own."

"I can ride Lagger, he has been my favorite, honey. I'll enjoy him."

She jumped on his back fast and straddled him and started off toward town. So I got on Blacky and told Dancing Bear as I shook his hand:

"Remember, you come meet my folks at the ranch south of Durango, bring your whole village if you can and stay a while."

Then I took off down the trail after Red Bird.

"Wait for me," I yelled.

"In hurry to see house, you hurry."

"It will still be there in two days."

There, we were married a week and already acting like an old married couple. That is true love.

That night we camped by a stream that worked its way down from the top of the mountain. We slept in each other's arms looking up at the stars. Then out of the blue we heard a crashing noise coming through the forest. The horses were raising Cain like I never had seen. I jumped out of our bedroll and grabbed my rifle and stood sure-footed, facing the direction that the noise was coming from. Then out of the woods it came face to face with me.

Chapter Twelve

The big grizzly stood straight up in the air, must have been two feet above my head; I fired point blank and hit him in the lungs. But not before he hit me one good blow to the arm which caused me to go flying in the air and hit a tree about ten feet above the ground.

"Red Bird, Red Bird, you all right? Be careful he may not be dead."

"Buck, how are you? You hurt?"

She came running over to me and bent down.

"Your arm; it's hurt."

I looked down and blood was running down my arm and dripping off my fingertips onto the ground. At least it wasn't my gun arm.

"Get me a rag out of my saddlebags."

She ran over to our bedroll and got the rag and came running.

"Tie it above the cuts and pull it tight as you can. If I should pass out, loosen this every hour to let the blood get to my hand. Think you can get the horses saddled and get me to town?"

"Sure, honey, you just watch me."

She had them horses ready to go in no time. She loosened up the bandage, then tightened it back. She helped hefted me up and we took off for town.

"I'm sendin' someone back for that skin. It'll look handsome in front of the fireplace."

"You're crazy, is that all you can think of with your arm nearly torn off?"

"It's not that bad, sweetheart; I'll live and that means you're stuck with me."

"Oh, Buck Taylor, don't know about you."

We were coming into town the next day in the afternoon.

"Look, go over, there's Bill, he'll get the doc."

We rode over to him. "Bill, Bill, . . . Buck hurt, says to get Doc."

Bill came over and took one look at my arm and yelled at two men in the street.

"Tim! . . . over here, help me; Jim go get the doc, it's Buck. He's hurt, hurry."

Tim came over and helped Bill get me off the horse and into the mining office. They laid me on the couch.

"What happened, Silver? She already cut you up?"

"No, did not; grizzly got him!"

"He's only jokin', honey. Ain't you, Tim?"

"Why, sure, ma'am, wouldn't want anything happenin' to this good old boy."

"He man, my man proves it at night."

Tim just shut his mouth; every time he opened it he put his foot in it as far as Red Bird was concerned. Then Jim came in with the doc. He took off the bandage.

"Get me some water and clean cloths."

Bill went to the backroom and brought some cloths and a pan with a pitcher of fresh water. Doc bathed and cleaned the wound; the bleeding had stopped long since. I could see four claw marks on my forearm. Then the doc spoke up.

"You're lucky it's not too deep; didn't cut into the muscle. You'll have a scar but no permanent damage. I'll sew it up and you'll be good as new in a month to six weeks."

Doc finished up and left. He gave me some pills in case I got a fever, then told Red Bird to clean it every day and put on a clean bandage. I called Jim over.

"Jim, have one of your men go out and get that bear skin. I'm not goin' to lose it after him leavin' his mark on me. It's about a day's ride toward Dancing Bear's village. Don't you think it a look good in front of our fireplace?"

"That all think about, Buck Taylor," Red Bird said.

"Sure be cozy to lay on in front of the fireplace this winter with you by my side."

"Maybe you right, go get bear, Jim."

"Yes ma'am."

"Have your man take Blacky and Lagger to carry the skin. It's a big bear . . . about eight and a half feet upright. Tim, would you rent a buggy and take me and my wife home? She wants to see her house."

"Sure thing, Silver . . . be right back."

Tim got back with the buggy and I got in back and lay down with my head in Red Bird's lap.

"Buck, I'll be out in a few days when you're settled; got some papers for you to sign," Bill said.

Tim took us off down the road to our new life on our new ranch. As we neared the ranch, I turned around to look at the house I hadn't seen it yet either.

But before the house was in sight, we pulled up and Tim said, "Look, boss, this was my idea. How you like it?"

"Well, never seen anything so large in my life."

There, on two huge poles that must have been twenty inches in diameter and twenty feet high, one on each side of the road sat a huge sign.

"What does it say, honey?"

"It says, 'SILVER BUCK RANCH. BUCK TAYLOR OWNER.'"

"Pretty sound, I want to learn to read, if live with white people should understand words."

"Why sure honey, never thought about it until now. We'll get you some lessons."

"Thank you, honey."

"Tim, isn't this where the Walters house was?"

"Sure was, but we gave the lumber away to people around town to mend their homes and such. Didn't think you wanted any of it in your new house. The ranch starts here where this sign is, and Jim and I thought the house should be set back a ways. You'll see over this next rise."

He got the horses going again. We were going up a slight grade and when we reached the top about twenty minutes later, there before us was the biggest house I'd seen in my life, even bigger than Jim Backo's back in Texas. Then there was a huge barn and corral; that barn was almost as large as the house. The house had a porch all the way around that looked to be twenty feet wide, with ten stairs going up to it on all four sides. There was a second porch on the second floor of the house that went all the way around also; it was about fifteen feet wide. There were doors on each side of the house, top and bottom with double doors, the likes of which that stunned me, on the front side. There were plenty of windows all around. Red Bird just looked at it without saying anything for a while.

"What you think of it, honey? It's kind of large, but we'll fill it up soon enough with our children."

"This is just for us? Big enough for whole tribe to live, never seen anything like this."

"Me either, to tell the truth. I always lived in a small home."

As we rode down the incline, I noticed the fine location of the house. It was built in kind of a valley that would protect it against the harsh winds that blew in the winter, and there were huge trees on three sides of the house with a small lake out in front about one hundred feet long. The front faced the southwest away from the harsh north winds. Then off in the distance about a mile away to the east, half way up the crest of the next ridge, was a house about halfway finished. I pointed it out to Red Bird.

"That over there must be my parent's house."

"Sure is," Tim said, "see off to the right of your parent's house?"

"Yeah,"

"That's the bunkhouse."

"Looks small."

"It's not really, it's big, but next to that big house it just looks small."

We drove up around the drive to the front of our house and Red Bird looked at the pond and back to the house.

"Long way for me to carry water."

"How about that, Tim?"

"No one has to carry water to this house. Wait till you see, we got ideas straight from Chicago. Things I never before heard of but they're here now. We even got all the furniture with the help of the women in town."

As we walked into the house through the huge double doors, it was a sight to behold. The floors were so nice and shiny that Red Bird got down on her knees and looked at her image in them. The stairs went up to the second floor. They were all of six feet wide all the way up. The living room was off to the right.

"Tim, I'm hurtin' a little, I'm goin to lay down on that new couch; we'll look later when I can admire it more."

Red Bird helped me over to the couch and sat down beside me.

"You can go ahead and look, Red Bird."

"No, wait for you. Too big; get lost."

"Tim will be with you."

"No, wait for you."

"All right."

Tim said, "Well, anyway when you get ready, the kitchen is over to the north there and back to the east is a play or game room and upstairs are the bedrooms. There's a basement too. Buck, I wanted to surprise you, but I better tell you there's no outhouse."

"What? What we supposed to do, go behind the trees like out in the forest and with all the cowhands around lookin'?"

He started laughing. "No, it's in the house . . . one upstairs and one down here, it's called a water closet. I'll come out tomorrow mornin' to explain it, but I guess the trees have to do till then. I better get now. It's near dark; can you make it to bed?"

"Sure can."

"There's lanterns, fancy, but there lanterns, all around, and matches when it gets dark. See you in the mornin'."

"Good night Tim," Red Bird said.

I laid there looking at Red Bird as she stared around the house until it was dark.

"Honey, see this? It's a match . . . now watch."

I took off the top of the lantern and lit a match and put it to the wick and it started up with a fine glow that filled the room with light.

"See that? now let's go upstairs and go to bed."

"Me sleep here tonight, see more of house with new sun."

"Well, all right, go see if Tim left our bedrolls, we'll sleep here on the floor. Take this."

"No, can see all right."

She brought the bedroll in and we went to sleep, as usual in each other's arms, but tonight she had to sleep on the opposite arm cause of my wound.

I woke up in the morning and Red Bird was not beside me. As I got up off the floor where we had slept, I noticed that the pain in my arm was better and I felt stronger but hungry. I smelled wood burning, it wasn't the fireplace. The large fireplace hadn't even been lit yet, so walking over to the door, I saw Red Bird outside with a fire going and cooking breakfast with what we had carried in my saddlebags. Then I saw Tim riding down from the ridge as I walked out on the front porch and down the stairs over to Red Bird. I kissed her good morning and was sitting down to eat as Tim rode into the yard.

"What you all cookin' out here for? Got a wonderful kitchen inside."

Red Bird looked ashamed, "I do something wrong, Buck?"

"No, you didn't, everything's fine. I love you. Tim, you should know not even I can get around a new-fangled kitchen, much less Red Bird."

"I'm sorry, should have thought, sorry if I hurt your feeling, Red Bird, didn't mean to."

"All right, Tim, have lot to learn of white man's ways. I'll try to learn."

Tim took us through the house showing us all the new things. Water that comes to the sink; he showed us how to use the water closet and the built in bath tub. We went back and sat on the couch and Red Bird just sat and was staring in a faraway look that I had never seen.

"What's the matter, honey?"

"I know why some white men think my people so primitive, we have none of this. But we are happy without all this. In time I will learn and make you happy."

"Red Bird, I do not mean to make you unhappy. And I don't need this to be happy. The only thing in the world that makes me truly happy is you and you only. I would give up all this and live in a teepee if that was what you wanted. I need none of this, just you. I love you."

"Tim, when is the next wagon comin' in from the mine? Oh, never mind . . . anyway, when it does come in tell Sam to bring Manuel with him and the extra mares we left at the mine and come to the ranch. We're heading for Santa Fe by the tenth of May to meet the cattle drive."

Tim left and I sat back and relaxed my arm, then took Red Bird upstairs to our new bed and we made love the rest of the morning. There was as much passion as there had been in the lodge last week.

"I love you . . . I just want to make you happy."

"Maybe you right, bed all right for love making. You take me like that all time I worry about nothing except pleasing you. I happy now, very happy."

"Just relax and take it easy and this place will grow on you."

"Maybe I like it," she said this with a smile and I knew she meant it, because she didn't know how to lie about anything.

The next couple of days were happy for us. Each day she would clean and bandage my wound and it was healing nicely. I showed her how to cook on the wood stove and use the pots and pans. Then the next morning Jim came riding up on Blacky. We went out to greet him. Then we saw he had Lagger behind him with the bear skin. Then his horse tied to Lagger.

"Hi, Jim, got the skin, I see."

"The man I sent had a time with these horses. They didn't want anything to do with this bear even if it was dead. He finally convinced them it was harmless."

Red Bird went over to Lagger and talked to him and then helped Jim get the bear skin off.

"Put right here . . . me do tanning . . . make last forever."

She spread it out in the hot sun and went to work on it.

"Honey, we're goin' to take the horses down to the barn."

"Go, I have work to do."

Jim and I walked to the barn and Jim pitched some hay into the new stales where he put Blacky and Lagger. Then gave them some oats. I rub down Blacky and Lagger and talked to them as I did so with one good arm.

"How's my folks' house comin' along?"

"Oh, it's fine, be done about in June sometime. Heard you going to meet them in Santa Fe."

"Yeah, about the middle of May. Think this arm will be all right by then. Doc's comin' out next week to take a look at it; until then I feel kind of useless around here. Not much to do anyways till we get the cattle here. In the mean time I'm teachin' Red Bird to use all the new things around here. You did such a fine job, thanks."

"You pay me to do a job and I did it the best I know how. Speakin' of work, I better get back and check on the men up at the new place before they put the water closet in the kitchen."

He was still laughing as he rode off toward my folk's house. I walked over and watched Red Bird as she cleaned and stretched the hide out in the sun with the head hanging down. As she worked, she paid no attention to me.

I was looking around and suddenly saw someone on a horse coming over the ridge. As the rider got closer I saw it was Bill. I hoped it was about the rest of the ranch. It was getting on to a month and a half and the cattle would be grazing on the grass south of here. Sure enough, it was Bill.

"Come on in here . . . got some papers for me, I hope."

"Sure do, it's taken a while but finally got all of it together. Some of the land cost a little more, especially along the river, but we had to pay the price because the rest isn't much good without a source of water. But you still got it cheap for what it will amount to."

"That's for sure, you need water. No ifs, ands, or buts." As he spread out the papers for me to sign, I asked him.

"Bill, you become a lawyer yet?'

"Sure did, last month, I took the bar examination and passed with flying colors. All because of you. I'm indebted to you for my life, really."

"Nonsense, I just saw a young man my age that was bright and eager to do a good job and gave you a chance. You did the rest."

I started reading the papers and signing them and handing them back to Bill. He put them back in the briefcase he carried around now. That made him look more like a lawyer than did the suit, tie and vest, all the mark of a man of the law.

"Bill, now that I own all that land, I want you to prepare a will. I have a certain division in mind, just in case, you never know."

"You're right, this much land and your part of the mine. There would be one heck of a fight over it. I can write what you want and draw it up when I get back to the office. Be a good idea you sign it before you go to Santa Fe."

"Well, Red Bird, I want her to have 30 percent in the mine. The rest to be split evenly among the rest of the shareholders. You know who has what. My folks will get twenty thousand acres includin' their house and land along the Los Piños River. The rest will go to Red Bird, that includes the land along the Animas River and her people can live on any part of her section. That's it. One other thing . . . do I need to register my brand?"

"It sure would help if any legal suits came up later."

"Then would you file the name Silver Buck Ranch? The brand will be a large B with a large S through the B. Would you have the blacksmith make about five brandin' irons up and have Sam bring them out when he gets to town."

I took out a piece of paper and drew the brand for him to give to the blacksmith. He put it up and we went out and he mounted up and headed north for town.

Red Bird came to me.

"I am done now, what we do?"

"How would you like to take Blacky and Lagger for a ride with me and look at some of our ranch?"

"Me like that, like wind in my face when ride Lagger. Good horse."

"Let's get goin' then, get some water and food to take, we might just have ourselves a picnic down by the river." She got the water and grub and went to the barn and saddled the horses. Then we took off in the wind across the grassy plateau that most of our ranch was built on. She made a beautiful figure on top of a horse, so slim with long black hair way past her waist flying in the wind and her long slender legs hanging bare on each side of Lagger. The slit in her dress rode up her leg until I could see her waist, her bare waist, for she still wore no under garments and if possible I never wanted her wearing any. As she rode, her bare breast under her dress rose and fell with the moment of the horse.

We came to a handsome spot on the river with large trees along the bank that hung out over the water, making a shaded patch half on the bank and half in the river. We stopped to give the horses a breather and to cut along this peaceful part of the ranch. Red Bird sat me up against a tree and told me.

"You rest arm and watch me, I take a bath in nice clean, cool river, tired of water in house."

With that she took her dress off and revealed that lovely body that I would never tire of looking at the rest of my life. Then she took out some soap.

"Like soap white man bathe with, smells good." She took the soap and jumped in the water and started swimming around, just having fun and playing. Then she waded over to the edge and started lathering her body with the soap. Washing every part for my benefit slowly, as though she was teasing me. Soon she was done and jumped back in the river to rinse off. Out she came to me with her body all wet and lay down next to me.

As we lay in each other's arms she said, "Now I go wash, you left me hot and wet down below. You come in with me, I wash you."

She removed my clothes the rest of the way and we went in together hand in hand. Good to her word, she washed both of us and we rinsed and got dressed and headed back to the ranch after heading east a few miles to see more of the ranch.

The next week was good and the nights were better. It was now May first, and I was expecting Sam to be coming any day now. My arm was nearly back to normal. The doc had been out and took out the stitches and said it should be back to normal in another week. He said just to keep working it more and more day after day until the soreness was out. Then on the afternoon of the eighth Sam came on a new horse and Manuel in a new wagon. Sam was herding the five mares into the corral as I came out of the house and went into the barn to get Blacky out and let him lose with the mares.

"Hello, Buck, what you doing?"

"Just keepin' a promise I made to him. Glad to see you made it. We leave in two days."

"We were waiting for the branding irons to be finished and Manuel had to get some things for the kitchen."

"Si, señor I know from what Mr. Gills said we would be needing some things, I hear there's water in the house. Much good."

"Manuel, when we leave in two days, I want you to stay here and get the kitchen fixed up like you want it and take care of the stock. If you need anything, just go to town and get it."

"Si, señor."

So on May tenth, Red Bird, Sam, and I rode south across the ranch, heading for Santa Fe to meet one of the largest cattle drives to come up this way. It took us all day to reach the border of New Mexico and the end of our ranch. We camped on our ranch that first night. Red Bird was concerned because she told me the Navajo tribe lived in all the area south of here.

"They see me and will take me captive for I do not belong here."

"They will not harm you as long as I live, that's for sure, honey."

The next two days we traveled and only crossed one river. It looked to be a dry spring, but if there was one more good river the cattle could make it. Then Sam broke my train of thought.

"Buck, you see what's on the ridge over yonder?"

We all turned and there were four Indians watching us.

"You know, we should try to make a deal for safe passage through here for some cattle."

Red Bird said, "Not make deal until have cattle with you, they will not believe you unless they see for their selves."

"Well then, we better get movin'."

We camped at night with a big fire because if we tried to hide they would think we were up to no good. But they may not bother us if they think we were just tracking through.

We were heading southeast the next morning, but we saw a mountain range far in front of us. I knew the cattle couldn't go over it, so we turned south for a day, then turned due east again. Then we hit another river. We jumped off our horses and led them into the middle of the river; we all put our heads down in the water and drank until our eyes were bulging and our bellies were full. We camped by that river that night and looked at the stars overhead. We slept good and got an early start before the sun got any hotter. But the coolness didn't last, by ten in the morning it was like an oven.

Then the next night we were among the mountain range. It wouldn't be much further now. The next day we came to the Rio Grande River and camped there overnight.

"Sam, you think the cattle can make it over what we just came through?"

"Sure, might lose a few head but we should make it. The longest stretch is three days without water. But I think most will make it through all right."

Chapter Thirteen

The next day we rode into Santa Fe. This was only the second town Red Bird had ever seen, but it was so much bigger than Durango that her eyes were wide open, drinking in all the sights. People looked at us funny, not knowing who we were.

"Let's stop in at the sheriff's and see if any cattle have been reported."

"I'll go get us two rooms at the hotel. I'll meet you all in the lobby."

"All right."

Me and Red Bird got off, and I saw her looking at the fancy dresses some of the women were wearing. I thought maybe she would like some new clothes.

We walked into the sheriff's office to report our arrival in town.

"What can I do for you, mister?" he said, looking up from his paper.

"I need to talk to the sheriff." He moved the paper down so I could see his badge.

"Son, you're lookin' at him."

"Well, Sheriff, my name is Buck Taylor and I came in to see if you've heard of a cattle drive up from Texas."

"Not a word . . . never been cattle this way."

"There will be soon, I'm expectin' some and we're headin' for Colorado. I have a ranch up along the border. We'll be at the hotel, would you let me know if you hear anything?"

"Sure, who's the girl."

"She's my wife, Sheriff."

"Well, some people around here don't take too kindly to Indians, even young and pretty. Best keep your distance from the saloon. Those cowhands get dunk, I don't know what they'd do. No offense, just a warning about the way things are around here, and you may not get a room either or food for her or you."

"Thanks, but I can handle whatever comes up. If I'm not around you can tell my man Sam if you hear anything. He'll be around the hotel or saloon, just ask for Sam."

"Will do."

We left the office and took the horses to the stable down the street. Then we went to the hotel and Sam was in the lobby waiting for us when we walked in the door.

"I already signed you in so you can go on up."

"All right."

We started up the stairs; Red Bird was on my arm when the desk clerk said, "Hey you, where you think you're going?"

"To our room."

"We don't allow Indians here and I don't remember you signing in."

"My man signed me in," I said as I came back down the stairs and over to the desk.

"What's your name."

"Mr. and Mrs. Buck Taylor," I said in a loud voice for everyone to hear. Sam here signed for us."

"I don't see, but a Mr. and Mrs. Silver Buck."

"That's us."

"You the one found that silver mine?"

"That's me, I want to see the manger."

"Yes, Mr. Silver."

He went to the back and another man came out.

"What's the problem here?"

"This man says I can't take my wife to our room."

The first man whispered in the manger's ear.

"Well I see, I guess in your case it's all right . . . here's your key."

I took the key and we went to our room. I put our things on the bed and turned to my beautiful wife and took her in my arms.

"Sorry, you have to see how some white men are. Why don't you speak up when we are around other people?"

"Not my place to speak when men are talking."

"In the white man's, world you can speak whenever you want to."

"No need, you, my husband, take care of me and everything else."

"You made your point. But it upsets me to see you treated that way."

"It's all right, I have you, and your friends are kind to me, and your parents will like me, I think, that is all I need."

"I saw you lookin' at the dresses the women in the street were wearin'. Would you like to buy some new dresses?"

"I did not like those, they look so funny and they are so tight, how do they breathe? You do not like what I wear?"

"Yes, I like what you wear and don't wear."

"What mean by don't wear?"

"Those women wear things to hold up their breasts and things to cover their bottoms and even legs."

"Why do they wear all that? I wear one dress and it covers all me need covered and keep me warm."

"I don't know why they wear all that, but I know some wear it to hold in the fat. You don't need any of that, your fine like you are."

"I glad you like."

"Let's go down and eat."

"But we will cause trouble."

"It's not us that cause the trouble, it's their minds."

So we went down and I saw the manager and I went over to him.

"Are me and my wife goin' to have any trouble when we eat?"

"No, sir, Mr. Silver, I'll explain to the waiter. I assure you, you won't have any trouble with my staff, but I can't guarantee what the other customers will do, you understand?"

"I understand, but don't condone the way people act to my wife and her people."

We walked to a table in the middle of the room among all the stares that were sent our way. But we ate in peace and went for a walk on the street before sundown. We saw Sam go into the saloon and come out just as fast. I called him over to see what was wrong.

"What happened in there, how come you came out so fast?"

"Not by choice, I assure you."

"Then why?"

"They threw me out when someone said that I worked for you. But I tell you one thing, I'd rather have friends like you and Red Bird than have a beer."

"I'm not goin' to stand for my men to be treated bad on my account. Wait here, I'm takin' Red Bird back to our room, be right back."

"Let it go, Buck, you'll be hurt."

"Don't worry, I'll be all right." I walked her back to our room.

"Lock the door and don't open it for anyone except me or Sam. Hear me?"

"Yes, but—"

"No, buts!"

I left and met Sam on the street and we went into the saloon. As we walked up to the bar I tried to spot the one likely to be the troublemaker. Put him down and the rest would back off. As I looked around the room, I spotted him, he was a great big man with a big belly and a long dirty beard and he was drunk.

"We'll have two beers bartender, right now."

The bartender looked nervous, as he looked at us then at the big dirty fella. But he got the two beers and brought them to us, then backed away, saying, "If I were you, I'd get out of here."

"Well, you're not me, are you? We just want to have a beer in peace, with no trouble."

Just then, I felt a tap on my shoulder. I started to turn and out of the corner of my eye saw the troublemaker.

"You the one found all that silver up in Colorado?"

"Sure am, but now I'm a rancher."

Everyone in the room was watching close at what was going to happen.

"You went and married that squaw. Why a white man go and do that?" He was steady, not as dunk as I had thought.

"'Cause I love her and she's more honest than some whites I've met."

"Well, I won't have a man say a Indian's better than any white woman."

As he finished the sentence I saw his fist coming at me. I ducked, and the blow missed and I came up into his fat belly with my right hand as hard as I could. He stumbled backward, trying to catch his breath. I walked over to him and hit him under the chin. This sent him back some more onto the top of a table, which made the table fall flat. I turned to walk back to the bar to finish my beer and leave, when I heard a click and at the same time Sam yelled.

"Buck, watch it, he's got a gun!"

But the warning came too late, I had already turned and at the same time pulled my knife free and threw it. Before he got a shot off, my knife had pinned his hand to the floor and he had dropped the gun. I walked over to him and kicked his gun away and bent over and pulled my knife out of his hand and wiped it on his pants. He grabbed his hand in pain. I looked at him.

"You asked for that, mister. I could had killed you if I wanted. Just remember that, 'cause next time you won't need the doc, you'll need the undertaker."

I looked around the room and spoke to everyone.

"I do as I please; I don't break any laws. If you don't like it, you can just leave me to my business or go straight to hell. I don't care one way or another. But the first way is your choice, but you mess with me or mine and I'll put you in the second."

I turned and walked to the bar and me and Sam finished our beer. Later we walked out of the saloon and back to the rooms. I said good night to Sam and went to my room.

"It's me, Buck, let me in, honey."

She threw the door open and threw herself into my arms and started kissing me all over my face.

"Me worry about you, you gone so long."

"See, I'm all right. Nothin' to worry about. We just had that beer that Sam wanted. Be back in a minute."

I went down and ordered up a bath. The bath came in a while and we bathed together, as we had at home since we've been married, washing each other with a little playing around. The earlier incidents had now been forgotten as we got out of the bath and dried each off and fell into the bed in each other's arms for the rest of the night.

The next morning we got dressed and went down to eat. I spotted Sam at a table, so we went over and joined him.

"Sam, after we eat would you go check on the horses? Make sure they're gettin' proper care, around here you never know."

"Sure thing. You know, Buck, I never seen anyone as fast with a knife as you are. Bet you're as fast with that gun."

"Well, don't go spreadin' that around. We don't want any more trouble if we can help it."

"I know, but I won't have to say anything, it's all over town about last night."

I spotted the sheriff coming over to where we were eating.

"Hello, Silver Buck, why didn't you tell me who you were when you were in my office?"

"I did, my name is Buck Taylor, that other was stuck on me by my good friends."

"Heard about what happened last night. The bartender told me you could had killed him and would had been in the right."

"I don't kill for the pleasure, but if I'm pushed I can. If that man would had made another move for his gun he would be dead."

"Glad it didn't come to that, and I want to apologize to your lovely wife for the way some people act. Not all of us are like that."

"Thank you for your kind words, Sheriff, but they're not necessary. I choose to marry and love a white man and I will be beside him until I die and no words or acts will alter that," said Red Bird.

"That's a fine speech, little lady, and I know you mean every word of it. My hats off to you."

He backed off with his hat in his hand, then turned and walked out the door.

"You want to take a walk, dear? See some of this town before we have to leave?"

We got up and left and were walking down the boardwalks along the shops. We had been walking a few minutes when Red Bird said, "Look, Buck, that woman over there."

"What about her?"

"Is she an Indian?"

"No, honey, she's a Mexican like Manuel that came to the ranch with Sam. What about her?"

"I like her dress, it looks nice and comfortable to me."

"Well, let's go ask her where she got it."

We walked across the street to where the woman was standing in her colorful Mexican style dress.

"Excuse me, señorita."

"Me, señor?"

"Yes, my wife was admiring your dress from across the street. I would like to know where we can buy one like it."

"I make this, but there is a place down here in the Mexican part of town where one can buy a dress like mine. You keep going down the street this way, then turn left and you should see it. It has dresses in the little window."

"Thank you, señorita."

We were off to buy some dresses. We came to the street and turned left and right away we saw the little shop. We went inside and a pudgy little woman came out of the backroom.

"May I help you, señor, señorita?"

"Yes, my wife likes your dresses. We would like to buy some."

Red Bird was looking over the dresses hanging around.

"Si, just look over here, these look to be her size. She is small and large up here on top. These are the skirts and these are the blouses. When she finds what likes she can try them on back here."

"Thank you, señorita, we'll look around and let you know."

"Honey, just pick out what you want and I'll buy it for you."

"These are so colorful and pretty."

She picked out four or five skirts and blouses and we went in the back for her to try them on. They fit her nice with her little waist and nice-size hips and large breasts. They were bright colors: reds, greens, blues, and yellows. All of them looked nice with her color skin and her black hair and dark eyes. She put on her dress and we went out to the front.

"We'll take these four sets."

"These are nice, I noticed them on her. She looks good in them, but she wears no under things."

"I not need any, too tight, body needs to breathe like leave on a flower."

"I like her like that anyway. We only been married five weeks."

"I bet you do!" she said as she figured the price. I paid her and we left for lunch and an afternoon nap.

We had been in town a week and Red Bird was becoming used to things. We were sitting on the front porch of the hotel on the swing when Red Bird came out and said. "I study people in town since we been here and they not to different than my people. They dress different, talk funny, and live in buildings and have work I do not understand. But most look to be honest and not too many want to fight. Growing up, I thought white man like to kill all time."

"You grew up around Jeb and Foster and then you met me. You knew we were good."

"Yes, but I thought you three different, that why you nice."

"There are bad whites also as well as Indians. But both our people condemn all for what a few do."

"That's it, true for both sides. We need to learn to live side by side in peace."

"I hope someday our children will see this happen, they will be of both worlds. We must teach them both sides."

The sheriff came up on the porch one afternoon.

"Some men rode in this morning from the south. They said there was a cattle drive heading this way about two days out. Maybe two, three thousand heads. They talked to an older man. They noticed a woman with them. Thought I'd let you know."

"Sounds like them. We'll probably head out in the mornin' to meet them."

"There's another thing; that man you had the run in with. He's been saying around that he's going to find you when his hand gets well. So keep a sharp eye out and close to this pretty woman. He might take her, out of spite. If possible, try to turn the cattle around town and don't let the cowhands come in all at once."

"Fine with me. We're turnin' northwest, south of here and let the cattle water and rest a day or two before headin' on to that dry section. If that's all right."

"Fine with me, nice meeting you two, I'll say so long case I don't see you again."

"Good-bye, thanks."

"Well, honey, looks like you're goin' to met my folks in a few days. I tell you, you sure look downright beautiful in that new store bought dress."

"I'm afraid, Buck, they will not like me."

"Honey, that's plum crazy. My dad takes one look at you and he'll be in heaven as I was, and my mother will love you for your honesty. Just be yourself and don't try to change one bit. I love you like you are. Now go and pack our things, I'll go find Sam and tell him we'll leave early tomorrow."

She ran off to our room and I went to the saloon where I knew Sam was sure to be. Sure enough, when I walked in, there he was belly up to the bar. I went over and ordered a beer and Sam turned to me when he heard my voice.

"Why, hi, boss, come to do drinkin' with me?"

"Just one beer, that's all. Come lookin' for you to tell you we're headin' out early. So sleep it off, 'cause we go to work tomorrow."

"I'll be ready, you can count on me. You know they named you right, you're a silver of a boss. Most fun I had in years here in this town. See that little gal over there? Had her in my room every night we been here. Boy, she knows how to have fun."

I finished my beer and told Sam, "Get to bed."

Then I left and went to the stables and gave the horses some feed and hay, then left to my room.

Red Bird had everything packed and ready, so we went to bed. Lying there, I heard Sam come up the stairs, singing an old cowboy tune at the top of his lungs. Then heard another voice say, "Be quite, Sam, you'll wake the dead." I knew he had the woman from the saloon with him again. I rolled over and hugged Red Bird, who was already asleep, and I went to sleep.

That night my dream returned as lifelike as the other two times I had it. There I was riding up to the ranch house after a long day's work and there on the porch was Red Bird and two small children. One boy about three or four that looked like me and a girl about two or three that looked like Red Bird, one on each side of her legs. The three of them were waving at me as I rode up.

Next thing I knew it was morning and we were down at a table eating breakfast.

"I best go up and get Sam a movin'."

Going up the stairs, I heard Sam coming down.

"'Bout time you be up and around."

"Sh, sh, my head's going to fall off," he said in a whisper.

"Got your breakfast waitin', come on."

"My head, Buck, can you talk a little softer, please?"

We went to the table and Red Bird waited as we finished our vittles. I sent Sam to get the horses ready. Red Bird and I sat and drank our coffee waiting for Sam to bring the horses.

"How you like the white man's food here in town?"

"Not as good as could be with more seasoning, but will fill the belly. That's what counts, doesn't it?"

"Sure is, but wait till you taste Manuel's food, it's like heaven."

Sam rode up in front of the hotel holding his head, and Red Bird and I went out and we mounted up and headed south to meet the cattle drive.

We were well out of town when the sun was high enough to warm the day as we followed the Rio Grande River. I knew we were sure to run into them by the river. You couldn't hardly miss three thousand heads of cattle, even if you were blind.

I began to worry as we got farther downriver because there was less and less water in it. If it was shallow this far north, what was it like in west Texas? Then I remembered the sheriff saying the men had talked to an older man and saw a woman and the cattle. So my worried thoughts started to fade. When dusk came there was no sign of them. We camped beside the river and was gonna be sleeping under the stars again.

"Bound to run into them tomorrow, don't you think, Sam?"

"If what those men said were true, we should."

"No reason for them to lie."

"No, maybe they came on to some good grass and stayed in one place awhile."

"Could be, how's your head now?"

"Still hurts a little, but a hot meal and a good night's sleep and I'll be back to normal."

We ate and turned in, but my mind was on watch as I sleep light when out in the wilderness and I knew Blacky would wake me if anything came around as he had done many nights before. The warmth of Red Bird's body kept me warm in the cool night of the desert. What I would have given to have her warm body next to me on those cold winter nights in the cave with Foster. That had been a year and a half ago. How fast time goes by.

As dawn came upon the desert we were mounted and on the move across the semidesert. It had been two years since I had seen my folks and ranch friends; friends that I used to go hunting with and work all the long hot summer. I used to go to barn dances and hay rides. As I thought back, it seemed like ten years instead of two. I was a kid then; now I was a married man.

About ten in the morning Red Bird stopped Lagger in his tracks.

"I will not go on."

"What's the matter?"

"We should meet them soon, right, honey?"

"Sure, not too much past noon for sure."

"Then take me to river. I want bath and my new dress on. I will not meet your mother and father with dust all over me."

"They won't mind."

"Buck, I mean it."

"You better listen to her, Buck. Looks to me even Indian women can be stubborn."

"Okay, Sam, you ride on and scout away from the river."

"Gotcha!" He rode off to the east. I took Red Bird to the river, and she undressed and jumped in. When she came up I threw her a bar of soap. As I watched her, the beauty of her body gave me a funny feeling.

"Red Bird, think I'll take one too."

"That good, you need one."

I got out of my clothes and in I went head first. I came up under her and touched that body I loved. I reached up and got the soap and lathered up her body all over. I came up and did her upper body. Then she took the soap from me and lathered me up all over and we washed each other's hair and rinsed off. We got out and dried our bodies off, then she washed my clothes. I felt better from the bath, at least cleaner but not satisfied physically, but we had the rest of our life to please each other. Red Bird got dressed in one of her new dresses. I got dressed after the hot sun had dried my clothes.

As we mounted up, Sam came riding in like a tornado with dust all around him.

"What is it, Sam? What's a matter?"

"They're here, about two miles over the next ridge."

Sam turned and started back from the way he had come and we were right on his tail. As we came to the top of the ridge there was a sight that I would remember the rest of my life. We paused on top of the ridge to drink in the magnitude of the moment. This was the largest herd ever brought through west Texas to Colorado when we reached that point. There they were spread out for miles with cowboys all around them. Those beautiful, hardy longhorns. What magnificent herd they made. Some of their horns had a four-to-five-foot spread. I scanned the herd once more trying to spot my father, but it was my mother in the chuck wagon that caught my eyes first. She looked fine and fit just as I had left her. Then my eyes fell on my father as usual on the point of the herd. He was looking mighty fit and happy. I just hoped they would like their new life with the harsh winters. It was too late now to worry about that. We sat there watching the men working the cattle. Then Sam spoke up.

"I never have seen cattle like that in Colorado. What they called?"

"Those, my man, are longhorns, the most hardy steer there is alive. That's why I thought they could make it this way. They been wanderin' around Texas since the Spanish brought them over on their ships. They survived in South Texas without any help from man for a few hundred years."

"We goin' to ride in."

"Yeah, but I don't want them to stop in the middle of the day. But I'll get my dad's attention and he'll ride up."

We rode along the ridge for a while until we were toward the front of the herd. I took my hat in my hand and started waving it back and forth to attract attention and it worked as my dad scanned the horizon, in front of the herd as he always did when he was riding point. He yelled to the other rider on the left point and took his hat off and pointed toward us. The man shook his head to indicate he understood. Then my dad took his hat and hit his horse on the rump and let the reins out and high-tailed it to the chuck wagon and pointed our way again and my mother turned the wagon in our direction. She moved the wagon fast as she could as not to scare the cattle and cause a stampede. My dad rode right beside her cause he knew mother would be mad if he took off without her.

As they moved away from the cattle, they speeded up their approach, and I got off Blacky and Red Bird got off Lagger, and came over to me and I put my arm around her.

My dad jumped off his horse before it came to a complete standstill and came to me and put his hand out to shake mine. As I took his hand, he pulled me into his arms and gave me a big hug.

"Glad to see you, boy, we can't call you that now. When you left you were a boy, but I can see you're a man now. You have the look all around you. This must be Red Bird." He took her in his arms and gave her a big hug as mother got down from the wagon and came over to us wiping her eyes. She threw her arms around my neck and I rose up and her feet came off the ground.

"Been quite a long time, son, glad to find you well."

She let go of me and went to Red Bird.

"Don't even have to ask, I can see it in your face, you all are already married." Red Bird spoke up.

"Yes, you right, been married one and half moons. We much happy. Love my man much."

"She's so lovely, Buck, how'd you get so lucky?"

"Well, Mother, since I been in Colorado luck has found me so many times it's unreal."

"Look how clean you two are and look at me with all this trail dust all over me."

"We took a bath in the river over there just before Sam spotted you," I said.

"It's 'bout time to bed down the herd for the night. I'll go tell the boys. We'll have a talk tonight."

"All right, Pa." He mounted up and headed for the herd.

"You know your pa, he thinks those cattle can't move without him there. You still didn't tell me how you roped this little gal, Buck."

"Honey, you tell her."

"Knew Buck great-grandfather since I was a little girl. Like him very much and his friend Foster brought Buck to village of my father. Saw Buck first time at sister wedding and liked him as soon as I saw him."

"I thought she was so beautiful the first time I laid eyes on her."

"He ran off to take bath and after wedding Foster took me and I met him and he was in the water, so I washed his clothes and put over fire to dry. When he came out of the water, I know he made for me when I saw his hardness."

My mother turned red and covered her face with both hands and laughed out loud.

"Me say something wrong, Buck?"

"No, honey, you didn't, it's just she's not used to your honesty but she'll get used to it. Mother, that's one thing I love about her, she'll always says whatever's on her mind. So when she tells you anything, you can believe every word of it."

"That's just great, I love her too. That's the only way to be, Red Bird, never change."

Sam got off his horse and came over.

"Mother, this is one of my best friends and a partner in the mine. This is Sam, Mother."

"Howdy do, ma'am, glad to meet you."

"How you do, Sam? Sorry my husband didn't meet you but you know how an old cowpuncher is. Cows come first to everything."

"Yes, ma'am, I'll meet him tonight."

"Now, men, go tend to business. Red Bird, you show me where to get this dust off me. I'll bring her back in a little while. You won't die, will you, son?"

"No, but you be careful, had some trouble in Santa Fe and the sheriff thinks the man might try to get even with me. So be on the watch."

"You know me son, when I'm on the trail I always have this with me."

As she got upon the wagon she pulled her rifle out of the boot. As I helped Red Bird up to the wagon I said, "We'll be close by . . . any trouble, fire one shot, we'll come a-runnin'."

Red Bird pointed toward the river and they rode off. I felt a little empty. This was the first time we'd been apart since we got married. Sam and me, we mounted up and rode into the herd. The men were bringing them to a stop for the night. As we rode around, I introduced Sam to the men I knew, which was just about everyone. It was like my Texas home had come to me. These men were ones I went to school with and rode the range with the older men.

The cattle finally settled down and all the cowhands gathered at the side of the herd toward the river. Everyone came and shook my hand and slapped me on the back.

"Dad, this here is my good friend Sam. He's goin' to be workin' with us on the ranch."

"Glad to meet you, Sam. Where's the rest of your men?'

"Well, I didn't know how many men you were bring so if you think we'll need more, we can hire some in Durango. It's about five miles from the house and about one mile from the front gate of the ranch and about eight miles from your's and mother's house."

"That sounds like a Texas ranch. Is it big as it sounds?"

"It is, we got all we were after, so it will support a few thousand heads more than you brought. That's twenty acres for one cow with a calf. It's around 110,000 acres. It's all paid for too."

"I never dreamed it was that large, we'll need some more men, all right."

"What I liked is it's west and east borders have rivers runnin' the full length. But don't get too happy, in the spring the rivers are full and over full with the snow melt, but by late summer they remind me of South Texas with a small creek runnin' by. But I got some plans. I'll show you when we get there. Now, how was your trip?"

Before he could answer mother and Red Bird came running up in the wagon, dust flyin' all around them.

"What is it?"

"Big ugly man with beard came up to us. Scared us, we took off. He had four others with him."

I told dad what had happened in Santa Fe and what the sheriff said.

"This is the man, so you better tell the men to be alert from now on, we sure don't want a stampede." Red Bird came to me and put her arms around my neck.

"It's all right, honey, I'll take care of you."

The men were put on alert and then the five of us sat around the fire drinking coffee and then my dad started telling us about the drive up from Texas.

"You know, Buck, you picked a fine trail, we had water until around El Paso. Then it was two days before we found a little cause we were away from the runoff from the mountains, but we must be gettin' closer to more mountains cause the river has been gettin' fuller. What's it like up ahead?" "Well, there's water now except about three days after we cross the Rio Grande south of Santa Fe.

After the mountains, it gets dry but we have to move fast as possible cause as it gets hotter the smaller streams dry up. No more snow, so they dry up. But I think we can make it. We saw Indians too, in the dry section, but I think we can deal with them by tradin' some cattle for safe passage."

"Can't Red Bird talk to them?"

"They not of same people, enemy of my people."

"See, Dad, we think all Indians are alike, but these Indians, if they found out we had the daughter of a Ute chief, they would attack us no matter what we gave them. Then they would use Red Bird to get to her father Dancing Bear. So she is takin' a risk to come meet you. But with her new clothes she can pass for a Mexican girl from a distance."

"Well, I guess I'm never too old to learn. Just thought all Indians fought together."

My mother spoke up. "Then your father is at peace with the white man."

"Yes, Father not like war. He hopes my marriage will make a better and long-lasting peace. I could see it in his eyes when he marry us."

My mother choked on the coffee she was drinking.

"Mother, don't die, we were married by a preacher from town also."

"Yes, we had a double wedding, Indian and white man, see, I just love my ring you sent Buck for me to have."

"Did he tell you how long it's been in the family?"

"He said over one hundred years, also say I give it to our daughter when she marry."

We all turned in for the night. All went well that first night and we were up and the cattle were on the move by dawn. I left Red Bird with mother and rode out to talk to my dad. He stopped as I rode up.

"I have a map here, made it on the way down. It may be rough but it will give you an idea of where we're goin'. See here, I thought we can cut the Rio Grande south of town. Plenty of water and grass. We can let the cattle fill up a day or two before we hit this dry part. Give the boys a chance to see Santa Fe. But the sheriff said only five or six at one time. Should be to the cut off spot by tomorrow afternoon."

"Can I keep this to keep me in line?"

"Sure."

"What's this above the border . . . this large area?"

"That's our ranch, Silver Buck Ranch."

"Where you get that name?"

"The men gave me that name when me and Foster found the silver mine."

"Is it a rich one?"

"Well, when we left the total was up to $250,000 and the stockpile from winter hadn't gone down much. That's minus the ranch and pay for the men and the cattle. Then there's the house, ours and yours and barns and bunkhouse. We still have enough in the bank and more comin' in."

"We'll get the ranch paying for itself in no more than two years."

"Speakin' of the ranch, I didn't bring the brandin' irons with us 'cause we don't have time for it out here but it's a big B with an S over the B, stands for Silver Buck."

"Well, son, I'm right proud of you, you did a heck of a job. And let me say I had my doubts about you and Red Bird gettin' hitched, but now that I see her and know her better, I have no doubts. You picked a fine gal with looks to match her mind."

"Thanks, Dad, glad you approve. Well I better get and see about her before she embarrasses mother too much."

I rode on back and untied Lagger from the wagon. Red Bird jumped on his back and we took off waving so long to my mother.

We rode slow, along the top of the ridge overlooking the herd.

"What you think of them?"

"You look like your father. He's proud and strong man, like you. I like much. Mother proud but different type. She proud of her husband and son. I think she likes me but afraid I take your love for her away. That will pass as time pass and she find my love for you is like hers for your father and your love for her like for you for your father, a family love not a man to woman passion love."

"You are too much; I think you hit the nail on the head. I don't know how anyone could say it better than that. I love you."

"I love you too, Buck Taylor. Now take me behind big rock and lay with me, I need it now, big man."

That night we camped a few hours from the cutoff point. I told my father, "Can you spare a couple of men tomorrow? I want to ride to town and see if my bearded friend who likes to scare women is there, and the men can get a few hours to have some drinks."

"Sure, take Jake and Tom, they're good men, and Sam of course."

"Fine, Red Bird, would you stay here with my folks? They'll take care of you. It will make me feel better knowin' you're safe."

"If it make you worry less, I will stay. Your mother is my mother now."

The next day about noon we crossed the Rio Grande and the cattle were drinking and eating their bellies full. Me and Sam and the other two men headed for town. We rode up to the saloon and sure enough there were five horses tied up in front that looked like they had been well ridden. They were all worked up into a lather.

"Keep your eyes open. Let me take care of him, you just make sure his friends stay out of it."

We walked in the saloon and the four men spread out. My men went right up to them. I heard them tell them.

"You keep out of this, it's their business. We have twenty more men out there that will be happy to come after you, if you interfere with this."

The man with the beard said, "Don't worry, boys, I can take care of this one. He's nothin', then we go get that woman of his."

He stood up and pulled the table and chair out of the way. Everyone behind me moved out of the way.

"What you want, little boy?"

"I want you to stop botherin' my wife and my mother."

"Who, me? Oh yeah, remember that woman we saw takin' a bath in the river boys? Why she's just my type and my boys can take care of that squaw of yours. She don't know what a real man feels like inside her, not with this little boy for a husband."

Jake said, "Tom, this man's a fool, he doesn't know he's facin' the fastest gun in Texas."

"Guess he doesn't even know that he won't get that gun out before he has a bullet in his head."

You could see the sweat break out on his dirty beard, and his fat belly started moving with laughter.

"I know, but it won't work, you're just tryin' to scare me."

"No, we're tellin' you for your health."

"Now, Silver, you know I was just a-funnin' you."

"Only my friends call me Silver, and you're not on the list. If you don't believe me, you can ask Brady, formally of Durango, when you reach hell."

He reached for his gun, but my bullet was already out of my gun and into his head before his gun cleared leather. He fell to his knees looking into my eyes and then fell face-first on the hard wooden floor. Sam pushed the man he had been watchin' over to where the body lay in a pool of blood.

"It's your turn, mister."

"No, not me, we didn't want any part of it. When those women yelled we hit the trail for here. Bob there wouldn't go in without backup. So he turned and ran with us."

"All right, boys, let them go. My ranch is south of Durango, Colorado, and these men of mine are goin' to remember your faces, and if one of them see you anywhere near Durango he has orders to shoot you on sight. Understand?"

"Yes, sir." They all agreed and lit out the door for their horses.

As we heard them ride off down the street I told the men, "Men, the drinks are on me."

I sat down with Sam and the boys and had a beer in my hand when the sheriff came in.

"See you got the best of old Bob there." He called two men over to carry the body away, but they had to get two more to get the job done.

"Sheriff, Sam, you know, these other two are my men from the drive. They're goin' to have a few drinks and we're goin' back to camp."

"Remember what I said about too many men in here at once?"

"I'll be lettin' five or six at a time come in and we'll be gettin' on our way home in two days."

"That's fine."

The bartender came over.

"Sheriff, it was a fair fight. Old Bob didn't have a chance . . . this Silver so fast I didn't see his gun come out."

"See you later, Silver, that's all I wanted to know."

"Well, boys, I'm not much of a drinkin' man, so I'll see you later. Goin' to light out for camp."

"Silver, think I'll stay and get to know the men better now that I'm goin' to be workin' with them."

"That's good, Sam. You all have fun, not too late, the other boys are waitin' their turn, here."

"Right, boss."

I rode Blacky out of town. It was coming on to dusk when I reached camp. I found Red Bird sitting by the fire. When she saw me she ran and kissed me for a full minute. The boys around us were kidding.

"Would you look at that?"

"Hope I catch me one that likes lovin' like that."

"Don't think I've seen a hug like that since that bear got ahold of me."

"You all boys can get you a gal when we get to Colorado. In the mean time, eat your heart out."

Everyone started laughing, even my folks, as I carried Red Bird to our bedroll away from the crowd and into a night of pleasing pleasures.

The two days went by and all the men had made it to town for some drinks and a good time.

Chapter Fourteen

We were now on our last leg home. The cattle were full of grass and water; the men were full of drink and whatever else they had managed to get into. If everything went right we should be on the ranch in two weeks. There was one more river before the dry spell came, if it hadn't dried up yet, which was possible this time of year. We would just have to wait and see.

At night, mother would talk to Red Bird and me, and father would sit around the campfire with the men I had grown up with, telling stories from my boyhood. It was always cold at night and hot during the day.

The next day we went between the two mountains. The river would be coming up. The grass, if it could be called grass, was very poor and the cattle wouldn't have much to do with it. I rode ahead to the point, to have a talk with my dad. As Blacky rode up there was a cloud of dust around us. This dust was different; it was a fine powder that managed to get into every part of one's clothes and body.

"You think the men can handle the herd awhile?"

"What you got in mind?"

"The last river should be comin' up and I thought we could ride ahead to check on it."

"I'm ready . . . just hope it's not full of this alkali. If it is we'll have to find a way around it. This stuff will kill them if they drink it. "When we came through here, this river was the one that was salty, but still drinkable."

We rode over to the point rider.

"Tom, can you handle it? We're goin' to check on the next river to make sure it's good."

"Sure, I'll take charge."

We rode out into the desertlike surroundings. As we got farther away from the cattle, the alkali dust seemed to diminish. We rode for an hour and the ground began to look like ground should. As we came over the next rise, there was the river. It still had water, but I could tell it was much lower than it had been when we came through earlier.

"It's much lower than it was. Hope we can get all the herd watered."

"I think there will be enough, but from the looks of this place there won't be much grass for them."

I walked Blacky over and got down and tasted the water. I spit it out.

"We better get back and hurry them along. This water is much saltier then when we were here. We may have to drive them until we can't see and start them before the sun comes up. Get here by early tomorrow. Another day and this water might be too bad to drink."

As we rode back, my dad asked, "How far to the ranch from that river?"

"It's around a hundred miles."

"We better drive them like you said. It will be better to lose a few now than to lose them all out there half way to the ranch."

When we reached the herd we rode around telling the men to keep them going until it was completely dark, and move them out before sunup. We drove them late and by dawn our dust was gone from where we settled that night. By noon with the hot summerlike sun straight above us, we came to the river. The cattle drank their fill, for even this slightly- bad water tasted good. As each bunch of cattle came out of the river and were turned northwest, another bunch of thirsty cows came in the, by now, ankle deep river and had their fill of the salty water. But they seemed not to notice the taste, for out in this wasteland any type of water was heaven-sent. As the chuck-wagon came across the river the men put what good water was left in one barrel and filled the rest of the barrels with the salty water from the river.

Red Bird and my mother went upriver while I watched over the wagon. There they took a long cool bath and washed all the alkali off their bodies and out of their clothes. We were out on the trail again in an hour. But this time ma took to the south side of the herd, so the dust would be blowing away from the chuck wagon.

The days were growing longer and this was to my liking, for we could drive the cattle a little longer in the evening. I kept to the front of the herd with my father during the day and with Red Bird at night away from the fire. Somehow we managed to keep warm. Then one morning I got the shock and reward of my life.

We were sitting and eating breakfast when my mother came out with, "Say, son, what you going to name my grandson?"

"What did you say, Mother?"

"You heard me. Haven't you noticed the glow on her face?"

I looked over at Red Bird, who hadn't been eating much of a morning, but I was thinking it was because of the hard times on the drive.

"Been feeling bad in the morning and missed my last moon cycle. Think we made baby in honeymoon lodge."

"Well, I'll be, what you know, me a father?"

"Your son, man of few words now."

I had a big grin on my face and felt like I was floatin' on a cloud.

My father woke me up, "Come on, Daddy, we have some cows to herd."

I woke up and said, "All right," and kissed Red Bird and patted her tummy, then jumped on Blacky's back and took off beside my dad. I couldn't get it out of my mind, a baby, a baby. Red Bird a mother and me a father. It was exciting to me. Did every new father feel this way? I was on cloud nine for two days; it snapped me out of it when we came to two dry creeks in a row. My mind got back to the trouble at hand.

"Buck, is it going to be this dry all the way?"

"It may, see it's like this, the two rivers that border our ranch are runnin' all right, but one runs southeast and the other southwest after leavin' the ranch. This middle part dries up out here. About two more days we'll be all right. The cattle are thirsty but by tomorrow they'll smell the water from the north and I hope that will keep them movin' even faster."

"I sure hope so, I can see now why you wanted us to start early. Two weeks later and that river back yonder would be dry. That might just make the difference."

Late that afternoon we spotted some Indians watching from a high ridge to the north. I said to my dad, "Look over yonder," as I pointed to the north."

"You got a plan?"

"Kind of, the Indians don't know how to raise cattle out here, so I don't think they will ask for more than they can eat, but I think we'll be lucky even if we give them twenty. To get safe passage, it's worth it. They'll come down after they watch us awhile."

Sure enough, that same afternoon I saw the Indians heading our way.

"Pa, get the men together in case of trouble and find someone that might know some kind of sign language."

"All right."

He rushed off and I watched as the Indians came closer. By the time they came up we were all spread out in front of the cattle. He had found one man that understood a little sign language and he was beside me and pa as they started their sign.

"Do you understand them, John?"

"Sure do, I guess they all have the same signs."

"What he sayin'?"

"Buffalo gone . . . our people hungry . . . need food."

"Tell him we need good water, if he knows where good water is, we trade fifteen steers for water for the herd."

"He ask if we stay here."

"Say no. we go north out of their territory where grass grow tall and plenty water for cattle."

"He says good, then show water for twenty head of cattle."

"Tell him it's a deal, if we have his word we pass safe through his land and my men pick out the twenty heads to be traded."

"He says you have his word you pass safe and your men pick cattle."

"Tell him I agree also."

I gave orders for four men to round up twenty head that looked like they wouldn't make it even with water. They went to work and in an hour they had them up with us.

"Tell him these are the twenty head and my men will help take them to the village cause they know how to handle them and he would have one of his men lead us to the water."

"He said good."

He picked one man to lead us and my four men took off with the Chief and the twenty head of cattle.

"Men, go back to your work and head the cattle behind us."

My father asked me, "Buck, you trust these Indians?"

"You can go back and ask Red Bird, any Indian gives his word and he'll died before he breaks it. I don't think they know how to lie."

"All right, you been up here longer than I have."

"Wait until you meet Red Bird's father, he's real friendly, and I invited him to come meet you and mother and stay on the ranch awhile. We'll have one heck of a party."

The brave led us about five miles west of where we were. We came to a formation of rocks that jetted into the blue sky, like they were spears being thrown up to the heavens. The brave stopped and pointed to the base of the rocks. Pa and I rode over and got off our horses and looked but didn't see anything wet. The brave and John came over

"Boss, he says to dig down a little way at the bottom of those cliffs in the shade there."

"John, go get a shovel out of the chuck wagon."

While he was gone the cattle started moving in closer and closer to us.

"Look at them, there's water around here all right."

John came back with the shovel and I dug down about two feet and hit wet sand. Another half foot and water came up. I dug out more and soon there was a whole pool of water and the cattle were forcing their way in to get a drink.

"Boss he says he go now, and to cover the pool back up. He says there's an underground spring and if left uncovered will soon disappear."

"Tell him to thank the Chief and we will cover it back."

He rode off to his village and we started to bring the cattle into the water., about thirty at a time. Then I told the men to get the cattle heading north after each bunch finished. As night fell across the desert the four men came riding in from taking the cattle to the village. The men ate and got the fresh water in their canteens and headed north with the next bunch of cattle that left. It took all night to get all the herd watered, but it was worth a sleepless night to know we were going to make it to the ranch with most of the cattle. It had added a day to the already long trip, but it was also worth the time.

The next night everyone except the night riders fell asleep earlier than usual. Late tomorrow we would be pulling into the south end of the ranch and over to the river to let the herd have their fill of grass and water.

The morning came early and we got started at sun up. By noon everyone could tell we were coming into a better region. The sand of the desert was behind us now and the green plateau ahead. I was up on the point with dad, when he pointed north.

"What is that up ahead."

"Dad, that's the Rocky Mountains. The ones we been passin' are ant hills compared to those up there. The foot hills start just north of Durango. Our plateau that the ranch is on is about five to six thousand feet up, but you don't notice it cause from here it's a gradual incline, but you get up where Red Bird's family lives and it's fourteen thousand feet up and there's some pretty rough country. Some places people haven't even gotten to yet. Just wait, we'll go huntin' when we get things runnin' smooth."

"Any bear?"

I pulled back my shirt and said.

"Yeah, this was done by a bear that hit me after I shot him. Nearly took my arm off. You'll get to meet him, his skin and head is in front of our fireplace."

"Well, I'll be doggone."

That evening we were camped on our land. The cattle drive would end soon. We were sitting around the campfire as the cattle were eating our good green grass, then I told my dad.

"You know, Dad, I have a plan for this ranch, that will assure us of water, plenty of water all year long, and water the grass."

"What plan do you have?"

"First we have to plant hay on a few hundred acres closest to the ranch houses. This will assure the cattle of feed all winter when the snow is deep. Second, before next spring we dig canals leadin' to big ponds or holdin' tanks. When the spring melt comes, instead of losin' most of the water, we open the gates that led to the ponds and capture this overflow of water. When the ponds are full we simply close the gates and the rest goes as nature intended. This holdin' pond can be covered with canvas to prevent evaporation by the sun. This water could water the cattle and be used for irrigation when it gets hot in the summer and the grass starts dyin' out. You think it will work?"

"Sounds good, but when we get to the house you can lay it out for me on paper. I'm just an old rancher no . . . engineer." He let out a big loud laugh.

"Tomorrow we'll head northwest until we hit the main river, from here it's about fifteen or so miles to you and mother's new home. The river on the west side of the ranch is the Animos River and on the eastern side is the Los Pinos River. We can let the cattle roam anywhere between those two rivers and as far south as here and the north side is right past the ranch houses."

"We better hire some more men right away, cause we're going to need at least two line camps along this southern border with two hands at each camp to watch for rustlers, Indians, and to keep back the cattle that want to roam south."

Later me and Red Bird went to bed. We were lying there and she said.

"Me glad to get to my house and sleep in our big bed."

"I didn't think you liked the house or bed."

"Me like house all right but bed is best, fun to make love to you on. I like."

"Me too, but this isn't too bad." With that I took her in my arms and we made love under the bright moon and stars that were in the open skies of our dear beloved Colorado. It is this place our children will grow up.

Early the next morning I went to Sam.

"Go into Durango and tell Bill that we should be home this afternoon with my folks and twenty-two cowboys from Texas and twenty eight hundred head of cattle. The first cattle ranch in southwestern Colorado is about to get started."

"Silver, I think I'll stop by and tell Manuel and maybe he can have a mess of food ready for us. I hate to admit it, but I missed his cookin', it grows on you."

"Sure does, we might surprise everyone. Take a steer with you and tell Manuel to fix a real Texas style barbecue and then invite the whole town. Tell them about five O'clock. All these cowhands will be tired but it will make them feel more at home, and don't tell any of the men. We'll surprise them and my folks too."

"What do I tell them when I take the steer?"

"Just say you want to show them a longhorn. The townspeople never seen one."

"Will do. I'd better be getting."

The boys and my dad and me headed the cattle out toward the river. We just kind of let them spread out along the trail to the river because all of this was their new home and their noses would find the water when they were thirsty enough. The cattle liked the grass and some stopped along the way to graze.

About three o'clock we reached the river and I gathered the men and Red Bird and my folks and made a little speech.

"You men have been through a lot together and now this is the end of the trail. You all will have a job here if you want it. It's different here than in Texas for the snow sometimes gets five feet deep here, but the pay will be worth it. Now I'm goin' to take my folks and wife to our house. I want all of you to get in that river and clean up and get to the house as soon as you can for a surprise I have in store."

"But how we know where to go?"

"Just head north, when you see two of the biggest houses you've ever seen, you're there."

"We'll be there."

Red Bird and I mounted up, and my folks drove the chuck wagon. In less than an hour we came into our front yard. My mother couldn't believe it.

"It's so big, Buck, and fancy."

"Red Bird, show Mother the inside bath so she can clean up; I didn't tell the boys but the townspeople are comin' out and we're havin' a party tonight."

Then Manuel came out.

"Hello, señor, nice to have you back. I have things already cookin' and they will be ready."

"Fine."

The women went inside to get gussied up for the party and I took Dad to the bunkhouse so we could clean up.

Most of the townspeople showed up and I introduced my dad and mother to everyone and we had a gay old time with plenty of food and drink for everybody. I took Red Bird by the hand, and got up and made another speech.

"I want you all to know that come next winter me and Red Bird are goin' to be parents."

Everyone yelled for joy, and then they started dancing. "I'm goin' to send a message to Dancing Bear and the mining camp and we're goin' to all get together and have another party in three weeks. So y'all be ready. We're all goin' to work together and make Durango one of the finest towns in the West. And we owe it all to my great-grandfather Jeb. Here a toast to Jeb."

Everyone raised their glass to toast Jeb. Then Bill got up.

"Here's to Silver Buck . . . one of the finest young men in the West, and to his beautiful wife, Red Bird. We owe them both so much."

Everyone raised their glass again. Then my father got up:

"I thought Texas people were friendly, but y'all have out done them, so here's to you and my family's new home in Colorado. Thank you all, me and my wife and the boys, for havin' us as your neighbors."

Again everyone toasted.

That was the end of the party that night, but in three weeks we had a bigger and better one, with all the miners and the whole Indian village. We had a gay old time. This is when I took Red Bird and Dancing Bear to the side and talked to them.

"Dancing Bear, you are part of my family now and I wanted to tell you in front of your daughter and my wife, that we both love you very much. I promise that if your village ever needs a new place to live, or your people need food, you come to me and I will help always. If I should die, it is in white man's law that I put there that the land south of here to the end of Colorado will belong to you and your people and no white man can make you move. Bill Gills will fight for you if anyone tries."

"I know not what to say, you, Jeb, Foster, and your father are unlike any white men I have ever known. I thank you and my people thank you. Same goes for me if you ever need any kind help. You send for me, and me and my people come help."

We shook hands and gave each other a big hug.

Chapter Fifteen

Everything at the mine went well the whole year, and by the end of the year we had as much in the bank as before I bought the ranch and built the houses. My folks were overjoyed with their new house. It was more than my mother ever dreamed of. My father was happy with the everyday needs of the ranch. The ranch was his life. I told him he didn't have to work but he insisted on taking care of every problem that came up. He supervised the building of the canals and ponds and the idea had worked fine. We still had water left by the time the snow started falling in late November.

Me and Red Bird were happy and spent almost all our time together waiting for the baby to arrive. We ordered all our baby things from St. Louis. Then on January fifteenth, in the middle of a blizzard, our first son was born. He was a handsome boy, and Red Bird said he looked just like me, but I didn't think so. We named him Buck Taylor Jr., but everyone called him Little Silver. After a couple of months without Red Bird, it was nice to enter her again and we enjoyed each other more than before. Then she was going to have another baby. We were as happy as the first time.

When Red Bird was a few months along the doc made her quit riding Lagger. She was upset by this because we loved to ride to our little spot on the river and be alone and enjoy each other in the pleasant surroundings. I spent more time on ranch duties because it was hard being around Red Bird all day and not being able to enjoy each other as we pleased, but at night I enjoyed her warm body next to mine.

Well, anyway the months went by and even Sam became rich from his small share in the silver mine. The town of Durango was growing by leaps and bounds from all the wages the ranch and mine paid out. Then the day before Christmas Red Bird had our second child, a darling tiny little girl and we named her Lady Bird Taylor. Red Bird had a hard time having her and the doc said she would not be able to have any more children. Red Bird was depressed for a while, but I told her I loved her and we had two beautiful children. Nothing else mattered, and when we were able to enjoy each other as we had since being married she saw I was right and began to enjoy our life again.

When Little Silver was two I started taking him to his grandfather's village to learn the Indian way of life as well as the white man's. I wanted him to know the kind of people his mother belonged to. When we came, Dancing Bear would drop anything he was doing and spend all his time with us. Dancing Bear was happy I let him teach Little Silver the Indian way of life. Dancing Bear would take him out for hours on the white stallion, showing him the types of plants and what kind of animals were good and which were bad.

When he turned four my father gave him a pony and would take him out and ride along with the cattle. He showed him how we put our brand on the cattle so people would know they were ours.

Then late one afternoon I came riding in from the range on Blacky, and there on our big front porch was Red Bird, shading her eyes from the sun, as beautiful as ever with four-year-old Buck Jr. on her right and little three-year-old-doll Lady Bird on her left, and I was happy.

This was the dream I had three times over the past five years. But this was not a dream; this was my life. This was the day I found out that dreams can come true.

End

Edwards Brothers Malloy
Thorofare, NJ USA
March 26, 2015